MW00682817

IN THIS SIGN

SR. MARY MARTIN JACOBS, OP

To Isabella

From Sr. Mary Martin, O.P.

2017
DNS PUBLICATIONS

In This Sign
by Sr. Mary Martin Jacobs, OP

Printed in the United States of America

DNS PUBLICATIONS

Dominican Nuns of Summit
543 Springfield Avenue
Summit, New Jersey 07901
www.nunsopsummit.org

ISBN-10: 0999243209
ISBN-13: 978-0999243206

Cover Artwork by Cecilia Lawrence

CONTENTS

CHAPTER 1
IN THIS SIGN

Eleven-year-old Patsy Morgan reached for the package of cigarettes lying on the living room end table and scanned it intently. She had early developed the habit of reading everything in sight and besides, needed something to allay her boredom during the TV station break. "Say Daddy," she exclaimed suddenly, "What does this mean?"

"What does what mean?" Mr. Morgan pulled his head out of the evening paper and glared at her. "This, at the bottom of the package." She read it carefully: "IN HOC SIGNO VINCES. What does that mean, Daddy?"

"I don't know. Just some advertising garbage. And don't get any ideas about smoking. You're too young." He sank back into the depths of the paper and Patsy sighed. Sometimes she wondered why she even bothered.

But curiosity would not let her rest and, next commercial break, she stealthily opened the end table drawer, pulled out a pencil and piece of scrap paper, and began to copy the mysterious words. "I said leave those cigarettes alone!" her father snapped from behind the paper.

"Yes sir," she said hastily and turned back to her TV program. But she had finished copying and the precious slip of paper rested securely in her jeans pocket.

That was Friday evening. On Monday morning she carried the paper to school with her. Maybe Mrs. Denton would know what it meant. She loved Mrs. Denton; all the sixth-graders did. Only that semester she had begun to teach at Linn Street School and everyone, parents as well as children,

1

had warmed to her. She was short and plump, with gray hair, which neatly framed her small oval face and a pair of gold-rimmed spectacles that would never quite stay on her nose. She had dignity and discipline, but her eyes sparkled with fun and never, in after years, could the children remember her raising her voice to correct them. When she appeared on the playground at recess, they would flock around her like chicks around a mother hen. Even shy Patsy joined the crowd, but she usually hung on the fringes, content to have the beloved teacher smile at her, and say, "Good morning, Patricia."

But today it was different; Patsy simply had to know. So, when recess came, she wormed her way through the circle of jostling, laughing kids, until she arrived breathless and determined in front of Mrs. Denton, grasping the precious slip in her hand. "Why, hello Patricia!" The little lady beamed at her with motherly affection. "What can I do for you?"

Patsy gulped. "Uh, Mrs. Denton, do...do you know what this means?" She handed her the crumpled scrap of paper and waited anxiously for a reply.

"What's it say?" cried Steve Miller, jostling Patsy for a better view. Linda Byrne and Sally McKeever peered around Mrs. Denton's shoulders from behind. The little woman adjusted her glasses with a habitual gesture and read aloud: IN HOC SIGNO VINCES. Then she looked at Patsy with keen interest.

"This is Latin, Patricia. It means: 'In this sign you shall conquer.' Where did you see these words?"

"On the bottom of my father's cigarette package," she replied.

2

"Oh," Mrs. Denton sighed, half to herself, "are they putting it on cigarette packages now?" Then she said to Patsy, "Do you know what this refers to?"

"The emblem on the package?" guessed Patsy.

"No, dear." Mrs. Denton sighed again. "Do any of you students know what the words 'In hoc signo vinces' refer to?" The children looked at one another and shook their heads.

"Well," began Mrs. Denton in her usual story-telling tones, "in the year 312 AD a Roman emperor named Constantine was fighting to subdue his enemies and unify the empire, which was ruled at that time by several men." She paused as if trying to remember and Patsy noticed her fingering a silver crucifix that hung around her neck. "The enemy drew up in battle formation," she continued, "at a place called the Milvian Bridge. Constantine was fearful, because everything depended on his winning the victory.

"The night before the battle, as he stood at the entrance of his tent, suddenly a great cross appeared in the sky and with it the words: *In Hoc Signo Vinces:* 'In this Sign you shall conquer." Mrs. Denton paused again and held up the small crucifix, so that all the children could see it. "Constantine immediately ordered this Sign of the Cross to be emblazoned on his imperial standard. Next day he led his troops forth to battle and won an overwhelming victory against his enemies. Thereupon Constantine embraced Christianity, professing his faith in the Cross of Jesus Christ."

"Oh," interrupted Steve, "I know all about Jesus Christ! We read the Bible every Sunday in Sunday school. But I never heard that story."

"You won't find that story in the Bible, Steven," said Mrs. Denton with a smile.

But Patsy said nothing. Suddenly she felt uneasy and disappointed. "Just a lot of superstitious nonsense," Daddy had dismissed her question about why people went to church. "Somebody they tell kids about to make them behave," Mom had replied when asked who was Jesus Christ. Patsy thought this was very funny; jesuschrist was one of Daddy's favorite swear words. Now she realized that Mrs. Denton was gazing at her intently. She lowered her eyes and said quietly, "My folks don't believe in God or religion."

"Don't believe in God!" gasped Sally, her eyes wide with astonishment. But Patsy ignored her.

"What does it mean to have faith in the Cross of Christ?" Her voice was almost pleading, though she did not know why. The little teacher's eyes met hers and they were alight with compassion and understanding.

"Patricia," she said, "to have faith in the Cross simply means to believe that Jesus died to save all people, that he rose from the dead and that, by his power symbolized in the Cross, all evil shall be overcome." The bell clanged, signaling the end of recess and Mrs. Denton gave an affectionate gesture of dismissal. "Go now, children, don't be late." She started to follow, then suddenly turned back to Patsy, who had remained standing there. "Patricia," she said, laying a hand on the little girl's arm, "would you like to have my cross?"

That afternoon, Patsy ran all the way home from school, her flame-red curls flying in the breeze, the precious silver crucifix bouncing against her chest. "Mom, Mom!" she burst in the back door. "Look what Mrs. Denton gave me!" Her freckled face was beaming with joy and pride.

4

Mrs. Morgan replaced the iron carefully on the ironing board and crossed over to her smiling. "Hello, Patsy dear." She kissed her on the cheek. "Now take a deep breath and tell me slowly. What did Mrs. Denton give you?"

"This," she replied, holding up the crucifix for her mother's examination. Mrs. Morgan's smile faded slightly.

"Well, dear, that's very nice," she said slowly, "and I'm sure your teacher meant well. But I wouldn't let your father see you wearing it, if I were you."

The light died in Patsy's eyes. "But, Mom!" Her fist closed tightly over the crucifix. "Mrs. Denton gave it to me. I love Mrs. Denton. What's wrong with wearing it?" Her voice choked with tears of disappointment. "Daddy can't be that mean, he can't be... I don't believe in her silly old Jesus anyway," she sobbed as she turned and ran from the room.

Nevertheless, she removed the crucifix and hid it in her room, so her father did not see it that evening. Next morning, while she was dressing for school, she took it out from its hiding place. "I don't care," she thought fiercely. "I don't care what he says. Mrs. Denton gave it to me and I'm going to wear it!" She pulled the chain over her head with a defiant jerk and marched off to breakfast.

However, Mr. Morgan scarcely looked at Patsy during breakfast and might never have noticed what she was wearing, if the car hadn't refused to start. From the kitchen doorway, where Patsy was collecting her books and deciding whether to wear a coat or not, she could hear the motor coughing and her father's muffled profanity. "Patsy!" he bellowed finally.

"Yes, Daddy." She bounced down the steps into the garage, without her coat.

"I can't get this ___ car started. You'll have to walk to school. And put a coat on; it looks like rain. Say, what's that thing around your neck?"

"It's.. It's just something my teacher gave me," Patsy suddenly felt her courage melting away under his belligerent gaze.

"Well, I don't care who gave it to you. Take it off! I won't have anything like that in my house. Your teacher, huh? I'll have her reported to the school board and fired. Foisting off religion onto unsuspecting kids!"

"Jim, dear, please," a quiet voice interposed as Mrs. Morgan appeared in the doorway. "Here's your coat, Patsy. You'd better get started or you'll be late." She gave Patsy a quick kiss and a gentle push in the direction of the driveway. "Jim, for heaven's sake, it's not going to hurt her any..." Her voice trailed off as Patsy hastened down the drive, only too glad to get away.

"Can't he ever understand?" she thought angrily as she hurried along. "I only took it because Mrs. Denton offered. He just never cares enough to listen." But such thoughts brought her dangerously close to tears, and pride would never let her come crying to school. So Patsy pushed the matter to the back of her mind and glanced anxiously up at the sky. He was right about one thing; it looked very much like rain. "April showers bring May flowers," she repeated grimly, but the rhyme had no power to cheer her. Neither did the fresh spring grass, the delicate newly leafed trees, the daffodils nodding along Mrs. Banks' front walk. As she turned the corner of the last long block, a great drop of rain splashed on her nose, followed by another and another. Patsy began to run. Down the sidewalk they pelted together, the rain and

Patsy, faster and faster. Now she was opposite the school. The pedestrian light was turning amber; she could just make it. As she dashed into the street, a shout rang out behind her, but she did not hear. There followed a screech of brakes, which she did hear, but too late. The next thing she knew was blackness.

CHAPTER 2
THE KINGDOM OF ARENDOLIN

Patsy opened her eyes, then promptly shut them again, as the sun shone full on her face. She lay there on the pavement, basking in its radiant warmth, feeling the rays burn orange against her closed eyelids. The sun? Her eyes flew open abruptly and she sat up in bewilderment. But it had been raining! Shielding her face with both hands, she stared in disbelief at the cloudless blue sky, dominated by a single disc of midmorning brilliance. What had happened? She pulled herself to her feet and looked around. To her left, a massive stone wall towered over her, so high she could barely see the top of it. Linn Street School had no wall like that. To her right rose a thickly planted, neatly clipped hedge, taller than Patsy herself. None of the neighbors had such a hedge. "Where am I?" she asked herself. Then her gaze fell on the sidewalk and she nearly cried aloud with dismay. It was not a sidewalk at all, but a flagstone path, smoothly laid and so well kept that not a blade of grass grew between the stones. "Where am I?" She did cry aloud now and her voice echoed harshly in her ears. For a moment she nearly panicked. Her heart pounded wildly; tears rose to her eyes and sobs to her throat. But then a familiar sound came floating down to her from over the hedge. Children!

Patsy swallowed her sobs and listened. Yes, kids playing! At least they would be able to tell her where she was. She turned to follow the path in the direction of the voices, hoping to find a gate or some sort of opening in the hedge. The effort of walking brought her completely to her senses and she realized for the first time that her coat and books were gone. "The cross!" she thought, but it was still there, hanging from its silver chain about her neck. Oddly reassured by the discovery, she clasped it in her fist, clinging to the ornate silver form as if it were her last link to a vanishing reality.

Ahead, on her right, Patsy at last spotted a gate of double-arched finely wrought iron. She jerked to a halt in front of it, breathless and trembling. Beyond the gate lay a garden, with beds of strange and brilliant flowers, which formed spiral patterns of blazing scarlet, deep rust and tawny gold. The flagstone path continued through the gate and wound in rhythm with the flowers until it formed a circle, in the center of which a tree-shaped fountain splashed and rippled.

Patsy gazed in astonishment at the unexpected beauty that lay at her feet. Her trembling ceased and her breathing became calm and even. She gave the gate an experimental push and, to her amazement, it swung open smoothly and noiselessly. Tiptoeing in, she closed the gate behind her and took several hesitant steps forward. Then she spied the children.

They were playing around the fountain: a girl about Patsy's own age, wearing a long sky-blue gown of some rich fabric; a boy, two or three years older, dressed in forest green breeches, leggings and tunic; and another boy, several years younger, in a grass-green suit of the same style. Patsy stared, her whole face wide open with mingled horror and fascination. Their hair! They had silver hair! Not merely blonde, not even platinum, but silver! "Like Grandma Morgan's," thought Patsy as she rubbed her eyes in disbelief. They did not seem to notice her, although she was close enough to hear their conversation clearly.

"I will not be the dragon!" the girl stomped her foot emphatically and shook her long silver locks so that they shimmered with sunlight. "I shall be a princess and you shall carry me across the moat."

"But Rilya, you're too big to carry!" protested the younger boy. He waved a long wooden sword vigorously in her direction. "The dragon's more important than the princess anyway."

"No it isn't, Landon! And I am going to be the princess, so there!" She turned to the older boy who was lounging against the fountain, indolently skipping pebbles into its sparkling waters. "Condin, why don't you be the dragon for a change?"

"Because someday I shall be a great prince and I must not lower my dignity." Condin drew himself up with a superior air. "Besides, these games are childish and I'm growing too old for them. He grimaced with disgust at the wooden sword in his left hand.

"O, Condin!" Rilya cried with hurt and dismay. "Rendil was never too old..."

"Rendil! Rendil! Beware the dragon!" shouted Landon, as he whirled unexpectedly and charged down the path toward Patsy, brandishing the wooden sword over his head. She had been watching them, fascinated, longing to join in their game, yet rooted to the spot in an agony of shyness. Now she would have turned and fled, but simultaneously with Landon's shout, a voice from behind cut across her loneliness.

"Who are you, little girl, and whence have you come here?" Patsy's heart stopped cold. She might have fainted had Landon not tumbled to a halt two paces in front of her, pointed his wooden sword at her chest, and cried, "Who goes

10

there, friend or foe?" Suddenly the whole thing seemed ridiculous. She burst into a fit of hysterical giggling that was nearer to tears than laughter. Landon and Rilya stared at her in astonishment, while the voice behind her joined in the laughter, an adolescent voice but decidedly masculine. Only Condin lingered by the fountain, his gaze fixed intently on his boot tops, the wooden sword dangling in his hand.

At last Patsy got hold of herself, and, wiping her eyes, turned to look at the owner of the voice. He was about sixteen, tall and graceful in bearing, clad in rich purple with a real sword, golden hilted, hanging at his side. Once again, Patsy gripped her own little silver cross and, summoning her courage, looked up into his face. He was still smiling as he surveyed the scene before him, and Patsy noticed, to her surprise, that his silver hair was turning black at the temples. "Just the opposite of us," she thought. Then his eyes fell on hers, eyes that were a deep midnight blue, the blue of a night alight with the full moon and a thousand stars. The very sight of them somehow consoled her, although she gripped the cross harder, to keep her hand from trembling.

"Well," young Rendil the Prince said at last, "what is your name and where have you come from?" His tone echoed with surprise and plain boyish curiosity.

"I...I," Patsy stammered, her mouth dry and her throat constricted.

"See here, now, speak up!" cried Landon with a grand gesture of his sword which narrowly missed Patsy's left ear. "Are you friend or foe?"

"Landon, stop it!" hissed Rilya fiercely. "You'll frighten her."

Patsy swallowed hard and tried again. "My…my name is Patricia Morgan and I live at 282 Vine Street, Kingstown, Ohio." She hesitated, then added doubtfully, "United States of America."

Rendil frowned. "You speak our language," he said, "but the sound of your name and your land ring very strangely in my ears. How did you come here?"

"I…I don't know. I was crossing the street on the way to school and it was raining and next thing I knew, I was lying in the middle of the walk on the other side of that hedge and it wasn't raining any more." Patsy shuddered, recalling her panic. "Where am I, anyhow? What's the name of this place?"

"This 'place'," said Rendil, drawing himself up to a greater height of dignity, "is the lordly castle of Celdondol, ancient throne of the mighty kings of Arendolin."

"Rendil is going to be king one day, aren't you?" Rilya's face glowed with pride and affection for her eldest brother. Patsy simply stared at him.

Rendil blushed and made a self-conscious bow. "In the name of our royal Mother and all the worthy court, I welcome you to the Kingdom of Arendolin, my lady…" he hesitated, groping for her name. "Patricia," Patsy supplied.

"My lady Pa…Patis…Paris…" Rendil frowned again.

"Palissa," Landon intruded. "She said Palissa!"

"She did not!" Rilya rejoined crossly, smacking him on the shoulder.

But Rendil ignored her and bowed again to Patsy, who was feeling less frightened and more embarrassed by the minute. "Well, my lady, if you will forgive us, I am afraid we shall have to call you Palissa. As for how you have come to

12

this fair Kingdom, if you cannot enlighten us, then neither can we enlighten you."

"Perhaps Dol has sent her in answer to our prayers," Condin put in unexpectedly, his voice laden with sarcasm. He sauntered toward them, deliberately indifferent to Rendil's sharp glance of surprise and hostility. "Well, you confessed that you had no explanation." Even Patsy found his smile infuriating. She had the impression that, although his eyes were the same deep blue as the others', they were somehow overshadowed with storm and darkness.

Rilya broke the uneasy silence with a strange excited gasp. "Condin! Rendil! Yes, don't you see? Her hair! Her hair is like the light of fire, like the leaves on the Gelfin Tree!"

"I do not look like a tree!" Patsy flashed indignantly. "And I'm sick of being called fire-head." The angry outburst came as a relief after what seemed an eternity of fear and uncertainty. But Rilya recoiled as if struck and Patsy immediately felt ashamed.

"The Gelfin Tree," Condin haughtily informed her, "is the sacred symbol of Dol, god of fire and light, special protector of our land. No one," he added, "in all the realm of Arendolin has hair like yours." He smiled triumphantly, pleased at the unexpected confirmation of his original remark.

"Yes, perhaps you are right." Rendil seemed reluctant to make the admission. "My lady Palissa, I think we had better take you to our Mother." Without further ado, he turned and led the way up the garden path toward the castle.

Patsy squeezed the silver cross until it bit into her hand. "Oh," she thought miserably, "I'm really in for it now." Blind with dread, she turned to follow him.

CHAPTER 3
OUR MOTHER THE QUEEN

The massive stone walls and high vaulted ceilings of Castle Celdondol utterly dwarfed the band of children as they paraded through, while the vast torchlit corridors echoed and re-echoed with their every footfall. Patsy stared about her, open-mouthed, her mind benumbed by sheer immensity. Even the maids and chamberlains, pages and guards, that tended to their affairs with a kind of cheerful bustle, seemed like so many ants by comparison. Many of them smiled and greeted the children in passing, and one or two of them gaped at Patsy in frank curiosity. She was becoming acutely self-conscious of her personal appearance. All the ladies, even the least important looking, wore long, swishing skirts of rich linen and satin and brocade which made her own jeans and battered sneakers seem shabby indeed. And her hair! Why, oh why, did she have to have red hair? "No one, in all the realm of Arendolin, has hair like yours." In her imagination, all eyes were fixed on her, every echo whispered of her. Patsy wanted nothing more than to crawl into a corner and hide.

But then she felt Rilya's arm about her shoulders, and Rilya's skirts brushing against her legs. "Don't be afraid," the girl whispered in her ear, "Mother is always very kind."

Patsy warmed instantly. "Thank you," she said, managing a thin smile. She felt more ashamed than ever for her outburst in the garden and wanted to say something polite that would make up for it. "I like your dress; it's such a pretty color."

"Oh!" Rilya beamed with pleasure. "I'm glad you like it. It's one of my favorite dresses for every day. If you want, we can give you one of the same material."

"Can you? Oh, thank you!" Patsy really smiled this time, a great, beautiful smile, and her whole body relaxed. "What's your name?"

"My name is Dolanya Rendilya Claris, first daughter of Rendol, lady-heir of Celdondol, princess of Arendolin." She paused for breath and grinned at the other girl's expression. "But everybody calls me Rilya."

Patsy giggled. "I'm glad. It's so much easier." With that she bumped into Rendil, who had stopped unexpectedly in front of her. "Oh, excuse me! Are we...what's happening?" She glanced around her in confusion.

They were standing in what looked for all the world like a waiting room. A low wooden bench padded with bright colored cushions stood along one wall. In the far corner, a scribe sat at his writing desk, his quill flying over an important looking parchment. Opposite the children loomed a heavy wooden door, tightly shut and flanked by two armed guards. Their helmets and breastplates flashed and dimmed in the flickering torchlight.

"Where are we?" Patsy asked, but Rilya did not answer. Her eyes were fixed on Rendil, who seemed to be hesitating, unable to make up his mind. At last he squared his shoulders, set his jaw, and started for the closed door.

Instantly, the scribe leaped from his stool with a muted cry. "My lord Prince, you must not go in there!" He gulped and went on more calmly. "Her Majesty is in council with the Lord Gendol and has left orders not to be disturbed under any circumstance."

15

"But Helfon, this is a matter of great importance." Rendil's voice cracked and he flushed with embarrassment. "Besides, I should have been called to the council also."

"That may be, your Highness, that may be, but orders are orders, and your mother the Queen is not to be disturbed." Helfon shot a half-contemptuous glance at Patsy and seemed about to add something. However, he thought better of it, snapped his mouth shut and returned to his writing desk.

"I think he is right." Condin sounded amused at his brother's discomfiture. "Maybe we should take our guest to her quarters and see that she is more suitably clothed before presenting her to Mother."

"No," said Rendil stubbornly, "we will wait here." With that he retired to a corner of the antechamber opposite the forbidden door, and stood there glaring at it sullenly.

Patsy wished with all her heart that he had accepted Condin's suggestion, but she dared not say so. Instead, she followed Rilya to the wooden bench, plopped down on one of the cushions, and settled back against the wall to wait.

"Lord Gendol is chancellor of the kingdom and commander of the King's armies," Rilya whispered to her.

"Oh," answered Patsy, feeling curiously unimpressed. A dull, tense stillness fell upon the room, broken only by the scratching of Helfon's quill. Patsy stole a glance at him. He had quite ordinary-looking brown hair, turning slightly gray at the temples and a few gray streaks in his neat little beard. Just like anybody else, she decided. She ran her eyes over the shelves behind his desk and was longing to know the contents of the scrolls stacked on them, when a sudden loud snort turned her attention to Landon.

He also had been watching Helfon, waiting for the secretary to become re-absorbed in his work. Cautiously he sidled over to one of the guards at the door and said, in what was meant to be a conspiratorial whisper, "What can I give you, if you'll let us into Mother's chamber when he's not looking?" He jerked a thumb at Helfon.

"What can you give me?" the huge, burly man roared. "What can you give me! Listen here, little prince, I'll give you forty whacks with the broad side of my sword if you dare take another step toward this door!" Landon backed away with such a startled look on his face that the second guard laughed. His companion too began to chuckle, and soon everyone in the room was laughing, even Helfon. Rendil's smile flashed like a glimpse of sunshine on a stormy day, and Condin gave his small brother a good-natured slap on the back.

"Say, fellow, you had better be careful or you won't live long enough to become a great warrior!" Landon grinned sheepishly and took refuge next to Rilya on the bench.

"Honestly!" she whispered, her face red with mortification, but she got no further because, at that moment, the forbidden door opened.

Instantly, everyone stood up and the guards snapped to attention. A tall, dark haired man strode forth, then paused and turned back, as if remembering one more thing. "I think, Your Majesty," he rumbled in a voice strong and stern, "that upon consideration, you will find my plan to be best, after all." With a bow and a flourish of his scarlet cape, he closed the door softly behind him and continued his stride as if nothing had interrupted it. He seemed scarcely to notice the children staring at him, but as he passed, Patsy caught in his face, just for a moment, a look of such anger and disgust that it made her flesh creep.

"I don't like him," she thought, but it was the only thought she had time for. Now it was her turn, and Rilya was taking her by the hand and leading her to the door.

Patsy's knees turned to jelly and she very nearly threw up. "What do I do?" she whispered, swallowing hard. "I've never met a queen before."

"Why," said Rilya with surprise, "you just curtsy when you are presented and then wait for Mother to address you."

"She makes it sound so easy," Patsy thought miserably to herself. "I wish I knew how to curtsy." She groped for the silver cross, but even that seemed strange and comfortless now.

Rendil had already entered the audience chamber, with Landon close at his heels. Condin waved the girls through the door, then followed after, closing it behind him. They paused just inside the room and Patsy was startled to see brilliant rays of sunlight streaming through windows high up in the opposite wall. In the dim stretches of the torchlit castle, she had forgotten that it was day.

"Yes, my children, what is it?" The low, musical voice sent chills down Patsy's spine, so that she dared not look at the speaker.

"My Lady-Mother," said Rendil, stepping forward and bowing, "we beg your pardon for approaching you unannounced in this fashion, but we have found a person who may be of the utmost importance in the endeavor to save our Kingdom from its foes. We met this lady just now as we were strolling in the garden. Her name and the name of her land are strange to my ears, she wears a strange symbol about her neck,

18

and she does not know how she has come to be here. And," he added triumphantly, as if it were all his own discovery, "her hair is as the light of fire and the leaves of the Gelfin Tree."

"We think maybe Dol sent her," Condin interrupted coolly.

Rendil shot him a look of intense annoyance, but the Voice said, "Do you, my son?" in a tone of unruffled serenity. Then she called majestically, "My lady, come forward."

Patsy, who had all this while been shrinking back against the door in mortal terror, now found herself being gently propelled in the direction of the Voice. She stumbled forward and then, for the first time, forced herself to look up. Her eyes fell upon a throne, wrought of alabaster and inlaid with gleaming gold. Upon the throne was seated a woman, graceful of form and robed in a gown of blue and silver. Her gaze rose further, until she beheld the face, fair and comely, of the Lady enthroned, and her hair, black as the raven's wing. Her gaze at last came to rest within the gaze of the Queen, and was caught and held by her midnight, starlight eyes. Patsy forgot all her fears, all her shyness and embarrassment, and surrendered herself to the tranquil depths. She experienced a sadness therein that made her want to weep, and yet a gaiety that made her heart leap with joy.

"What is your name?" the Queen asked her.

She replied, "Patsy; Patsy Morgan. But your children call me Palissa."

The Queen smiled. "Then I, too, shall call you Palissa, with your consent." Patsy beamed and nodded gladly. "Well, then, my lady Palissa, what is your native land?"

Patsy hesitated, frowning. "Earth, I guess," she said at last. Somehow, the dawning realization that she was no longer within her own universe did not hold any fear for her.

"That indeed is a place beyond my knowledge," the Queen replied. Her countenance grew very grave and once again she drew Patsy into the depths of her gaze, tranquil and sad. Her eyes rested a long while on the silver crucifix. Then she asked, "What do you know of Dol, god of fire, protector of our realm?"

"Nothing, Ma'am," Patsy answered.

"Well spoken, my lady." The Queen inclined her head in affirmation. "You know not of Dol, nor were you sent by him. A far greater One has sent you, and of his light only dimly have I seen." The music of her words flooded Patsy's being like the waves of the sea, then ebbed and flowed back into the depths, leaving only silence.

For a moment Patsy stood motionless and dazed, her mind so overwhelmed that she could not even think in words the questions welling up within her. None of the other children dared to speak, although Condin shifted uneasily from one foot to the other and glanced longingly at the door.

"My lady Palissa," the Queen herself broke the spell with tones of warmth and friendliness. "You are welcome to the Kingdom of Arendolin."

"Thank you, Ma'am," Patsy answered and, remembering her manners, bowed awkwardly.

"Children," the Queen continued, "take our honored guest to your quarters and see that she is treated with all courtesy."

"Ooh!" cried Rilya, bubbling suddenly to life. She clapped her hands with delight and ran to hug Patsy, who smiled somewhat bemusedly as she returned the embrace.

Rendil stepped forward and bowed again to his mother. "My Lady-Mother, we are most grateful for your kind reception of the Lady Palissa. We hope that our hospitality will not be unworthy of her great dignity." Patsy wondered offhand why he was always so formal, but quickly erased the thought as he turned to her and smiled. "Come," he said, with a grand gesture to them all, "your room awaits you."

Landon banged on the door with his wooden sword. "Open!" he cried, "Open in the name of the Lady Palissa, honored guest of the Queen!" The door swung open and he marched through with the others following.

Just as Patsy was leaving she heard the Voice again. "Rendil, my son."

"Yes, Mother."

"Stay a moment. I would speak with you."

CHAPTER 4
THE MYSTERY OF THE KING

The children's quarters occupied the whole northeast tower of the castle, only a short distance from the Queen's private chambers. Breathlessly they tugged Patsy up the steep and winding stairs, with Landon shouting, "Make wa-ay! Make wa-ay!" as they clattered along, and laughing gaily at the sound of his voice bounding and rebounding in the stairwell. At the second level Rilya halted, motioning Patsy to follow her, while the two boys stumped on to the top floor. As they turned into the doorway, Patsy collapsed against the nearest wall, gasping and heaving.

"Do you do this every day?" she finally managed to ask.

Rilya laughed. "Of course, many times. You'll become accustomed to it. Come in now and meet Galna. Will she ever be surprised."

But Galna, the plump and pleasant nursemaid, seemed not a bit surprised and took Patsy in hand as if welcoming young strangers were an everyday affair. She and Rilya dove into the wardrobe room, emerging in a matter of minutes with armloads of petticoats and a gown of moss green silk so beautiful that Patsy could hardly believe they would let her wear it. She stood unprotesting as they whisked off her old clothes and proceeded to transform her, at least outwardly, from a skinny little girl into a charming young lady. Finally, they led her to a mirror and stood back, beaming with pleasure. Patsy looked, blinked, and looked again. They had even brushed her hair until it lay almost smooth! A smile twitched the corners of her mouth, then grew into a grin, which spread until it engulfed her whole face and finally became joyous, irrepressible laughter. Her new friends laughed also and Galna gave her a motherly hug.

"Dear, dear," she clucked at them as she collected her wits and began hustling about, "their Highnesses will arrive any time now for lunch and I haven't a thing prepared."

They were about to leave the room when Patsy remembered. Her cross! She had nearly forgotten it in her pleasure and excitement over the beautiful new clothes. Dashing back, she snatched it up and pulled the chain once more over her head. The crucifix nestled against the soft green cloth as if the two were made for each other. Patsy sighed with relief and joy.

Even Rilya smiled when she saw it. "It's very pretty," she said, fingering the small silver form. "Is it an image of your god?"

"I…uh," Patsy was taken completely off guard. She groped wildly through her mind but could think of no reply whatever. Finally she heard herself saying, "Yes. Yes, it is." To her relief, at that moment Landon trooped noisily in with Condin close behind, and all four of them sat down to dinner.

Under cover of a general conversation and the business of passing the portions, Patsy managed to get hold of herself. Why had Rilya asked such a question? Why had she answered yes instead of no? "But then," she defended herself mentally, "how could I ever tell them that I don't believe in God?" She thought of the Queen's mysterious words about a "far greater One," but could not comprehend what they meant.

Suddenly, she felt a gentle hand on her shoulder. "My lady, are you all right? You haven't touched your food." Galna was bending over her anxiously, while the others looked at her in alarm.

"Oh!" she exclaimed. "Oh, yes, I'm fine." Hastily she plunged her fork into the meat on her plate and then into her mouth. The fine seasoning made her forget everything else and she swallowed several more mouthfuls in rapid succession.

"Now that's much better!" Galna laughed as the other children also relaxed and resumed their meal.

"I think it is a fine idea to conduct Lady Palissa on a tour of the castle this afternoon," said Condin, "but we are due for history lessons, and I'm sure Old Wirebeard will not let us off without a formal command from Mother."

"Oh, bother with Old Wirebeard!" exclaimed Rilya in annoyance. "Can't we just sneak off and let him worry about why we're not there?"

"Last time I did, he caned me." Landon's voice quivered at the memory. "He made me go to bed without supper. And when Mother came, I wasn't there, so she left without giving me a blessing. I hate Old Wirebeard!" he added passionately.

"If you mean Sir Pandil," put in Galna with a meaningful glance at Landon, "you needn't worry about him. He took to bed this morning with an attack of rheumatism and is not likely to be up until day after tomorrow. So you're free for the afternoon." Her "I forgot to tell you" was drowned by the cheers of all present, including Patsy, who thought she would much rather see the castle than listen to a history lesson.

"Just think," cried Rilya, "we can show you the parapets and the courtyards and the great gates and…"

"and the soldiers marching," interrupted Landon, "and the armory and the horses…"

"and the city beyond the walls," Condin continued, caught up in their enthusiasm, "and the river with its ships seaward bound and…" And Patsy began to laugh for sheer joy, all her perplexity forgotten once again in her excitement over this marvelously unexpected adventure.

She found that the ancient walled fortress of Celdondol embraced even more splendors than she had imagined. The children led her out through the garden and along the path between the hedge and the wall, which she had followed earlier that day. Then they ducked into one of the massive stone guard towers that punctuated the fortress walls, and skipped up another endless flight of circular stairs, emerging finally onto the battlements. As they paused to catch their breath, Patsy stared open-mouthed at the panorama which lay before her.

The afternoon sun, like some fiery Midas, had touched the cold stone parapets of the castle, turning them to molten gold. Silvery-white doves wheeled homeward to their nests in the gilded niches, circling in a stately minuet with the many-colored banners of Arendolin. Far below them, in the castle yards, soldiers drilled in perfect formation, their helmets plumed with scarlet and gray. A troop of horsemen, clad in the same rich livery, guided their mounts toward stables in the distance. "Isn't it splendid?" demanded Landon, his midnight eyes alight. Patsy nodded in mute wonder.

"But that's just some old soldiers," Rilya exclaimed impatiently. "Look over here!" Patsy turned at her bidding and, standing on tiptoe, gazed over the battlements toward the wide world outside. A deep moat surrounded the castle, its waters dark and sluggish. Beyond the moat, grassy flower-dotted meadows sloped gently down to the banks of a swift-flowing river, the sound of whose rushing waters echoed in the distance. The river descended on its course from rolling wooded hills that piled up, more and more sharply, until they became mountains of misty purple, vanishing into the horizon. Patsy felt that she could drink their beauty forever.

"Oh, why do you always look over there! I can't see anything over there!" Landon was gripping the top of the battlements with his chubby little hands and trying desperately to hike himself up by digging his toes into the cracks in the wall.

"Never mind, fellow," said Condin, boosting him up with a laugh. "Trees and meadows and hills are only for girls anyway. We men shall go down by the city, to see where the ships are docked."

Nevertheless, Landon lingered on his perch, gazing intently across the hills. "Condin," he asked as he finally slid down, "are those mountains where Father was killed?"

"Of course they are!" Condin snapped his voice suddenly taut with emotion. "How many times do I have to tell you that? Why don't you just shut up and stop asking questions!"

"Condin!" Rilya gasped, but he stormed on, unheeding. "Quit asking me, I say. I don't know any more than you do. Why should they tell me anything? And stop sniveling like some little brat. Crying won't bring him back."

By this time Landon was sobbing aloud, his round face streaked with tears, but Rilya had recovered her voice and came charging into the fray. "Condin, you perfect beast! How can you be so nasty to your little brother? What would Father say if he were here? I think…" Her voice broke, but she swallowed and went on. "I think you didn't love him at all, you've been so mean since he died." Tears gushed forth and dropped unchecked onto the front of her dress. Condin glared at her with murderous fury, but words had failed him. Fists clenched and face contorted, he turned on his heel and fled back into the guard tower, the clatter of his boots on the stairs fading as he descended them.

For awhile, no sound could be heard on the battlement but the muted sobs of the two stricken children. Patsy stared at the pavement, trembling with shock and anger. At last she ventured an embarrassed glance at Rilya, who was struggling both to master herself and to comfort Landon. Their eyes met and the younger girl murmured brokenly, "I'm sorry."

"I'm sorry too," said Patsy, then added rather inanely, "I didn't know your father was dead." Rilya nodded, her eyes filling again. Patsy waited while she wiped them and blew her nose. "Was he the king?"

"Yes." Another awkward silence followed, during which Landon blew his nose loudly and mopped his ravaged face. Finally Rilya spoke, addressing him rather than Patsy. "Would you still like to see the ships on the river?"

"No," he gulped, "let's go back."

So Rilya took his hand and led the way, through the tower, down the winding steps, and out along the path to the garden. For awhile no one said anything, until, Landon pulled away and ran on ahead. Then Rilya turned to Patsy and began to speak quietly. "Last summer, we were told that the enemies of our Kingdom were amassing troops on the northern border, even though they hadn't attacked us in many years.

Immediately, Father mustered his army and marched northward to meet them. A terrible battle was fought and Father was killed, but Lord Gendol rallied our men and drove the enemy back into the mountains." She paused, drew a deep breath and let it out slowly. "That's all I know. Maybe Rendil knows more; Mother certainly does. But what I…we…none of us can understand is why Father died. A King cannot be killed unless he forsakes or betrays his enchantment, and Father would never have done that." She shuddered and her eyes grew suddenly wild and fierce. "What happened to him?" she demanded. "I want to know! What happened to him?"

Patsy stood speechless, a wave of cold fear raising goose flesh on her arms. An enchanted king who could not be killed? But that only happened in fairy tales! She felt the old panic flooding and choking her. "Where am I?" her mind cried out. "How can I know what happened to the King when I don't know what's happening to me?"

But Rilya had recovered herself again and was watching Patsy with undisguised concern. "Oh," she moaned, "I'm so sorry, I've alarmed you. What a terrible way to treat a guest!" She took her hand. "Come, supper will be ready shortly and meanwhile I can show you where you'll sleep." Patsy followed her numbly. The sun was already sinking low in the west as they approached the entrance of Celdondol. Its huge stones had suddenly turned gray and cold.

Chapter 5
The Darkness Within

Galna refused to lay supper on the table until Condin arrived, but, when it was almost dark and he still had not made his appearance, she finally relented. The children's faces told her more plainly than words that they had been quarrelling, but she asked no questions and made no rebukes. Patsy was glad that he had stayed away and glad also that no one seemed inclined to conversation.

They were nearly finished with their meal when, all at once, the door burst open and Condin rushed in. When he saw them staring at him, he stopped short, pulled himself up, and walked to the table with an air of dignified nonchalance. But they only continued to gape in astonishment. His clothing was torn, his boots muddy, and his grimy face streaked with tears. He avoided Galna's eyes as he addressed her in his politest tones. "I beg your pardon for being late, but I was unavoidably delayed. May I have my supper now?" Rilya opened her mouth to make a sarcastic reply, but snapped it shut again under Galna's piercing gaze.

"Yes, your Highness," the nurse answered, as if nothing at all were wrong. "Come and sit down. I've kept it warm for you."

Patsy fixed her attention on her plate and managed to choke down the remaining mouthfuls of dessert, but, out of the corner of her eye, she could still see Condin sitting near her, eating slowly. She did not want to see him, or to understand what he might be feeling. An unreasonable anger surged within her that anyone so hateful could at the same time

29

be so pathetic. As Galna at last cleared the dishes away, she said to Condin, "Her Majesty will be here shortly. I would advise you to go and change your clothes."

"Yes Ma'am, he replied meekly, rising from the table. "Thank you."

She smiled sympathetically and gave his shoulders a squeeze. "Don't forget to wash your face," Patsy heard her whisper as she escorted him to the door.

The others got up and went over to the fireplace, where a crackling blaze dispelled the evening chill. Rilya plopped herself down on a cushion by the hearth and muttered in disgust, "Look at him, putting on as if it were our fault." Patsy nodded emphatically in reply, although somehow the remark seemed rather unfair. Seating herself next to Rilya, she thoughtfully smoothed the folds of her precious new dress. Rilya smiled fondly. "You look well in it," she commented.

"Thank you," replied Patsy, shyly returning the smile.

For awhile they gazed into the flames, saying nothing. Suddenly Landon, who had not spoken all evening, yawned noisily and said, "I wish Mother would hurry up and come."

Patsy's heart leapt. "Your mother is coming? When?" she cried.

"Why, any time now," answered Rilya. "That's what Galna meant when she told Condin to go quickly and change."

"Oh," said Patsy, "I didn't understand. Oh, I'm so glad!"

"Mother comes almost every night," Landon told her. "She blesses us with the protection of Dol, so that the darkness won't hurt us. But I'm not afraid of the dark anyway," he added, "even if she doesn't come." The girls smiled, knowing from the tone of his voice that just the opposite was true.

Condin returned shortly after but did not dare to join them at the fire. Instead, after some hesitation, he wandered over to the window and, throwing aside the heavy brocaded curtains, moodily scanned the stars. Tension crackled in the air, more loudly than the logs in the hearth.

Then the door opened again, so quietly that they almost did not notice, and the Queen stood among them, unannounced and unattended. Her presence filled the room with light and warmth, as if she herself were a fire. "Mother!" cried Landon, and, running, he flung himself into her arms.

"Well!" she laughed as she gently disengaged herself. "Would that the Queen were this welcome to all her subjects." She caressed each of her children in turn with a tranquil gaze; then she knew.

"My children," she said with a kind of immense sadness, "you have been quarrelling again." Patsy turned away in confusion, unable to bear the pain of her reproach. Rilya hid her face in her hands and tears flooded Landon's round eyes. Even Condin could not meet his mother's gaze, but bowed his head in shame. "Royal children of the Silver Hair…" Her voice was low and gentle, yet Patsy would have almost preferred her father's angry shouting. ".. You are destined to bear the enchantment of Dol, and do you not yet understand? The enemy we are striving against is not the darkness of night, nor even the armies of the North. No, my children, the great enemy is within, in selfishness, suspicion and jealousy. You have learned that the enchantment will not make you good. Instead, you must become wise and good, so that you can use its powers in the service of our people. And if you turn to evil, these same powers will become weapons of horror for our destruction. All will be lost, and you yourselves will likewise be destroyed." Her voice trembled slightly. "Your Father knew this well…"

She paused for a deep breath, then, with a sudden effort, shook herself loose from the grip of sadness. "Oh, enough of this! Come, let me bless you." Immediately, Landon bounced forward to kneel at her feet, and joy once more lit her face as she tousled his silvery curls and cupped his head in her strong young hands. "May the light of Dol protect you, my son, from the terror of darkness and give you sound sleep," she intoned solemnly.

"May it truly be so," he answered, seizing her hand and kissing it.

"Rilya, my daughter." Her voice was tender and forgiving. Rilya came forward slowly.

"I'm sorry, Mother," she whispered as she knelt. Her cheeks were wet with tears. The Queen embraced her, wiping the girl's face with a fold of her gown.

"May Dol see in you compassion and understanding, and so find you worthy of his favor."

"May it truly be so." Rilya also kissed her Mother's hand, then retired.

"Condin." Her eyes searched his face in vain for some sign of warmth or contrition. He hesitated, then came forward reluctantly and knelt, not daring to look up. "Condin, my son." Her voice was pleading now, as she clasped his shoulders and bowed low over his silver head. Still he did not raise his eyes, but held himself still and unresponsive. "Oh, my son, may Dol rescue you from the powers of darkness and bring you safely into the light of peace."

"May it be so," he replied tonelessly. At last he lifted his eyes to hers; they were dry, dull, aching with misery. "May it truly be so," he repeated. Then abruptly he rose and returned to his place, without kissing her hand.

All this while Patsy had been edging further and further away from the group. She felt lonely and out of place in this family conversation which did not concern her. Even so, she could not help overhearing, and what she heard made her still more uneasy. All of them, including the Queen, seemed to take the matter of Dol and his enchantment seriously. If even she really believed it, Patsy concluded, maybe it was true after all. At the thought, a queasy little knot of fear bounced up and down in her stomach. But mingled with the fear was also a certain embarrassment. From her earliest years, she had heard religious dogma and ceremonies ridiculed, until the attitude had become deeply ingrained. Besides, she was not yet sure that she really believed in the Jesus whose cross she wore; and she was quite sure that she did not believe in Dol, whoever he was supposed to be. Still, Patsy could not help wishing that she were somehow part of that intimate family circle, and not alone outside.

"My Lady Palissa." The low, musical voice startled her out of her reverie and, once more, sent chills down her spine.

"Yes, Ma'am?"

"My Lady, we have treated you shamefully, affronting you with our ill behavior and now turning our backs on you in neglect. Please accept our apologies."

"Why, I…" Patsy stammered and blushed with confusion.

"Will you not come and join us?" The Queen extended a friendly hand.

Patsy's heart did a somersault of joy. She leaped forward so eagerly to take the proffered hand that she tripped on her long skirts and nearly went sprawling. The Queen caught her up with a laugh and gave her a quick reassuring hug that made her laugh too, though somewhat breathlessly.

"Oh, Mother, bless her too!" Landon exclaimed.

"Oh, yes, Mother, why don't you?" added Rilya, obviously delighted with the idea. Patsy scarcely heard or understood the suggestion, so carried away was she by her sudden proximity to the great Lady.

The Queen looked down at her with gay amusement. "Yes, perhaps Dol will bear her up and steady her footsteps lest she fall."

This Patsy did understand and her temper flared. Cheeks blazing, she was ready to blurt out a rude refusal, when the Queen checked her with a contrite gesture and a tiny, puzzled frown. "O, little one, we did not mean to offend you. Again, I am sorry. But I do not understand. Although Dol is not your god, still…" Pausing, she lifted up Patsy's silvery cross in the palm of her hand and contemplated it for a moment. Patsy stood quietly, waiting. She was ashamed of her temper, yet suspicious and not wholly mollified. No, they were not mocking her; they were far too kind. But she would not, could not, kneel and be blessed in the name of someone else's god!

Finally, the Queen turned her gaze from the crucifix to Patsy and once again drew her into the tranquil depths where all suspicions and hatreds were swallowed up in light. The child could not comprehend what she read therein, nor even give a name to the love and joy that overwhelmed her. She felt the Lady's hand upon her head and heard the Lady's words low in her ears. "Very well, little one. May your own God, the great One who sent you, himself bless you and strengthen you and give you courage for your mission." Then, before Patsy could even stammer a reply, the Queen raised her head and looked round at them all. "Good night, my children," she said quietly.

"Good night, Mother," cried Landon. The other two joined him in chorus as the door opened and shut. She was gone.

Patsy blinked, open-mouthed, half-afraid that the Lady had vanished into thin air. But the others seemed not in the least perturbed by her sudden departure. Instead, Rilya went immediately to her brother and took his hand. "Condin," she said firmly, "I'm sorry. Please forgive me."

Profound surprise flooded Condin's face, but he managed a small, twisted smile and a stiff nod that signified both acknowledgment and mutual contrition. Pulling free from her hand, he turned almost shyly to Landon. But the little boy was already at the door, bouncing up and down with impatience.

"Come on, Condin, hurry up or we'll be late for bed! I'll race you up the stairs!"

"Oh, will you?" Condin broke into a wide grin. "I'll whack you with a pillow if you beat me!" With that he flung the door open and the two of them pounded out, the clatter of their boots and the melody of their laughter dying away into echoes as they ran.

Patsy climbed into bed that night armed with a grim determination to try and understand what was happening to her. Was it only than morning that she had run to school in the rain? Where was she now? And what sort of people were

35

these, with their strange gods and stranger enchantments? But the goose-down pillow was so soft under her head and the embroidered coverlets so light against her body and Galna's glass of warm milk so satisfying in her stomach, that, mercifully, she slept.

CHAPTER 6
AN EQUESTRIAN INTERLUDE

Next morning during breakfast, Galna announced that, since Sir Pandil was still under the weather, it had been arranged for them to take their guest riding in the fields by the river. "Hooray!" whooped Landon, banging his fork on the table. "Galna, you're wonderful!" Blithely ignoring her frown, he turned to Patsy. "I'm so glad you're here, Lady Palissa. Now we don't have to suffer Old Wirebeard." Patsy giggled in spite of herself and Condin also chuckled at the innocent effrontery.

But Galna was not amused. "Turn around and eat your breakfast like a gentleman!" she snapped. "Sir Pandil will be about this afternoon and then you will make up for lost time." Her voice was threatening, but seeing their downcast faces, she relented with a twinkle. "But meanwhile, you will have His Highness Prince Rendil to keep you company on your outing."

"Oh!" It was Rilya's turn to gasp with delight. "Come on, let's hurry and finish, so we don't keep him waiting!" She and Landon dove into their breakfast with renewed gusto, while Patsy followed suit. Only Condin looked unhappy at the prospect of spending the morning with his elder brother. He finished his meal in sour silence and, rising abruptly from the table, left without waiting for Landon. Rilya sighed wearily at his departure and gave a helpless shrug of her shoulders.

But Patsy was too occupied with her own difficulties to be very sympathetic, for it had suddenly occurred to her that "riding" meant "horseback riding" and she had never ridden on a horse's back in her life. Her fears were confirmed when Rilya and Galna hauled her off to the wardrobe and began outfitting her in soft leather culottes and matching jacket and knee-high boots with thick heels. To her dismay, Rilya was so filled with anticipation of the morning's activities that she chattered on incessantly and Patsy could not find the opportunity, much less the courage, to admit her problem. So she nodded and laughed and let the other girl's enthusiasm catch fire in her until she nearly forgot that she could not really share it.

However, when they arrived, breathless, at the stables and found Landon and Condin already mounted and waiting impatiently, the depth of her predicament became painfully clear. Landon spotted them first. "Here they come," he cried, trotting out to meet them. "Hurry up, you turtles, or the morning will be over before we even leave the grounds."

"We had to find proper clothing for Lady Palissa," Rilya rejoined with a prim toss of her head. "Where is Rendil?" she added as Condin rode up. She stroked the nose of his chestnut gelding and kissed it fondly.

"Rendil is in the stables," he answered, "arranging for your horses. In fact, I see him now. He has obtained one of the finest mares for our guest." Patsy gulped when she heard this and turned to look where he was pointing.

The young prince was striding swiftly toward them, his purple cloak streaming out in the breeze. "Fair ladies, good morning!" he hailed them from a distance and stopped to make a playful little bow. Rilya giggled and curtsied, but Patsy contented herself with trying to force a nervous smile. "I trust you are hale and fresh and ready to chase the winds," he continued gaily. "And for you, Lady Palissa, we have the finest horse in all Arendolin, saving only the Queen's." He gestured toward a slender, snow-white mare being led out by one of the grooms.

It was now or never. Patsy closed her eyes, took a deep breath, and blurted out, "But I don't know how to ride."

Her announcement was greeted with a moment of shocked silence. Then Landon exploded. "You don't know how to ride! Oh, no! That means we'll have to take a carriage. You can't do anything in a carriage!"

"Will you keep quiet!" Condin turned on him furiously.

"But I...Oh gumfiddles!" He kicked his pony in despair and the poor animal bucked, running off across the corral and leaving his rider in the dust.

"You deserved it," said Rilya vindictively. She threw a reassuring arm around Patsy's shoulders. "Never mind. You can ride pillion with me. Can't she, Rendil?" She looked beseechingly at her older brother. "It wouldn't be too much for Stala the White if we rode her together, would it?"

Rendil knit his brow in thought for a moment, then smiled fondly at his young sister. "No, the noble beast would bear ten of you and feel no strain. But I have another idea. You may ride Stala alone if you wish. Lady Palissa," he bowed to her with utmost courtesy, "would you do me the honor of riding before me on my own mount?"

Patsy was struggling so desperately to keep back her tears that she did not understand his question, but she sensed that he expected some sort of reply. She raised her eyes to his and found that they were warm and clear and dark, so like his mother's that she was moved to a shaky "Yes."

"Oh, how wonderful!" Rilya hugged her impulsively. "Thank you, Rendil, thank you." She hugged him also, to his amusement, then ran to where the coveted mare stood waiting. Patsy watched in stinging envy as she leaped into the saddle and the groom adjusted the stirrups.

"My Lady, are you ready?" Patsy started and looked at Rendil stupidly. Another groom had handed him the reins of a magnificent black charger, fleet of foot yet tall and powerful. "You have only to place your foot in the stirrup, so," he indicated patiently, ignoring her confusion, "and when I lift you up, grasp the pommel and swing yourself into the saddle." She did as he instructed, too frightened to protest. In a twinkling, his strong hands seized her waist and propelled her high onto the horse's back. She bit her lip and gripped the pommel for dear life, but within seconds he too was up and settling in behind her. "Ho, Fendal," he cried, "we're off!" Fendal lifted his proud head in response and trotted out of the corral, with the other horses following him.

Patsy gasped and screwed her eyes shut against the still burning tears. She was terrified of the horse's height and the speed at which they were moving. But a few moments later she flung them open again in surprise as the thud of horses' hooves on dirt became the ring of horses' hooves on stone. They had passed around the west side of the castle and were now crossing the great paved court in front of its main entrance. The first sight, which focused in her blurred vision, was that of an ancient yet majestic tree with leaves of blazing orange, full formed like tongues of fire. It stood alone in the center of the courtyard, encircled with a low fence of unhewn, translucent rock. "That is the Gelfin Tree," said Rendil, reading her unspoken astonishment. "Its leaves never wither or fade and it has stood sentinel over our land for many a generation."

They passed it in reverent silence and, slowing to a walk, approached the gateway of the fortress. There they halted, while a string of heavy-laden supply carts passed through ahead of them, amid a great din of whips cracking and mule drivers shouting. "They are carrying provisions to our troops on the northern border," explained Condin, who had reined in next to them. "And Lord Gendol himself is leaving tomorrow for the North, is he not?" he asked with a sidelong glance at Rendil. Patsy felt her escort stiffen behind her and wondered why he did not answer.

Finally, the last cart creaked and jolted through, followed by a small band of cavalrymen, and the children themselves drew up to the gate. The guards stood to attention and saluted as they rode by, under the massive stone arch and forth onto the drawbridge. Patsy caught her breath in fear, lest the thick wooden planks give way and they plummet into the moat. But soon they had crossed in safety, and turning away from the city which spread southward and east, they struck out for the meadows sloping away upriver toward the hills.

Once free of the road, they broke into a gentle canter and Patsy began to relax. The rhythm of the horse beneath her, the reassuring presence of Rendil behind her, the coolness of the breeze on her cheeks soothed her battered feelings and restored her wounded self-esteem. After awhile, Landon raced on ahead, bound for the woods near the river. "Hey-y-y!" he called back to them from the thicket's edge, "Come and see. Swans!"

Instantly, Rilya was off, the great white Stala bearing her forward with lightning speed. "Wait!" cried Condin.

"You'll frighten them away!" But he urged his mount in swift pursuit. Patsy, caught up in the excitement, waited eagerly for Rendil to follow them. When, instead, he slowed Fendal to a walk, she twisted around impatiently to see what was wrong.

To her surprise, she found him gazing moodily off into the distance, his face creased in an anxious frown. Turning back to follow his line of vision, she spied the supply train, a tiny line against the horizon, lumbering steadily northward. Patsy remembered Condin's earlier remark and her curiosity was piqued. She made up her mind to ask. "Is Lord Gendol really leaving tomorrow for the northern border?"

Rendil was startled out of his reverie. "I beg your pardon?"

"Rilya said there was a terrible battle on the northern border and your father was killed. Is that where Lord Gendol is going?"

He gave a short, bitter laugh. "Yes, he will join his army there."

"Why?" She was determined to pursue the subject. "Will there be another battle?"

"Yes." He heaved a great sigh. "In very truth, unless the gods prevent it, there will be another battle, and Dol only knows what will be the outcome."

"Do you mean we might be killed?" Patsy felt a sudden chill.

Rendil looked at her as if trying to make up his mind about something. Then he took a deep breath and said, "Allow me to explain. Our enemies who dwell in the mountains of the north have long been in league with the Dark One to overthrow us. Many ages ago, one of our royal grandsires, strong with the enchantment of Dol, dealt them such a severe blow in battle that, since then, we have lived on our land in peace. But, three winters ago, it was revealed in prophecy to our own Royal Father that the mountain dwellers had gained such power through evil enchantments that soon they would again make bold to attack us. Father was also shown a sign, the possession of which would guarantee victory for the forces of Arendolin.

"Immediately he set off in quest for the sign and, except for brief intervals, was absent from court for most of that span of seasons and the next, while our Lady Mother and Lord Gendol ruled the Kingdom in his stead. Finally, last summer, the summons to battle came, and, with the sign still unfound, our armies rode forth. The contest was fought to a standstill and the forces of light emerged, if not victorious, at least undefeated. But the inconceivable had happened. In the course of the struggle, our Royal Father, the invulnerable King, Enchanted of Dol, was killed and his enchantment dispersed."

"But how?" Patsy interrupted. "Rilya said he couldn't be killed. She said you knew what happened."

Rendil shook his head slowly and looked off into the distance. The supply train had disappeared over the brow of a hill. "No," he said, "I know only what Lord Gendol told us, namely that Father was leading the charge with his customary valor and audacity, when suddenly he drew up his horse, wheeled around and shouted, 'Fall back, fall back! It is a trap!' The troops, accustomed to implicit obedience, turned at once and retreated. By the time Lord Gendol had rallied them, Father had been overwhelmed and slain." He paused and Patsy saw him bite his lip to hold back the tears.

"Then he saved the rest of the army from being killed, didn't he?"

"Yes, but how or why did that constitute a betrayal of his enchantment?" He made a helpless gesture and hung his head in silence.

Patsy glanced across the fields toward where the two boys had dismounted and were thrashing about in the brush while Rilya watched from the vantage point of Stala's back. She felt acutely uncomfortable and wished that she could join them. Suddenly, Rendil spoke again, this time his voice strained with bitterness. "Mother will not allow me to accompany Lord Gendol. It is my duty to recover the lost enchantment and avenge our Father's death and she will not so much as permit me to leave the fortress!" He clenched his fist angrily. "As if I were a child and not a man! How can she hope that Gendol will vanquish the enemy without the enchantment and without the sign?"

His mention of the sign rekindled Patsy's interest. "What was the sign anyway?" she asked. "I don't think you ever said."

"The sign?" He looked at her with a strange, almost greedy, expression. "Yes, the sign. Father described it to me once only, but I have not forgotten: Two beams of silver, one upright, the other transverse. They hung suspended beneath a cloud of fire, like the leaves of the Gelfin Tree. And the words graven upon them were: In this sign you shall conquer."

Chapter 7

Night of the Full Moon

Patsy's heart stopped. For the space of two pulse-beats there flashed before her mind the gray hair and gold-rimmed spectacles of her beloved Mrs. Denton and the small silver cross in her hand. She heard her firm, quiet voice amidst the children's shouts and laughter: "In this sign you shall conquer." Abruptly, Patsy felt her heart begin pounding again. She shuddered, as a wave of dizziness and nausea passed through her; then she looked helplessly at Rendil. He was staring at her with the same strange, piercing expression as before.

"That's…" She choked, swallowed, and tried again. "That's my cross." Her hand closed over it protectively. "I mean, your sign is my cross. It's…"

"Yes," he said, too quietly. "So I thought. And so, I suspect, our Lady Mother thinks. I must confer with her!" He stirred with sudden animation. "Come, let us be off! There is not a moment to lose."

"Wait!" cried Patsy, gripping his arm in panic as he jerked sharply on the reins. "What about the others?" Casting about wildly, she saw, to her relief, Rilya cantering in their direction and gesturing reproachfully.

"Oh!" Rendil swallowed an expression of impatience, then thought better of it. "No, you are quite right. You need not come now. Join the others for today, at least." He held Fendal in check and watched tensely as she approached.

"...so long. We've been waiting and waiting for you." Rilya's words floated ahead of her on the breeze. "What's wrong? Has something happened?" Her tone changed to one of alarm as she drew near enough to notice the strain in their faces.

"No," answered Rendil. "It is quite all right. But I find that I must return to the castle immediately. I think you will not mind taking Lady Palissa on with you?"

"Of course not. But, can't you stay with us," Rilya wailed, "just a little while? I was looking forward to it so!"

"I am sorry," he said grimly as he dismounted. "This cannot be postponed." He gestured to Patsy. "You will have to get down." Numbly she complied, wincing as he caught her and, with almost the same movement, heaved her up behind Rilya onto Stala's back. Then he remounted and paused to look at the two stricken faces. "I am sorry," he repeated more gently. "Do have a pleasant day." He hesitated as if to say more, but changed his mind and, turning Fendal's head, galloped off in the direction of Celdondol.

Patsy most emphatically did not have a pleasant day. She was badly shaken by the unexpected discovery of her cross's significance and even more upset by Rendil's hasty departure. Although she did join the others, she could not share in their laughter and play, and eventually wandered off by herself. At first, Rilya had plied her with questions, but seeing that she could extract no satisfactory explanation from her, had soon given up. Patsy's obvious state of distraction put such a damper on everyone's spirits that as soon as they had downed Galna's picnic lunch, which she scarcely touched, they mounted their horses and rode for home.

That afternoon, true to Galna's prediction, Sir Pandil, the crusty old tutor, was well enough to give lessons. He announced his subject as "the cultural development of Arendolin during the reign of Rendol Hagendil the Fourth," and launched into what proved to be an interminable lecture. For awhile, Patsy was so fascinated with the stiff gray beard which thrust itself out from his wizened little face, that she actually found herself listening to him. But, as his voice droned on and on in a meaningless hodge-podge of names and places, her mind slipped back into its mood of churning perplexity. What would happen to her now? Perhaps they would force her to ride into battle at the head of their armies. Or maybe they would take from her the cross, which had begun, little by little, to be so precious to her. And where was Rendil? She wondered what had passed between him and his mother. Would the Queen let him go with Lord Gendol now? Why didn't they at least come and tell her their plans?

Through the open window she could hear the clatter of horses' hooves, the rattle of carriage wheels, the sound of men and women calling to one another. The nobles and their ladies, Condin had explained earlier, were gathering for a farewell banquet to be held that evening in the Great Hall of the castle. The Queen would preside from her throne on the dais and, he added in tones of genuine envy, Rendil would be there also, seated on her right. Patsy remembered now and reflected grimly that that was why they had not sent for her: they were busy getting ready for the banquet. But the thought of hanging in suspense until the next day nearly made her ill. Then she recalled what else Condin had told her: that when the feasting ended, Lord Gendol would spend the night in solemn vigil beneath the Gelfin Tree. "It is the night of the full moon and he must beg the blessing of Dol upon his great and noble mission."

The blessing of Dol! But did not the Queen bestow the blessing of Dol? Patsy had nearly forgotten the events of the previous evening. "Surely, if she's going to give him a blessing, she'll come afterwards and give us one too. Then I can ask her what they intend to do with me." This thought so buoyed up her spirits that she willingly endured the rest of Old Wirebeard's lecture and later downed a hearty supper.

After supper, they relaxed before the fire and chatted gaily, the other children picturing for Patsy the silver tiara with its single star sapphire which would adorn their mother's brow, as well as the silks and velvets, gold and jewels worn by the nobles and their ladies, and also the appointments of the Great Hall and the courses that were generally served at a banquet of this sort. She drank it in open-mouthed, scarcely able to imagine such magnificence as they described. But as the evening wore on and the Queen did not appear, she became more and more restless and impatient. Finally, when Galna pronounce it bedtime, she could contain herself no longer. "But your mother hasn't come yet!" she wailed. "Aren't we going to wait up for her blessing?"

Rilya looked at her with astonishment. "Don't you realize? She won't be coming tonight. She and Rendil are at the banquet and they certainly will not leave until late." Seeing her friend's grief and disappointment, she added reassuringly, "Never mind, tonight is the night of the full moon, when the enchantment is strongest. No harm will come to you tonight. Besides, we must get to sleep early, because we'll be expected to attend the departure ceremonies, tomorrow at dawn." Too crushed to protest further, Patsy obeyed, dragging herself to bed in a state of bitter loneliness and dread. Rendil had not returned, the Queen had not bestowed her blessing, she, Patsy, was tired, tired of it all, and yet she had to sleep because tomorrow at dawn the whole nightmare would begin anew.

In spite of her weariness, she lay for a long time wide-eyed in the dark, staring sightless at the bed canopy overhead, with the bed curtains drawn close around as if to afford herself at least some security, however external. Her mind, too, lay exhausted and still, until, after what seemed hours, a new thought struck her. Home! She sat bolt upright under the impetus of the idea. She would give them her cross, if that's what they wanted, and then she would go home! Her hand gripped the silver form in a moment of fierce possessiveness, then loosened again, hesitantly. No, they could have it; she was going home. Now. Tonight.

What time was it? She flung aside the bed curtains and blinked with surprise at the sight that met her eyes. Night of the full moon, indeed! It poised, flawless and free in the deep midnight sky, shedding its radiance over everything, suffusing the room with silver light, beckoning to Patsy through the wide open window. She stared for awhile in utter fascination, then tore her gaze away and shivered. Why had they left the window open on such a chilly spring night? Remembering Lord Gendol, she pitied him.

But she had a purpose and could not tarry for long. She had to find the Queen, give her the cross, and leave this place at once. Cocking her head, she listened intently but could hear nothing except peaceful night stillness. "The banquet must be over," she thought, "and the people gone home. That means the Queen will be in her rooms – if I can find them." Setting her face with determination, she climbed out of bed.

Cold stabbed through her bare feet as they hit the stone floor, but she left her fur-lined slippers lying there, for fear that they would scuff too loudly as she walked. Instead, she wrapped herself in a woolen robe and started out.

In the other bed, Rilya slept peacefully, the curtains drawn aside so that the moon shone full upon her. A shaft of light played in her hair, silver with silver. Patsy smiled as she tiptoed by. "I wish I could take her with me," she thought with regret. But she did not pause, padding on into the living quarters, where Galna snored gently on her cot by the fireplace. She picked her way with care, grateful that the moon afforded her enough light to avoid bumping into things. At last she reached the door and tried to open it. To her dismay, the old hinges creaked and Galna heard the noise. She stirred in her sleep and murmured incoherently, while Patsy shrank against the wall with pounding heart. However, she soon fell back to snoring and Patsy, with a sigh of relief, gathered enough courage to try the door again.

This time it opened far enough for her to squeeze through; wisely, she did not attempt to close it again. The stairs presented her with quite a different challenge. Except for a single torch flickering dimly, far, far down, they were completely dark. Patsy, accustomed by now to the brilliant moonlight, strained to see ahead into the abyss, but could not make out even the first step. By groping along the wall with her hands and the floor with her feet, she managed to find it and, taking a deep breath, began the perilous descent.

Slowly, carefully, step-by-step, she felt her way down. After what seemed an eternity of groping, when her feet were already numb with cold, she missed a step, and plunged headlong into darkness. She did not fall far, because it was the last step before the second floor landing, but she was bruised and badly shaken, and lay for a long time trembling on the rough stone floor. At last she found the strength to pull herself up and look around. It was lighter here; she could see the steps before her now as she started down the last flight. The torch at the tower entrance cast long shadows up the walls to meet her. She stared wildly at the eerie, dancing shapes and wondered if the old castle had any ghosts. Once or twice she stopped to listen but she could hear nothing.

Just a few more steps and it was over; she had reached the bottom. The arched tower entrance yawned before her, the torch flared harmlessly above her head. She glanced back up the way she had come and shivered violently, trying not to dwell on how she would return. "Maybe I won't have to," she thought, and the thought cheered her. Resolutely, she turned and plunged through the open door.

Suddenly, a huge shape loomed up at her side out of the darkness. Patsy screamed and hid her face in terror. For a long moment it seemed as if the world had come to an end and she would be eaten alive. Then a burly voice materialized out of the shape: "Say, little lady, where do you think you're going at this time of night?" The guard! How could she have forgotten? Half a dozen times at least she had passed him at his post and had even stopped to admire his scarlet cloak and gray tunic and his shining silver breastplate. Now she heaved a tremulous sigh of relief and uncovered her face to look at him. "Well?" he growled, pulling back the slide of his lantern and holding it up to her.

She blinked in its circular glare. "Please sir, I…I want to see the Queen." She squared her shoulders, stood to her full height and repeated her request. "I want to see the Queen."

"You want to see the Queen, eh? Well, little lady, you'll have to wait until morning for that. No one sees the Queen in the middle of the night."

"Please, sir," she began pleading now, "it's…it's important. It's about the sign and…and all. And I can't go back up those stairs again!" she nearly wailed.

The sentry was long accustomed to the ways of royal children but he had never met one like this. He gazed at her reflectively in the lantern glow: the tousled mop of orange curls, the pale, earnest face, all eyes and freckles, the slender, be-robed body, the bare feet. "You're that newcomer, aren't you?" he asked, "the one they seem to think is so special."

"Yes, sir. Please, sir," she summoned her most grown-up manner and vocabulary, "my mission is urgent. I must have an audience with the Queen. At once."

"Well…" he growled, "I'll probably be disciplined for this, but never mind. Come on, lass, I'll take you to the Queen."

"Oh, thank you!" She could have hugged him for sheer gratitude. He set off immediately, with her running behind to keep pace with his giant strides. She had stubbed her bare toes twice before they reached another sentry standing guard before the closed door of the Queen's private chambers.

"Who goes there," he rapped out in a clipped undertone.

"Radin from the northeast tower," answered the first guard, also in an undertone. "I have this kid with me…what's your name?"

"Pat…no, Palissa, Lady Palissa."

52

"…Lady Palissa, who wants to see Her Majesty on urgent business."

"At this time of night? You're out of your mind!"

"That's what I told her, but she insists. Listen…" he lowered his voice to conspiratorial whisper, "she says it has something to do with the Sign. Maybe Her Majesty will need to know before Gendol rides in the morning."

"Well," the clipped undertone responded, "I still think you're crazy, but let's see what Lady Calya says about it."

"Oh, no," Radin moaned, "that sharp-tongued shrew? You won't get anywhere with her. Too bad it's her turn to wait on the Queen."

"Shh," the other cautioned. "She's Lord Gendol's favorite niece and twelfth in line to the throne." He knocked softly on the door. After a breathless moment of silence and no response, he knocked again. Again, silence and no response. Patsy was beginning to despair when, suddenly, the door opened and a sleepy-eyed but indignant lady-in-waiting thrust her head out.

"What do you want?" she demanded, not bothering to whisper.

Radin snapped to attention. "The Lady Palissa desires audience with Her Majesty on urgent business."

"What? What do you mean, coming at this hour with such a request? Who is this Lady Palissa who would dare to disturb Her Majesty in the middle of the night?" The two guards stepped aside and motioned Patsy to come forward and speak for herself. But she only shrank backward, cowed by the woman's haughty manner. Lady Calya peered at her owlishly in the lantern light, then laughed with scorn. "You fools! This is no lady. This is just some peasant brat the children dragged in the other day from Dol-knows-where. They're amusing themselves by dressing her up and pretending she is a royal visitor from some strange land. Send her back to bed. Hurry up, before the Queen awakens and finds her here."

"Begging your pardon, my lady," Radin rejoined, "but she says her request has to do with the Sign."

"The Sign? Oh, yes," she smiled an infuriating smile, "I know all about that, too. Uncle Gendol says it is a lot of nonsense. But why waste any more time? Good night." With that she withdrew her head and shut the door firmly.

The two guards looked at one another and then at Patsy who was struggling in the throes of rage and humiliation. "Sorry, lass," said Radin, not unkindly, "but you heard the lady. You just go on back to bed now and try again in the morning."

Patsy nodded dumbly, too overcome to respond, and turned back into the darkness, without any idea of her direction. But she had barely trudged four steps when she heard the door open again and a familiar low voice filled the corridor with its music. "I was not asleep, good captains. You may send the child in."

CHAPTER 8
COLLOQUY BY MOONLIGHT

Patsy could not believe her ears. She whirled around and stared hard at the slender, white-gowned figure in the doorway. It was no illusion; yet when it disappeared into the room beyond, she fairly flew in pursuit of it, past the two guards, whose stiff military posture but ill-concealed their grins of pleasure, and past the Lady Calya whose deep curtsy well concealed whatever emotion she might have felt. The figure paused at the entrance to the inner chamber, silhouetted against the radiant moonlight within. "My Lady Calya."

"Yes, Your Majesty."

"You may close the door behind us."

"Yes, Your Majesty."

Once again the figure disappeared and Patsy stumbled after her in haste. Unexpectedly, a thick, warm carpet embraced her feet, drawing her to a halt. She blinked and looked about in bewilderment. Then her eyes focussed and she saw the Queen standing at the far end of the room by the window, gazing outward at the living, vibrant sky. She lingered there for a moment before turning around and beckoning to the little girl. "Come here, my child, and tell me: what is it that you want?"

Now that her quest was accomplished and she stood face to face with the Queen, Patsy suddenly felt overwhelmed with shame and reluctance. Summoning all her strength, she managed to blurt out, "I...I want to go home!" Then she did the one thing she had least wanted to do. She burst into tears.

Instantly, the Queen stepped forward, put out her arms and drew her to herself, clasping her to her bosom with words of tenderness and comfort. For a long time Patsy sobbed uncontrollably, until the pent-up tension and fear of the past two days had all poured out of her. Eventually, her tears subsided into loud, intermittent snuffling, and she stood back on her own feet, fumbling in her pocket for a handkerchief. The Queen gravely offered her a square of silk and lace which she took and used to blow her nose and wipe her eyes.

Then, as if the conversation had not been interrupted at all, the Queen asked, "And why do you wish to go home?"

"Because," she gulped, "because Rendil says my cross is your sign and there's going to be a battle and you can't win the battle without the sign and I don't want to be in any battle." She gasped for breath. "So you can take the cross if you want it but please let me go home."

"But my dear child," the Queen smiled with amused compassion as she sat down on the edge of the bed, "neither you nor Prince Rendil will be riding forth to battle."

"No?"

"No, and furthermore, I do not have the power with which to send you home."

"Oh." Patsy felt completely deflated; she did not know whether to be disappointed or relieved.

The Queen's smile played on her lips then reposed in gravity. "You see, I did not bring you here, nor did my god, but Another has sent you and you may not return until he allows you to do so."

"Oh." Now Patsy felt trapped and began unconsciously looking over her shoulder toward the door, as if to find some way out of her predicament.

"You have been given a great mission, little one, and you are free to accept or refuse it. Do you understand this?"

"No, Ma'am. If I'm free to refuse, then why didn't God ask me before he sent me here? Or at least tell me what I was supposed to do when I got here?"

"That is in his own wise counsel. But now that you are here, you must realize that you are free to cooperate or not. You may relinquish the Sign and then withdraw into yourself, leaving us to puzzle out its meaning and use, or you may bear in your own hands what has been entrusted to you and help us to wield it by your knowledge and strength."

"I…I can't; I don't know anything about the Cross; I can't even remember what Mrs. Denton told me." Patsy nearly began to sob again in rebellion and frustration.

"You know nothing about the Sign?" The Queen's countenance betrayed her astonishment. "But this is indeed strange, that the gods should send so small a child on so vast an errand and give her no knowledge whatever, even of themselves!" She stretched out her hands toward Patsy. "May I see your cross?"

Patsy removed the crucifix from around her neck and held it out to the Queen, who took it and raised it up by its chain to the moonlight. The silver form swung gently between light and shadow as if it were something alive. Together they gazed at it, until the silence grew still and deep. Then the Queen spoke, her voice like the whisper of leaves in a midnight wind. "It has been revealed to me by the power of Dol that this is the image of the Great One."

Patsy chilled and shivered with unaccountable terror. Then her mind cleared and she remembered. "He died to save all people," she declared loudly, starting at the sound of her own voice.

"He died? But how is it that a god can die?"

"I don't know, Ma'am. That's what Mrs. Denton said. My Dad told me there isn't any God, but I guess I'd rather believe you and Mrs. Denton."

"Who is Mrs. Denton?"

"Mrs. Denton is my teacher. She gave me the cross; it was hers. When I asked her what it meant, she said that Jesus died to save all people, that he came back to life again, and that by his power all evil would be destroyed."

"I see." The Queen fell silent as her gaze turned, not to the cross, but inward, to some invisible realm of vision and peace. The silence grew, louder and louder, until Patsy's very being throbbed with it and her head began to reel.

Then the Queen spoke again with accents of quiet solemnity. "Mighty indeed is the Great One, beyond all other gods, that he should become human and die in order to save all people from the evil that enslaves them."

"He did it because he cared," Patsy blurted. She was surprised at her own conclusion, but hastened on anyway. "Daddy says if there is a God, he doesn't care about the world, but Daddy's wrong. Maybe nobody ever told him about Jesus."

"Perhaps not. For surely this is a deed of love, and of such love as I have never before heard or imagined." The Queen's voice lightened with affectionate wonder. "Your elders have told you many strange and conflicting tales, little one. Have they ever told you that love is far more powerful than any enchantment?"

"No, Ma'am. Is it really? Daddy says there's no such thing as magic and that everything can be explained scientifically. Is love more powerful than science too?"

"Yes, my dear child." Laughter twinkled in the Queen's eyes, then disappeared. "You see, knowledge of the universe and its secrets is a great thing, giving people power to use nature for good or for ill. Great too is the enchantment bestowed on us by the gods, giving us a power beyond nature, to use for good or for ill. But love is the greatest power of all, for love is what moves us, love is what directs us to use those other powers for good. Even if someone had no power at all, if they had love, they would accomplish mighty deeds. I want you to remember this and think on it well. You are only a small child and truly powerless in the sight of others, but you bear on your breast the Sign of the Great One, of him who not only loves but who is Love. If you are faithful to him and cling to his love, there is nothing you will not be able to do."

"But what am I supposed to do?" Patsy burst out impatiently. "I don't understand. What am I here for? Can't you tell me"

"No, my child, it has not been revealed to me. You must wait quietly and in due time God himself will show you."

"I'm tired of waiting. And what about Rendil? Aren't you at least going to let him ride with Lord Gendol tomorrow?"

"No, I am not. He is young yet and untried. Nothing can be gained by exposing him to danger at this point."

"Oh." Again Patsy felt strangely let down, as if torn between two conflicting loyalties. Of course, the Queen was the wisest, best, most understanding grown-up she had ever met, and what she said had to be right. Why then did she feel so sorry for Rendil? She wanted to argue, to cry out that he was old enough and brave enough and that the battle was hopeless without him. Instead she bit her lip and said nothing.

The moon had all the while been sinking slowly toward the western horizon and the room was less bright than it had seemed before, but the Queen needed no exterior light in order to fathom Patsy's distress. "Child," she said gently.

"Yes, Ma'am?"

"May I explain? It is true that Prince Rendil has both a high destiny and a grave responsibility before him. He sees this and is eager to reach out and grasp what is his. I understand him well. He is noble and generous and brave like his father, but he is also impetuous and headstrong and little comprehends the magnitude of the difficulties, which lie ahead. These stem not only from his youth, for he is barely of age to rule, but also from the dispersal of the enchantment which he must recover before he can take his seat on the throne of Arendolin. He alone is able to do this; I cannot help him. But…" She paused, as if arrested by her own train of thought, and swept Patsy with a mysterious searching gaze. "But you can."

"Me?" Patsy squeaked.

"Yes. You see, one of the conditions laid down by the gods for the recovery of the King's enchantment is that only the rightful heir may claim it. No one may help him, unless he be especially appointed for the task. And now you have come…"

"But what about the battle?" Patsy interrupted nervously, still imagining herself thrust into the midst of it. "Rendil said you couldn't win without the Sign."

The Queen inclined her head gravely. "The battle is crucial, and when I invoke the blessing of Dol upon Lord Gendol in the morning, it will not be a mere formality. But I am confident that, with the help of Dol, he and his troops will be able to hold the enemy at bay, at least one more time. We have discussed the matter carefully and although I was at first inclined to let Rendil join him, he has persuaded me that this would not be wise. As for the Sign…" Here she paused again and, for the first time, it seemed to Patsy that she was genuinely troubled. "We have discussed that also," she continued slowly, "and are both agreed that a young girl has no place on the battlefield."

"Lady Calya says Lord Gendol says the Sign's a lot of nonsense," Patsy asserted.

"Yes, I am afraid that that is his opinion on the matter. His lack of credence distresses me, although I must admit that we have very little external evidence that your cross is the long-sought-for Sign. Yet, by the interior light of Dol, I know that it is and I know also that your mission is to assist my son Rendil in recovering the lost enchantment, and with it the throne of Arendolin. Are you willing to do this?"

Patsy stared at her, overwhelmed and terrified. She had sensed the coming question but had not expected it to be put so bluntly. Still, she knew in her heart of hearts that there could only be one answer, and, summoning her last ounce of courage, she gave it. "Yes, I'll…I'll try."

"Good, oh very good!" The Queen's smile burst forth with radiant beauty. "I am sure the Great One will not fail to give you the necessary strength."

Patsy breathed a huge sigh of relief, as if a mountain had been lifted from her soul. She felt so caught up in the other's gladness that, incredulously, she heard herself asking, "Ma'am, will you bless me?"

"Yes, if you so wish." The Queen grew even more radiant as she stretched forth her hands to lay them lightly on the child's head. "May the great God above all gods," she intoned, "grant you largeness of heart, keenness of mind, strength of will, peace of soul. May he protect you unfailingly and bring you safely to your home when your mission is accomplished."

"May it be so, " Patsy answered, and, for the first time that evening, she too smiled.

"Now, my child," the Queen's tone became brisk and bracing, "you must be off to bed. We have wasted half the night away with our chatter!"

"Yes, Ma'am." Patsy whirled about and trotted obediently toward the door. Then she thought of something and stopped. "Can I have a light to take with me? It's awfully dark out there."

"You may ask the guard to escort you to your quarters."

"Oh, thank you." She hesitated again. "Ma'am?"

"Yes?"

"Who is Dol?"

"He is a servant of the Great One. He will be your servant also when you need him.

"Oh. Ma'am"

"Yes?"

"May…may I kiss you?"

"Why of course!" The Queen laughed and the music of her laughter flooded the night. Patsy ran back, threw her arms around the Lady's neck and kissed her on the cheek. She felt the answering kiss fall into her tousled mop of curls, as, with a whispered "Good night," she tore herself away and pelted out the door.

CHAPTER 9
THE DEPARTURE OF GENDOL

Patsy had barely gotten to sleep when she felt herself being roughly awakened again. "My lady, my lady, get up!" Galna's voice was loud and urgent. "You must hurry or you will be late for the ceremonies!"

"Oh…" Patsy groaned. She had forgotten about the ceremonies and did not care to remember. "What time is it?"

"Nearly dawn. I overslept and did not call you. The boys are already dressed and waiting." The plump woman quivered with haste as she laid Patsy's clothes across the bed. "Please do hurry now," she pleaded.

Patsy yawned, fisted her aching eyes and looked around curiously. The drapes were drawn across the window but no moonlight shone through them. Rilya was already pulling her dress on over her head; Patsy thought she heard her mumble something through the thick folds of velvet. "Huh?"

"I said good morning sleepyhead!" Rilya's face popped out above an embroidered yoke. "I hope you're well rested."

"Well, um…" Patsy yawned again noisily and began to climb out of her nightgown. To her relief, Rilya merely grinned and continued dressing in silence. In a shorter time than seemed possible they were ready and had joined the boys on the tower stairs. Landon managed a drowsy "Good morning" but Condin merely nodded silently. He and Rilya both carried lanterns that threw out bobbing circles of light, but Patsy could not help shuddering as she recalled her adventure of a few hours earlier.

When they reached the tower entrance, they found an escort of four soldiers waiting for them. One of them was Radin and Patsy tried to catch his eye, but he took no notice of her. Indeed, everyone seemed unusually solemn. The guards moved off in quick step, with the children trotting along behind. No one spoke a word as they clattered and clanked through the halls. Patsy felt vaguely that something was different, and for awhile she could not imagine what. Then she realized. The castle was deserted! The familiar hustle and bustle of pages and courtiers, knights and common soldiers, highborn ladies and servant girls was stilled. Not a person was in sight; no sound could be heard but the echo of their footfalls as they passed.

Patsy chilled with apprehension. Maybe they were all still in bed, but then why was Lord Gendol leaving so early in the morning, with no one to see him go? She did not have much time to wonder about it, for they soon rounded a corner, walked a short distance down another corridor, and halted before two great bronze doors. Torches blazing in wall sockets high overhead illuminated the doors and cast strange patterns of light and shadow on their ornately carved panels. Grotesque yet noble figures of men and beasts seemed to leap out at them from the gleaming metal, then dart back into stillness again. The whole history of the Kingdom was depicted there in high relief, while on the center panel of each door was graven the Full Moon and Flaming Tree, ancient shield of the kings of Arendolin.

Patsy gasped in amazement, and then her stomach gave a lurch as slowly, slowly the doors began to open inward.

Rilya and Condin extinguished their lanterns and laid them aside, while the little party closed ranks, two by two, and marched through. At first as they passed, Patsy was aware only of more torches, hundreds of flaming torches, which shed a kind of muted brilliance over everything. As her eyes adjusted to the unaccustomed light, she realized that they were in an enormous hall, staggering in its proportions, its ceiling disappearing upward into blackness, its walls and floors, except for the torches, utterly bare. For a moment she felt overwhelmed by a sensation of plunging into nothingness, but the feeling died away as the soldiers did an abrupt right face, then another, and halted.

Before them on a high stone dais, approached by many steps, stood a massive throne of alabaster and silver, blood red with the reflection of the crimson hangings behind it, and burning in the glare of myriad torches. Seated on the throne, indeed filling it and the whole room with her majestic presence, was the Queen. Patsy rubbed her eyes and stared in awe. Was this the same woman, who, only a few hours before, had spoken to her with simple and motherly affection? Now she towered, an august figure in robes of midnight blue, her ebony hair swept up beneath the argent tiara upon her brow, her right hand gripping the scepter of royalty. At her side stood Rendil, tall and princely in the same deep blue. His brow was unadorned, except for the dark hairs of maturity beginning to show at his temples.

As the children and their escort halted, the Queen rose from her throne, and, gathering her robes about her, swept down the steps followed by Rendil and twelve attendants in scarlet and gray livery. Slowly they descended into the vast empty chamber with the children bringing up the rear. Patsy, stumbling along next to Rilya at the very end, tingled with excitement and fear. She yearned to ask her friend what it was all about, but Rilya frowned and shook her head before she could even speak. So, in prolonged, mysterious, and nerve-wracking silence the procession moved between endless ranks of torches, until their light and fire burned in Patsy's brain. At last, when she thought she could bear it no longer, they reached the end of the hall. Before them two other bronze doors stood already open and, from without, the welcome scent of chill night air greeted them. Abruptly, they passed through the doors and into darkness.

With the glare of the torches still in her eyes, Patsy stumbled blindly and would have fallen if Rilya had not steadied her. She felt herself being gently guided to the left and then made to stand, she knew not where. Only after what seemed ages of sightless staring did her eyes grow accustomed to the dimness and she recognized the Queen in front of her with Rendil at her right. They were on the steps before the main entrance to the castle, facing the great stone courtyard with the Gelfin Tree in its center.

Patsy turned her gaze toward the courtyard and realized, with a shiver of astonishment, that it was thronged with people. So that was where they all had gone! In the early dawn with a few pale stars still shining in splendor, she sensed rather than saw them, spread out in all directions to the very foot of the wall, waiting in silence, except for the restless pawing of a troop of horses directly in front of the gate. They waited, and the waiting grew unbearable, until the Queen raised her arms high above her head, and the ceremony began.

A blast of trumpets split the stillness into glittering fragments and the thunder of drums beat it down. Raggedly at first, then in greater unison and intensity, the people began to sing. Try as she might, Patsy could not understand the words of their song, although it rose and swelled like a mighty torrent in the clear air. Condin, Landon and Rilya joined in, even Rendil, until, out of all that vast assembly, only Patsy and the Queen were silent.

On and on the singing continued, in simple and virile strains, conjuring up hope and courage and trust. But at last, with a final long-held note of triumphant joy, the music closed and died. Again the trumpets sounded, and now the Queen stepped forward, raised her arms aloft as before, and began to chant. Her voice, clear, strong and melodious, soared into flight, carrying upon its wing words of power and prayerful invocation. Patsy thrilled to their beauty, even though the language remained the same: mysterious and incomprehensible. The prayer continued for some time, but not until it came gracefully to a conclusion, did she look away from the Queen and out toward the Gelfin Tree. Instantly her thrill died away into horror and she heard herself scream. For, with a flash of light and a rush of sound, the Gelfin Tree had burst into flame.

The crowd fell back before it with a wave of murmured awe as Patsy heard herself scream again. "Be still!" Condin turned on her fiercely.

"It's all right," Rilya whispered, putting her arms around her. "Mother has invoked the presence of Dol upon our gathering and he has manifested himself as he did when our Father first set forth."

Patsy nodded blankly, all the while staring in terror at the blazing Gelfin Tree. The figure of a lone man stood silhouetted against it and she forced herself to realize that it was Lord Gendol. To the slow, solemn beating of the drums, the murmur of the crowd welled up into another song as he advanced with deliberate pace across the courtyard and up the steps, until he stood face to face with the Queen.

Patsy wrenched her gaze away from the Tree and directed it toward Gendol. She could see him clearly now in the growing dawn light. He was dressed in the uniform of an ordinary soldier, gray tunic and leggings, silver breastplate and greaves, and long scarlet cloak caught with a silver clasp at the throat. His head was bare and the sole token of his rank was a silver medallion hung about his neck, bearing the image of the Flaming Tree. He seemed to Patsy exceptionally handsome and she wondered why she had disliked him earlier. He knelt before the Queen and the Queen laid her hands on his head in the now-familiar gesture of blessing. She spoke the words quietly, in the same unknown tongue as before. When she had finished, he kissed her hand, rose with graceful agility and turned once again toward the Gelfin Tree.

The drums beat insistently and the chanting of the people grew loud and urgent, as with unhesitating firmness Gendol descended the stairs again and strode across the courtyard. Patsy glanced at Rilya in wonderment. What was he going to do? But Rilya seemed not to notice her. Condin too had his eyes fixed on Gendol and his face expressed an admiration akin to worship. Closer and closer, the noble figure approached to the flaming-yet-unburned Tree. Now he was within a few steps of it, but still he did not slacken his pace. The chanting rose into a mighty, triumphant crescendo while Patsy unconsciously screwed her eyes shut and gripped her crucifix tightly.

Suddenly a gasp of astonishment burst from the assembly and the singing drew to a ragged halt amid confused exclamations of dismay. Patsy's eyes flung open again. What had happened? She looked at her companions, but they were staring in disbelief at the Gelfin Tree, Rilya white and trembling, Condin with his fists clenched, Landon simply uncomprehending. Reluctantly, Patsy followed their gaze and noticed to her surprise that the Tree was no longer burning. It grew as it had always grown, gnarled and serene, its leaves rustling faintly in the dawn wind. At its base stood Gendol, with his cheeks flushed and hair disheveled; he was quite unharmed.

Patsy heaved a sigh of relief. At least that was over! She had expected to see him devoured by the flames, consumed in some sort of monstrous human sacrifice. Instead, ignoring the agitation of the crowd and turning his back on the Tree, he strode quickly across the courtyard, mounted the steps, and stood, for the second time that morning, face to face with the Queen. Now he did not kneel and the words he spoke, while in an undertone, were clearly intelligible.

"Perhaps, Your Majesty, Dol the Protector does not find favor with me." He spoke curtly and with a tinge of sarcasm, as if blaming her for the humiliation he had apparently undergone.

"My Lord," the Queen replied, "you must realize that the favor of the gods cannot be bought by mere rites and ceremonies." She spoke mildly but her face betrayed deep pain and unexpected fear. "I do not understand why Dol has withheld the signs of his benevolence. Something is amiss, yet though I have searched my heart and begged for light, I cannot

70

fathom it. However, we have no more time now for hesitation and self-examination. We must go forward boldly and trust that our Protector will not abandon us." She squared her shoulders resolutely. "I will speak to the people."

Gendol nodded and stepped to her right as she advanced to the edge of the steps and held up her arms for silence. While the crowd began to compose itself, Patsy studied the Queen intently from behind. She did not understand either, although for different reasons. Why were they so upset because nothing had happened to Gendol? Maybe it was all some fake magic trick and nothing would have happened anyway. "Hocus pocus and mumbo jumbo" she could hear her father saying. But the Queen didn't think of it as hocus pocus or mumbo jumbo, and Patsy had come to believe deeply in the Queen. Besides, now that she had accepted her mission and the burden of the Sign, somehow it was her concern also if Dol withheld his favor from these people.

Patsy felt for the cross under her cloak, and for the first time her fingers became sensitive to the twisted, tortured figure upon it. Then she glanced curiously at Rendil, standing just opposite her, next to Gendol, on his Mother's right. He was staring sightlessly into the distance, his face a mask of anger and resentment. Neither he nor Gendol moved as, amid tense stillness, the Queen began to speak.

"My beloved people, we are gathered here, as you know, in this sacred place to invoke the blessing of Dol upon the person and mission of Lord Gendol, illustrious commander of the royal armies. You have witnessed how Dol has manifested his presence among us, which is, in itself, an evident sign of his care for us. However, for reasons that we cannot fathom, he has not chosen to bestow upon us the special sign of his protection."

A low, uneasy murmur arose from the crowd and, as the Queen again raised her arms for silence, something about Lord Gendol caught Patsy's eye. He wore a strange but vaguely familiar expression on his face and she found herself wondering who he reminded her of.

"But, my people, we must have courage," the Queen continued. "As you know, our situation is urgent. The enemy is amassing once more to attack us and we must advance to meet him while we still have time. Therefore, Lord Gendol will ride forth as planned, with unwavering trust that Dol the Strong…"

Unwavering trust! The words stirred Patsy to recognition. Not two months before, her parents had brought her with them to a wedding, a terribly dull affair where the minister had droned on and on about unwavering trust and fidelity. How her father had squirmed with boredom and irritation! Because it was his boss's daughter, he had had to attend. Patsy looked across at Gendol again and now she felt sure. He wore the very same look as her father had, of boredom, irritation, and something deeper: an undisguised contempt for the whole affair.

"He doesn't believe," she thought to herself. "He feels the same way about Dol as Daddy does about God." The realization stunned her. He did not believe but the others thought he did and they trusted him. She tried to persuade herself that it did not matter, that a brave general could fight his country's battles while despising his country's gods. But, as she watched the Queen give him the formal embrace of farewell and Rendil repeat the gesture, with teeth clenched, she realized instinctively that Lord Gendol's unbelief constituted a fundamental act of treachery.

She stood stock still, in a fog of confused apprehension, while some concluding ceremonies were performed and the troops mounted up. As they clattered across the drawbridge, the rising sun burst in splendor over the east wall of Celdondol.

CHAPTER 10
RENDIL'S PROPOSAL

The rest of that morning passed without further excitement. The children had class with Sir Pandil again, but the poor man knew that he was lecturing to four pairs of deaf ears. Condin stared moodily out the window the whole time and when reprimanded for inattention, answered so insolently that the old tutor caned him. Landon too kept bouncing to the window and back, whispering *sotto voce* to Rilya, "Do you think they're at the river yet?" and "How long until they come to the mountains?" and "Someday I'm going to be a soldier too."

Meanwhile, Patsy suffered in silence. She longed to be alone and to try and think through all that she had discovered in the past two days: the meaning of her cross, the nature of her mission, the unbelief of Gendol. But it was no use asking to be excused and besides, her head ached so badly that she could not think anyway. As morning wore on the headache worsened until, by noon, she could not help complaining to Rilya, who immediately informed Galna that their guest was ill. The good woman, in her turn, showered Patsy with motherly sympathy and hustled her off to bed, where she stayed, gratefully, for the rest of the day.

That evening, the Queen appeared, as before, to bless her children. Patsy heard her from the other room and, to Galna's dismay, came dashing out in her robe and slippers to greet her.

"Well, little one," the Queen laughed, "have you been making up for lost sleep?"

"I…" Patsy blushed, conscious of the presence of the other children.

"She had a headache," Rilya explained, "and went to bed early. I hope it's gone now," she added.

"It is, thank you." Patsy smiled at her.

"I am so glad to hear that." The Queen smoothed Patsy's tousled curls with an affectionate gesture. "May Dol preserve your head from further aches and keep it safe upon your shoulders."

"Is that my blessing?" Patsy was disappointed.

The Queen's smile faded away into sadness. "It is all I have for you tonight, my child. But may the Great One himself lead you swiftly to fulfill your mission."

"May it truly be so," Patsy answered wonderingly as she kissed her hand.

The next morning, Galna announced that, in her estimation, Lady Palissa would benefit far more from selecting material for her new dresses than she would from another session with Sir Pandil.

"Oh!" cried Rilya, clapping her hands. "May I join her?"

"Now, did I say anything about you?" Galna frowned at her with mock severity.

"But, but, you wouldn't do it without me, would you?"

"Eat your breakfast, Your Highness. You will be late for class."

"Oh…" Rilya pouted with disappointment and envy. "Lucky you," she said, turning to Patsy, "you are allowed to try on all the latest fabrics and we have to suffer Old Wirebeard."

"What's so interesting about a bunch of dresses, anyway?" put in Landon. "I'd rather hear about the Battle of Fendar Dil."

Condin laughed. "That's because you're a boy. You have to be a girl to become excited about dresses and such." He winked at Patsy. "Right now I wish I were one."

Patsy recalled the conversation later and grinned to herself. She did enjoy the look and feel and smell of the silks and satins and velvets and laces that Galna presented for her approval. They made her seem so rich and grown-up, so "Lady Palissa", that for the moment she almost forgot that she was plain Patsy Morgan with a mission to accomplish. A loud knock at the door jolted her back to reality.

Galna opened it and a young page, dressed entirely in scarlet, bowed ceremoniously and addressed himself to her. "His Royal Highness, Prince Rendil, asks leave to speak with Lady Palissa in His Highness's private quarters."

Patsy's stomach turned to water. She had been waiting and waiting to see Rendil again, but now that he had summoned her, she wanted to flee instead.

Galna was eyeing her curiously. "Well, my lady, I think that whether we like it or no, we shall have to comply with His Highness' request."

"We? Are you coming too? Oh, thank you! I mean…" Patsy hesitated, knowing that Rendil would not like it. "I mean, you don't have to come. I can go by myself."

"Go by yourself!" Galna threw back her head and laughed. "Why, child, don't you know that a lady never appears before the king or prince unattended? I would send Her Highness Princess Rilya with you, but I know Sir Pandil would object. So," she gestured with a flourish, "I will be your escort."

Patsy did not know what to say, so she smiled uncertainly and followed her out. The page led them to Rendil's apartments on the first floor of the tower and ushered them in with the announcement: "The Lady Palissa and companion, as you requested Sire."

Rendil was standing with his back to the door, intent upon some papers laid out on a table, but he whirled around immediately to greet them. "My Lady, good morning! I trust you are well this morning?"

"Yes, sir, thank you," Patsy answered shyly and curtsied as best she could.

"And dear Galna. I have not seen you for a long while. How are you?"

"Fine, thank you, your Highness." Galna beamed with pride at her former charge.

A short, awkward pause followed, during which Rendil seemed to be trying to phrase his next remarks. "My dear Galna," he finally began, "I do wish I could sit down and talk with you as in old times, and I appreciate your accompanying Lady Palissa according to the order of propriety, but…" He took a deep breath, "but I am afraid for now that I must speak with the Lady alone. You may wait outside for her if you wish."

Galna gave him the same curious, penetrating look that she had given Patsy earlier. "Very well, your Highness," she replied tartly, "but I think you are not so grown-up as not to need an occasional word of warning. Watch yourself!" She curtsied and turned to leave. "I shall wait for you in the antechamber," she said to Patsy on her way out the door.

Patsy did not know whether to be relieved or frightened at Galna's dismissal. She remained close to the doorway, looking first at the floor, then at Rendil, then at the floor again. He smiled ruefully and nodded in the direction of the antechamber. "She will not be hurt; she knows me too well. However, I daresay, she suspects me of some slightly dishonorable intention. Thank the gods, you did not have Rilya with you; I could never have gotten rid of her. But do come and sit down." He gestured to a chair near him by the table. Patsy walked over and sat down as bidden. She felt wooden, unable to think.

"You know of course why I wished to see you."

"Because of the Sign?" She fingered it hesitatingly, but it brought no security now.

"Yes. Mother has told me of her conversation with you and of her conviction that you bear the Sign by the will of the Great One."

"She also said I was supposed to help you get back your enchantment, but she didn't tell me how. Did she tell you?"

He laughed shortly. "All she told me is that by some design of Dol, I am not to accompany Lord Gendol into battle. Mother has spoken."

His tone was so sarcastic that Patsy felt moved to defend the Queen. "Well maybe she saw that inside herself, the way she saw about my Sign. I can't explain it, but you know what I mean."

Rendil appeared startled and somewhat ashamed. "Well, yes, I suppose I do. I am sorry." He was silent for a moment.

"I don't trust him anyway," Patsy remarked abruptly.

"Whom don't you trust?"

"Lord Gendol."

He looked at her sharply. "I find that very interesting. Why do you not trust Lord Gendol?"

"Because he doesn't believe."

"He does not believe? What do you mean by that?"

"I mean…" Patsy groped for a way to help him understand. "You see, my dad, my father, he doesn't believe. He thinks there aren't any such things as gods or enchantments or signs and when he has to go to a church service, he gets very bored and can hardly wait to leave. Anyway, I know what he's like, and Lord Gendol is the same way. I can tell by the way he acted yesterday. He doesn't care at all about your Dol, he thinks my Sign is nonsense, and…" Here Patsy was venturing into the realm of conjecture and realized it. "…and maybe he wants your enchantment for himself."

"Impossible!" Rendil interjected. "The enchantment belongs to the King alone. Gendol would have to liquidate the entire royal family in order to claim it for his own." The thought struck him dumb and for a moment he stared at her open-mouthed. Then he shook himself. "No, Mother trusts him. And Father trusted him too. Yet, Father was killed. But, no, Father could not have lost his enchantment unless he himself forsook or betrayed it." He paced restlessly to the window and back again. "Are you quite sure of what you are saying?"

"I'm sure of what I saw at the departure ceremony. I can't prove it or anything. I just know I don't trust him, even if your mother does."

"Perhaps it is true, perhaps he is planning some treachery. All the more reason then for going ahead with my plan, and as soon as possible."

"Your plan? What plan?"

"This plan. Listen carefully." Rendil darted to the door and locked it, then checked the window. No one was about. He returned to the table and began again, in a low, excited tone of voice. "Mother said that I was not to ride forth with Lord Gendol, but she did not say that I could not ride forth after him."

"I thought you told me she wouldn't let you leave the castle," Patsy interrupted.

Rendil frowned at her and continued, ignoring the point of her comment. "We must leave as soon as possible, in order to reach Moldan Gorge before he does. We shall have to go by way of the river in order to avoid detection and it will take longer."

"We?" Patsy interrupted again, nervously.

"Yes, of course. You will not be able to help me unless you are with me."

"Oh. Yes. I mean, we and who else?"

"Who else would you wish to accompany us?"

Patsy really didn't know, but she thought fast. "Some soldiers? How about Radin? I like him."

Rendil had to smile, in spite of his growing impatience. "Yes, Radin is a good man, but he belongs to the Queen's Guard and not to the army. Besides, apart from the Queen's men and a few soldiers hand-picked by Gendol to guard the fortress, there are no troops left in Celdondol. All the reserves have ridden with him to the front. No, I am afraid we shall have to go alone. Can you be ready to leave by tomorrow evening?"

Patsy drew breath so sharply that she swallowed down the wrong throat and began to choke. The ensuing moments of violent coughing gave her opportunity to gather her wits for further protest, while Rendil waited with annoyed concern.

"I'm all right," she managed to gasp at last, in response to his unspoken query. After wiping her eyes and blowing her nose, she continued. "I really want to help you if I can, but what good is it for you to follow Gendol if you haven't got your enchantment yet? Wouldn't it be better to wait here like your Mother wants, until things are safer?"

"Safer!" Rendil exploded. "Safer! How can I worry about safety when our lives are already at stake?" He restrained himself with visible effort and began again. "Listen to me. Carefully. The forthcoming conflict is of crucial importance; our whole Kingdom hangs in the balance. Whatever vision Mother may have had, I feel certain she is wrong to think that Gendol can triumph without either the Sign or the enchantment. We now possess the Sign, but he has refused to acknowledge it. If he has indeed turned traitor, that makes our task even more urgent."

He took a deep breath and hurried on before Patsy could interrupt once more. "You are correct in saying that my presence at Moldan will be of no use without the enchantment. But I cannot hope to recover the lost powers of kingship by hanging about Celdondol twiddling my thumbs! I must ride, and ride swiftly, trusting that Dol will see fit to bestow on me what I lack before I reach the end of my journey." He hesitated and looked at her almost shyly. "There is something else you must know if you are to help me."

"What's that?" Patsy asked, curious in spite of herself.

"I must undergo certain trials before the dispersed enchantment will gather to me. These trials have been foreordained by Dol from time immemorial and are embedded in our ancient songs and legends."

"Well, what are they?" Patsy demanded.

Rendil hesitated once more, then closed his eyes and began to chant softly:

> Rendil, Prince, the Rightful One,
> Ride, thy power to regain.
> Testings three thou must fulfill
> Ere in majesty to reign.
>
> 'Neath the silver bow thee down;
> Fire thy sister, friend thou call.
> Clouds command now: break and fly!
> Rain do cease thy wayward fall!
>
> Broken branch then succor, soothe;
> Listen! Silent Ones shall speak.
> Flame command now: flash and flare
> Cold be banished; warm the weak.
>
> Strong before the mighty stand,
> One alone the horde hold fast.
> Light command now: radiant rise!
> Dark moon, fall, thy spell downcast!

Ride on, Rendol, King to reign!
Glorious wield thy power won.
Check the haughty, lift the low;
Be thou friend to gods and men.

His voice died away hoarsely on the last line and, for a moment, both he and Patsy were quite still. She broke the silence first. "I don't understand it. Is it some kind of riddle or something?"

Rendil smiled a bit ruefully. "The words are mysterious, but I am afraid they were meant to be. I know, as every child of Arendolin knows, that the first two lines of each verse refer to one of the trials that must be undergone, while the last two lines refer to the power that is bestowed when the conditions have been fulfilled. I asked Mother for further elucidation but she said she could not give it. She told me that if I would read the ancient chronicles, I would discover that for every prince who has undertaken this quest, the conditions and their fulfillment are different, although the words of the song are always the same."

"Every prince? You mean there were other princes who did this before you? Then how come the song has your name in the first line?"

"Because every first-born son bears the name of Rendil. It designates our position as prince and rightful heir."

"Oh. Well then, did you read the chronicles? What did they say?"

Rendil sighed. "I have combed through thirty dusty tomes and fourteen brittle scrolls, some in the original script and tongue of our first forebears, and it is just as Mother observed. Therefore, I have no choice but to go forward blindly and let the signs and their fulfillment happen as they will. But you must come with me to help me. Can you be ready by tomorrow night?"

Patsy's heart skipped a beat. "Does your mother know about this?" she asked, stalling again. "We really should have her blessing before we go."

"No!" Rendil fairly shouted with exasperation. "Can you not understand? Mother knows nothing of this and you must not tell her. I will ask you once more only. Are you coming with me or not?"

"I...I...Yes!" Patsy gulped finally. She was trembling and nearly in tears, but she did not have the courage to refuse in the face of his anger.

"Very good," Rendil nodded with satisfaction. "You must return to your quarters now; it is getting late in the morning and Galna will be growing impatient. I have not worked out all the details of our departure yet, but in the meantime, you should prepare whatever you will need for a fortnight' s journey – in a small bundle please! – and also a blanket. I will arrange for food, horses and other such necessities. Come."

He strode toward the door and Patsy rose numbly to follow him. "One more thing," he said with his hand on the latch. "You must pretend to Galna that we have spoken of nothing important. And, I adjure you by all the gods, do not whisper a word of this to Rilya."

Patsy nodded and he opened the door for her. She went out without a backward glance, but as she passed, she heard him say, "Thank you." The words sounded hollow, but she no longer cared

CHAPTER 11
DECISION

Patsy was a coward and knew it. She felt ashamed of her cowardice: ashamed alike of the lack of adventuresome spirit that kept her from agreeing to Rendil's plan, and also of the cravenness with which she had given in to him under pressure. She wanted desperately to fulfill her mission and make the Queen proud of her, but, with equal desperation, she feared the risks involved. She sympathized intensely with Rendil's desire to prove his manhood in battle and adventure, but love and admiration for the Queen made her shrink from a course of action that amounted to outright disobedience.

"I have to help Rendil," she told herself, "I promised the Queen I would, and besides that's why I'm here." But this was not how the Queen wanted it done. "Well, what does she know?" Patsy argued with her conscience. "Didn't she herself tell Rendil that it was different for everyone?" And all the while, at the back of her mind, lay an unspoken resentment that Rendil had pressured her, that he had not allowed her real freedom to choose.

The most painful part of Patsy's quandary was that she could not discuss it with anyone. When she emerged from Rendil's chamber, Galna regarded her with a mixture of ill-concealed curiosity and frank disapproval. Although Patsy did her best to smile and make light of the situation, the old nanny was too experienced in the ways of children not to be suspicious. Patsy realized it, but could only hope against hope that she would not report the matter to the Queen.

Rilya proved easier to deal with, since she had no reason to suspect that Patsy had not spent all morning in the royal wardrobe. She plied her with eager questions about color and style, and Patsy, feigning an enthusiasm she no longer felt, gave her glowing descriptions of all the fabrics she had tried and which ones she had chosen. However, even this pretense became difficult to keep up, and after awhile she lapsed into moody silence.

But the Queen was the worst of all. Patsy dreaded having to face her, burdened as she was with the guilt of their contemplated defiance of her wishes. She toyed with the idea of confessing the whole sorry plot and taking refuge behind her authority against the wrath of Rendil. But sympathy for Rendil was steadily gaining ground in Patsy's mind and she soon abandoned any thought of betraying him. Instead, she began to picture herself mounted on Fendal with Rendil behind her in golden armor and flowing purple cape, and the two of them riding forth to victory against the forces of evil. The picture was not at all a disagreeable one.

By the time the Queen arrived that evening to give the children her blessing, Patsy had nearly convinced herself that the great lady was mistaken, that she and Rendil were in the right, that if it were not for his ridiculous prohibitions all misunderstandings could be cleared up by a simple explanation. But one glance of the Queen's gentle, laughing eyes shattered her illusions, and Patsy found herself dropping her own gaze and blushing in confusion.

"My child, is something wrong?" The Queen sounded surprised and somewhat dismayed.

"Why, no Ma'am," Patsy answered evasively, "I'm just tired, that's all." The statement was at least half-true, but it felt – and sounded – like a lie.

"Oh, child." The Queen's voice was heavy with sorrow. "You were not this way with me yesterday. Who has poisoned you? Has my son Rendil infected you with his bitterness?"

Patsy avoided her searching gaze and said nothing.

"Listen, child." The Queen gripped her shoulders tightly and her words carried more than a hint of anger. "By pride and rashness Rendil will never win the enchantment, nor will you succeed in helping him. If by some chance, he is able to wrest power from the Great One, it can only lead to his ruin and you yourself will not escape unscathed." She relaxed her grip and her tone became gentler. "I do not blame you and I understand your sympathy for Rendil. Do you remember what I told you the other night – that love is all-powerful?"

Patsy nodded forlornly and looked up at her from out a deeply troubled soul.

"Well then, remember this also: it is by love, humility, and compassion that your quest will be completed, and not otherwise."

"Yes, Ma'am. Please…" Patsy's voice broke but with effort she controlled it. "Please, will you bless me?"

The Queen sighed and placed her hands on the little girl's head. "May the Great One give you wisdom, courage, and peace, my child."

"May it truly be so," Patsy replied, and kissed her hand.

Somehow Patsy managed to sleep that night, but when she awoke in the morning, the full weight of her situation bore down on her again. In spite of all that the Queen had said, she still could not work up the courage to refuse Rendil. At the same time, she reproached herself for her cowardice in not wanting to go with him. She wondered what he would do if she did say no to his plan. Perhaps he would take her cross from her by force and leave without her. Remembering her talk with the Queen on the night of the full moon and what she had said about bearing the Sign in her own hands, Patsy removed the cross from around her neck and contemplated it gravely. Both the form and the figure seemed stiff and unyielding. "God," she said aloud, "why did you get me into this mess?" It was the first prayer of her life, but no answer was forthcoming.

Breakfast that morning was a hurried affair because Condin and Landon, with unexpected brotherly solicitude, had importuned the horsemaster to give Lady Palissa riding lessons, and he had agreed.

"Sorry, we didn't have time to warn you," Condin responded, rather shyly but with real pleasure, to her open-mouthed surprise. "He sent an orderly over early this morning to tell us it was all right."

Patsy smiled and thanked him, although she could not decide whether to be glad or dismayed. At least she would not be available if Rendil sent for her. All the children accompanied her to the stables, with Landon skipping back and forth, chanting "Lady Palissa will ride a white horse, ride a white horse, Lady Palissa will ride a white horse." Soon Patsy was laughing and joking along with the others, breathing deeply of the fresh spring air, and putting all her troubles far behind her.

The "white horse" turned out to be a dappled gray pony, gentle and plodding, and "riding" meant circling slowly around and around the exercise yard, but Patsy made no complaints. Instead, she gripped the reins and sat bolt upright, unable to get used to the feel of an animal moving beneath her. For awhile, the boys ran along beside her, whooping and shouting encouragement, but they soon tired of this and dashed off to another part of the castle, where some of the Queen's Guard were working out with swords. Rilya stayed behind, sitting on the fence and commenting cheerfully on Patsy's "progress" every time she rode by.

Patsy was just making up her mind that she had had enough of riding lessons, at least for that day, when she heard Rilya gasp and squeal, "Rendil!" Jerking her head in that direction, Patsy froze in dismay. Sure enough, there he was, clutching Rilya around the waist from behind and laughing as she squirmed and giggled. Before Patsy could think what to do, he noticed her looking at them and raised an arm in greeting.

"Ho, Lady Palissa! How are you this morning?"

"Fine, thank you." She managed a nervous smile as he vaulted over the fence and came striding toward her. From his attire, she surmised that he too had been practicing with the sword, and his next words confirmed her guess.

"Condin and Landon told me I would find you here. So you are learning to ride. Good!" He smiled pleasantly and stroked the pony's nose. "I am sure you do not wish to spend the whole morning circling the exercise yard. Would you allow me to lead you over to the fencing arena? I wager that you have never seen fine swordsmen at play."

"No," Patsy answered, studying his face. He seemed all innocence and good humor, and she decided to trust him. "All right," she added, "but what about Rilya?"

"Why, of course Rilya will come with us. Will you not?" He addressed his sister who had already skipped over to join them.

"Where are you going?" she asked, her face bright with eagerness.

"To the fencing arena."

"Oh, good! I was beginning to get dizzy, watching poor Palissa ride around in circles."

"Come, then," he cried, "let us not waste our time in talking!" He seized the pony's bridle and headed for the gate, much too quickly for the fledgling equestrienne's comfort. However, they had not gone six paces beyond the exercise yard, when Condin and Landon ran up, breathless and panting.

"Rilya, Rilya," they called, "hurry up, you're missing it!"

"Missing what?" she asked, puzzled.

"Wait 'til you see!" Landon answered, grinning broadly.

"Hurry up," Condin repeated, grabbing her hand and pulling her along. "It will be over before we get back there."

"But, but..." Rilya's useless protests strung out behind her as the two boys hustled her off. Soon they had rounded the corner of the blacksmith shop and disappeared, leaving Patsy to stare after them in amazement. Then she heard Rendil chuckling to himself.

"Now that we are alone, shall we discuss our plans?"

Patsy caught her breath with sudden realization and her temper flared. "You had them do that on purpose! You're mean!"

He chuckled again. "I thought myself rather clever, really. At any rate, we shall rejoin them presently. In the mean time, are you ready for tonight?"

"No!"

"No? What do you mean, no? You have not changed your mind, have you?"

Patsy struggled in vain with her anger. "What would you do if I told you I had?" she shot back defiantly.

"I would order you to hand over the Sign immediately and I would go without you." His temper was also rising.

"You can't have my cross. It's mine!" She clutched it tightly in her fist.

"No, it is not yours." His voice trembled now with fury. "By the will and design of the One who sent you here, and by the light of Dol who revealed your coming, the Sign is ours. I command you to hand it over, if you will not come with me."

Patsy opened her mouth to shout a resolute "no!" but the word would not come out. What Rendil said was true and she knew it. In a very real sense, the cross no longer belonged to her, nor did she belong to herself. Both the Sign and its bearer had become part of a larger reality. Tears of pain stung her eyes as she finally gave in. "All right. I'll go with you."

"Thank you," he answered grimly. "Now we must settle our affairs, quickly, before the others miss us. I will meet you on the second floor landing at midnight. Be dressed for riding as you are now and have your extra clothing and a blanket with you."

91

"How will we get past the guards?" Patsy recalled her adventure of a few nights before. It seemed so far away now.

"There is a narrow opening in the tower wall, originally for defense purposes. I tried the other afternoon and it is just large enough for me to squeeze through sideways. You should have no problem."

"But how will we get away from Celdondol on horses without anyone seeing us?" She didn't know why she even cared.

"Ah!" Rendil smiled triumphantly. "In the days of the Great Wars, when this fortress was often under siege, our ancestors had a tunnel dug, reaching from the stables, which were purposely constructed against the outer wall, down to the river. Condin and I explored it one time when we were younger. It is still in good condition and large enough for horses to pass in single file." He broke off abruptly. "We have talked long enough. Are you ready now?"

"Yes," she gulped, and shuddered.

An unexpected look of sympathy crossed his face. "I know you are frightened. I am sorry it had to be this way." He patted her shoulder awkwardly. "Come now, let us be off."

With a jerk on the pony's bridle, he led her away toward the fencing arena. As they passed the blacksmith shop a couple of waiting peasants pulled off their caps and bowed to Rendil who gravely acknowledged their greeting. None of them noticed a boyish silver head, which ducked around the corner of the building and disappeared at a dead run.

CHAPTER 12

DEPARTURE

Patsy began gathering her provisions together that afternoon, piling them on her bed behind the drawn curtains. By bedtime, everything was there: underwear, socks, handkerchiefs, her riding clothes and boots, comb and brush. So far, the whole affair was proceeding more smoothly than she had anticipated. Despite her nervousness and obvious preoccupation, neither Rilya nor Galna had asked her any questions. Apparently, they had begun to accept the strange behavior of their little guest, much as they accepted Condin's abrupt changes of mood. Early that morning at the exercise yard, he had radiated amiability and good cheer, but by the time Patsy and Rendil arrived at the fencing arena, he had withdrawn into his shell like a clam. Since then he had spoken only once, and that was after supper. Glancing out the window, he turned to Patsy and remarked with studied casualness, "Storm clouds are gathering. That's a bad omen."

"Huh?" she questioned blankly, not comprehending.

"It looks like rain," Rilya tried to explain, supplying for her brothers lapse into stony silence. "When it rains at night and the light of the moon is obscured, that means that the powers of darkness are abroad."

"Oh. But it has to rain sometime, doesn't it? At home, we're happy when it rains at night and the sun shines during the day."

"Yes," Rilya replied somewhat testily, "but in your world you are not governed and protected by the enchantment of Dol."

"That's true." Patsy reflected briefly that it was a pretty poor god who was afraid of the dark. Then she dismissed the whole matter as sheer superstition.

That was after supper. But now that the lights were out and everyone had gone to bed and she was sitting alone behind the drawn bed curtains, listening to the moaning of the wind and the occasional rumble of thunder, she wondered if perhaps it was true. After all, this was an entirely different world, where lots of strange things had already happened. At any rate, their journey promised to be a cold, uncomfortable one. She had become reconciled to it by now, with a kind of dull, despairing resignation. Whether Rendil was right or wrong, she had not much choice but to follow him as best she could and get it over with. She fingered the crucifix and the thought crossed her mind – how did he feel about what he had to do? But the thought passed quickly. She was grateful for one thing – the Queen had not come that evening. The other children did not seem to expect her, although no reason was given for her absence. Patsy knew that she could not have faced her again.

In the meantime, she had no way of knowing what time it was. Rendil had said to meet him on the landing at midnight. She strained her ears, but no sound of movement issued from Rilya's side of the room. In the distance, she could hear Galna's muffled snore. Quietly she began to dress, still sitting on the bed behind the curtains. When she had finished, she listened again, then picked up her bundle, her blanket, and her boots, and peered anxiously around the bed curtains. Rilya was asleep.

Fingering the cross one last time, she set out, tiptoeing across the room, her heart pounding so loudly that she was sure someone would hear it. But Rilya slept on. Galna too remained motionless; not even a long, distant roll of thunder served to disturb her. Miraculously, even the door did not creak this time. Once Patsy had gained the landing, she pulled her boots on and sat down in the dark to wait. For awhile her heart continued to pound and she trembled with nervous anticipation. But Rendil was long in coming, very long. In spite of everything, she finally began to doze.

A sharp pain in her leg and a heavy thud jolted her awake. Straining her bleary eyes, she made out a tall, shadowy figure setting itself upright beside her. It hissed something angrily. "Huh?" she asked, much too loudly.

"Shh! I said, what are you doing, sitting in the middle of the landing? I tripped over you."

"Oh. Sorry. What time is it?"

"Just past the midnight watch. The off-duty guards should be in the barracks by this time. Do you have everything?"

"I think so."

"Good. Come, then, take my hand lest you get lost."

Patsy picked up her bundle and groped for his hand. She found it after a moment, warm but damp with perspiration. Her own hand felt small by comparison and very cold. Quickly and quietly they proceeded down the stairs, but before they reached the next landing Rendil halted.

"What's wrong," Patsy whispered.

"Nothing is wrong. This is where the opening is."

"Where?" Although Patsy's eyes had grown accustomed to the dark, she could not see any aperture in the wall.

"Up there." He reached up with his hand and indicated a narrow, protruding ledge some way above his head. "I will have to lift you up first, then I will follow."

Patsy watched with growing apprehension as he uncoiled a long rope from his belt and knotted it securely around a torch holder on the wall.

"All right now, take this," he said, handing her the coil of rope. "When I lift you into the window, you must drop the rope down the outside, then lower yourself by it to the ground."

"Lower? How?" she squeaked.

"Hand over hand, of course," he answered impatiently. "Use the stones in the wall for toeholds to help yourself along."

Patsy began to shake with fright, but she had no time to protest, as Rendil had already grabbed her around the waist and was boosting her up to the window. She grasped the ledge to pull herself up and, in so doing, dropped her bundle. "Oh, my things," she moaned.

Rendil muttered something to himself as he stooped to retrieve them. "Here," he growled, "throw it out the window before you. When we reach the stables, I will strap it on your back, so you will not have to carry it."

"All right." Patsy did as she was told, casting her bundle into the windswept outer darkness. But she could not bring herself to follow it. "What do I do?" she whispered shakily.

Rendil drew an impatient breath but the pathos in her voice made him pause. "Very well," he said at last, "take the end of the rope and tie it around your waist. Then hold on and I will lower you down. When you reach the ground, untie yourself and tug sharply on the rope, so I will know you are safe. Do you understand me?"

"Yes." Patsy wished she were dead. Her knees knocked and her stomach churned, but all the same, she fumbled to obey. When at long last she had tied the rope about herself as best she could, she mumbled, "Okay." Rendil braced himself against the inside wall and nodded encouragingly. There was nothing left to do. Crouching in the narrow aperture, she grasped the ledge and slowly let herself out.

As she did so, a flash of lightning rent the darkness, followed by a loud clap of thunder. For a moment she clung to the ledge in sheer panic. But her grip began to give way, bit by bit, and finally with a small, frightened cry, she had to let go. Instantly, the rope tightened, sliding up under her armpits and biting into them with the force of her own weight. She clutched at the taut line, trying desperately to keep it from slipping off over her head. Rendil had already begun to pay out the rope with rapid, jerking movements, but the downward motion only increased her discomfort. She found herself bouncing and scraping against the tower with such force that soon her arms and legs were bleeding and her clothes torn. Endlessly, the nightmare went on as down she lurched, jolting and jerking, until at last her feet touched the ground and she collapsed in a small, sobbing heap.

So exhausted was she that for a long time she simply lay there, forgetting all about Rendil in the tower. Presently, however, another clap of thunder roused her and she bestirred herself to get up. To her amazement, she saw Rendil already halfway down the wall, climbing on the same rope to which she was still tied. Clumsily she tried to undo the knot, but her hands were so sore that she could not manage, and in the end she had to pull it off over her head. Within seconds Rendil was beside her on the ground. "Oh," he lamented, rubbing his chafed fingers, "the rope has burned my hands. I did not know you were so heavy. Do you have your things?"

"I don't know," Patsy gulped.

"You…? Ah, by all the gods, I ought to go without you! Where are they?" Casting about impatiently, he spied them on the ground a few paces off and darted over to snatch them up. "All right," he said, "we must be off. We have no more time to waste." With that, he seized her by the arm and strode off at a rapid pace. He did not make straight across the castle yard, but through the garden, close by the hedge, then under the shadow of the outer wall, well out of sight of the guards on the ramparts. Patsy stumbled along after him, so tired that her legs would hardly move. By the time they reached the stables, she was sobbing again, breathlessly.

"Hush!" Rendil hissed. "What is the matter with you?"

Patsy snuffled and wiped her eyes on her torn sleeve. "I banged against the tower all the way down and got all scraped and skinned." She snuffled again with indignant self-pity. "And the rope burned my hands too."

Rendil sighed. "I am sorry. I forget that you are younger and a lady, unaccustomed to such adventures. We cannot stop to tend your wounds, that must wait for later. Now we must get on and be very quiet about it so as not to disturb the horses or wake the stable boys."

"Won't they be disturbed anyway, with all the thunder and lightning?"

"Very likely. It will cover whatever noise we make. Come." He took her arm again and led her toward a low window in the side of the stable. To his obvious surprise, it was standing open. "I unlatched it this afternoon," he murmured under his breath, "but I did not leave it ajar." Stealthily he peered inside, but there was neither light nor movement. So he swung his legs over the sill and climbed in, turning back to help Patsy over.

The stables smelled almost overpoweringly of hay and horses and manure, and Patsy was not at all happy when Rendil closed and latched the window behind them. But she reflected that they would soon be out in the open air again, seated on Fendal's back. Then at last she could rest.

With sure instinct, Rendil began to pick his way between the rows of stalls. "Here we are," he whispered at last, pausing before one of them. Fendal snorted a low greeting to his master, but just as Rendil was making his way into the stall, a brilliant flash of lightning turned the darkness into midday. He gave a loud gasp and backed away, not from fear of the elements, but because there, directly in front of him, illuminated by the glare, stood his brother Condin.

"Well," said the younger boy, with a triumphant smirk, "we do meet in strange places. What happened? You are late – I've been waiting for hours."

"What are you doing here?" Rendil demanded, forgetting to whisper.

"I'm going with you, of course. Did you think I didn't know you were planning something, after that cheap trick you played on Rilya this morning? I doubled back behind the blacksmith shop and heard your every word."

"You are not going with us!" Rendil's voice was harsh with rage.

"I am and you dare not try to stop me!"

"You are not!" Rendil leaped for him and the two boys went over in a tangle of arms and legs inside Fendal's stall. His saddle came crashing down on top of them and the horse neighed and backed away. The other horses began snorting and moving about restlessly, and Patsy cried out, "Stop it, you two, stop it!"

Just at that moment, lightning flashed again and she heard the tramp of heavy feet and a deep voice calling, "Who goes there?" Casting about in a panic, she spied some bales of hay and dove behind them. As the door flung open at the far end of the room, a loud clap of thunder temporarily drowned all other sounds. From her hiding place, Patsy could see the dim glow of what she guessed was a lantern.

The stablehand called again, "Who goes there?" but no answer came back except the low, nervous whinnying of the horses. "Sure I heard something," he muttered, bringing his lantern glow a few paces closer. "Ho, Pon old boy, what's bothering you? Is it the storm? Dundil, quiet now! Phew! Sure is a bad one. The Dark Ones walk tonight and that's for certain!" The lantern glow swept the room and Patsy crouched lower into her corner, while the hay scratched and stung her sore legs. "Well, I don't see anything. Guess it was just thunder. Won't none of us sleep much tonight, horses nor men." He swept the room with his lantern once more for good measure. "Well, guess that's that. Now, all you horses, you just take it easy. Old Taf's right here in the next room and nothing's going to happen to you." With that, Old Taf turned on his heel and stomped out, closing the door behind him and plunging the room once more into darkness.

Patsy eased out her breath in a long sigh of relief, but did not stir from her hiding place. Presently she heard stealthy movements in the direction of Fendal's stall, then whispers.

"Is he gone?"

"I think so."

"Thank the gods!"

"Yes, but I'll have him back here in an instant if you won't take me with you."

"You filthy little brat!"

"Tch, tch, brother. Make up your mind, quickly."

"All right, you can come with us."

"Very good. Hurry up and get Fendal saddled. I have Burdil all ready and the entrance to the tunnel uncovered."

Rendil ground his teeth in reply, but another streak of lightning revealed him, disheveled and begrimed, hastening to comply.

"Where is Lady Palissa?" Condin asked somewhat anxiously.

"Right here." Patsy popped up from behind her bale of hay.

"Good," said Condin. Rendil said nothing, but gave a last vicious jerk on the saddle girth and began backing Fendal out of his stall.

"Aren't you going to tie my things on my back like you promised?" Patsy knew immediately that it was the wrong thing to say.

"Keep still and carry them!" Rendil snapped.

"I'll be glad to do it," Condin purred all too helpfully.

"Later," Rendil growled. "We have no more time to lose."

Condin shrugged elaborately and motioned Patsy to follow them. Rendil led the way to an empty stall, the wooden floor of which had been carefully removed, plank by plank, to reveal a yawning hole and stairs descending steeply into blackness.

"All right," Rendil whispered, assuming his most commanding air, "I will go first. Lady Palissa, you follow me so that you do not get lost. Condin, you bring up the rear. Come, Fendal!" He tugged on the horse's reins and began to steer him toward the hole. But Fendal snorted and backed away nervously. "Hush, Fendal old boy, you must not be afraid. It is only a little way and no harm will come to you." He stroked the horse reassuringly and tried again to lead him into the dark tunnel. This time Fendal slowly and reluctantly followed him. "Good boy, good fellow," Patsy could hear Rendil murmuring as he and his mount disappeared into nothingness. She turned and looked at Condin in terror.

"Go on," he motioned with his hand. "Don't follow too closely, or you might be stepped on if Fendal backs up. You can't become lost in the tunnel anyway and I will be right behind you. If Burdil will cooperate, that is."

Patsy swallowed hard and, with quaking knees, descended the first two steps. But she had nothing to grasp for support and hesitated, feeling desperately that she would lose her balance and fall.

"Go on," Condin hissed again.

"I can't," she quavered back. "I'll fall."

"Crouch down, step by step, until the wall is high enough to support you."

This seemed like good advice, so, summoning her courage, Patsy stooped and inched her way down, until she was able to feel the wall of the tunnel, cold and damp, under her hand. From there she proceeded with greater confidence, down, down into the dank and musty-smelling earth. At first she could hear Condin behind her, urging on his horse, but after awhile, as the tunnel leveled off into an alley of smooth, hard-packed clay, she could hear nothing at all. "Rendil must be far ahead already," she thought, and hurried on to catch up with him. But several minutes of hasty groping forward did not bring him into view.

She slowed down then and listened for Condin behind her. No sound. She strained her ears. Still no sound. All was blackness around her. Where was she? "Help!" No answer came to her, not even an echo, in the close and all-absorbing earth. Panic-stricken, she began to run, forward or back, she did not know which. Fortunately, she had not gone very far when she crashed, full tilt, into Condin.

"What's the matter?" he demanded, setting both her and himself upright. "Where are you going?"

"I'm lost," she gasped. "Where are we? Where were you? It's dark in here!"

"Calm down, calm down. You're not lost. This tunnel only runs in one direction. Just keep going forward. We're already halfway through."

"Oh," Patsy moaned and flopped against the wall in a state of exhaustion.

"Come on," Condin prodded impatiently, but she did not move. He waited a moment, then seized her arm and, pushing her ahead of him, propelled her along the path. They went on that way together for some time, until Burdil snorted suddenly and they heard Fendal's answering snort directly ahead of them.

"Rendil?" Condin called softly.

"Here," he replied. A dim glow of light illuminated him momentarily, followed by a loud rumble. Patsy rubbed her eyes in perplexity.

"Where are we?" she asked him.

"Near the bank of the river," Rendil replied. "Do you not hear it?"

Yes, Patsy did hear it, rushing swift and deep, swollen with the many waters of spring. She listened and inhaled gratefully the rain-pregnant air. It made her feel calm and refreshed.

"Well," Condin broke in, "what are we waiting for? Time is getting on."

Rendil took a deep breath and let it out very slowly. "Yes," he said at last. But still he hesitated.

"What's the matter?" Condin taunted. "Are you frightened?"

"No!" he retorted angrily, but Patsy sensed some struggle within him. At length, he stretched out his arms toward the hostile darkness and chanted softly: "Rendil, Prince, the Rightful One, Ride thy power to regain." Then he squared his shoulders and stepped forth from the tunnel. As he did so, the storm broke and, with a mighty roar, the rain swept down.

CHAPTER 13

DARK ONES WALKING

Rilya did not sleep very well that night. Every time she began to doze off, another peal of thunder would rouse her. She pulled the bedcurtains close around so as not to see the lightning, and clamped a pillow tightly over her head to shut out the noise. But it was all in vain. Once she thought she heard Lady Palissa moving about, but decided it was only her imagination. Then, a little while later, she heard footsteps again, this time not Palissa's soft tread but the stealthy, deliberate scuff of heavy boots on the stone floor. Rilya froze with dread. "The Dark Ones are walking," she thought. "Oh, why tonight, of all nights, did Mother send word that she was not coming?" Another crash of thunder sent her burrowing deeper under the covers, but as the sound died away, she found herself listening in spite of herself, listening once more for the footsteps.

There! She heard them. They were drawing nearer! Or were they? She felt that she must scream from sheer uncertainty. "I have to get hold of myself," she thought. "I am Dolanya Rendilya Claris, first daughter of Rendol, and I must not be afraid. Is not Dol my protector?" The idea gave her courage and she sat up in bed, listening yet again. The footsteps were nearer now, hovering somewhere by her bedside table. Was that the sound of someone searching through her things? She drew a deep breath and cried out at the top of her voice: "Begone, Dark One! Dol is my protector!"

Instantly, the searching noise stopped and the footsteps turned and clattered across the floor in the direction of the window. Rilya thrust her head out from behind the bedcurtains just in time to see a shadowy figure disappearing over the ledge. She did not follow, but sat quite still, waiting tensely to see if it would come back. When, after several anxious moments, it did not reappear, she heaved a huge sigh of relief and flopped back on the bed, savoring her triumph. Then she thought of Lady Palissa. Sitting up again, she poked her head around the curtain and called softly, "Palissa! Palissa, are you all right?" But she got no reply. "She must be asleep," she thought. "Poor thing, she seemed so down hearted. I won't awaken her." With that, she lay down once more, but it was a long time before she was able to sleep.

Patsy did not sleep at all that night. She and the boys had set out in the teeming rain, following the river upstream. Rendil led the way with Condin after him, carrying Patsy tandem on the back of his mount. She was stung to the quick by this final insult, but felt too tired and humiliated to protest. True to his promise, Rendil had tied her bundle to her back, but with no great grace, and had heaved her up behind Condin as if she were another piece of baggage. Then both boys proceeded to ignore her. When she complained that she was going to fall off, Condin sighed wearily and told her to hold on to the saddle. They had not gone very far before her fingers ached from holding on to the saddle and her legs ached from spanning Burdil's broad rump. To make matters worse, neither their hooded leather capes, nor the canopy of leaves overhead, could keep out the rain for long, and soon they were soaked to the skin.

Their path was narrow and slippery, and Rendil had frequently to dismount and pick his way through the rocks and trees. The rushing stream sounded dangerously close in the darkness, making Patsy shiver, much more from nervousness than from cold. Still, neither boy seemed willing to consider stopping or turning back, and Patsy knew better than to suggest it. She could only endure in misery as, hour after hour, they traveled on.

At last, despite the wet and the chill, her eyelids began to droop and her head to sag against Condin's back. Dimly, through her drowsiness, she heard him say, "Listen to the birds. It must be nearly dawn." It was the first full sentence anyone had spoken all night and, in spite of herself, she did begin to listen, as first one, then another, then a whole chorus of chirping voices joined in the morning song. Lifting up her heavy head, she looked all around but, to her disappointment, it seemed as dark as ever. Gradually, however, the trees became more and more visible, then the muddy, rocky path, then the river to their right. Still they traveled on, until by the gray light of full dawn, they saw a large outcropping of rock, rising sharply to their left. At its base, a wide, shallow cave offered shelter from the rain.

"Let us turn in here and rest awhile," Rendil said.

Patsy's heart leaped. She had almost despaired of their ever stopping; now his words seemed too good to be true. But turn aside they did and after a few minutes of steady climbing, they reached the cave. At last the moment came when they halted and Rendil lifted her to the ground. To her dismay, her knees buckled under her and she fell forward with a cry of pain and surprise.

"It's all right," said Condin as he dismounted, "you're only stiff from riding. So am I," he added ruefully, rubbing his legs to restore the circulation. He and Rendil helped her up, but they had very nearly to drag her into the cave. There she collapsed again, exhausted and too soaked to appreciate the small comfort of a dry patch of ground. Soon the boys had their horses unsaddled and rubbed down as best they could. Then they embarked on a search for dry wood, which occupied them so long that Patsy was afraid they had abandoned her. Finally they returned with enough to build a fire at the entrance of the cave. All three of them removed their boots and spread out their capes before the fire to dry. The boys took off their shirts as well, while Rendil produced a dry blanket from his saddlebags for Patsy to wrap herself in. They breakfasted on salted meat and some brown bread, which Condin had filched from the castle kitchen. Before long, lulled by the warmth of the fire and the satisfaction of food, Patsy dozed and slept.

The dawn trumpet, sounding muted and uncertain through the still-pouring rain, awakened Rilya from her uneasy sleep. For awhile she lay quite still, listening to the steady dropping of water and wondering why. Not since Father was killed had it rained at night like this. The thought filled her with momentary panic. Had Lord Gendol suffered defeat already, even before the night of the Dark Moon? "Dol is our protector," she repeated to herself firmly. Besides, Mother still had her enchantment and Rendil would soon recover his, and with it his rightful place as King of Arendolin. This idea was more consoling. She smiled as she envisioned her favorite brother seated on his throne in the Great Hall, crowned with silver and sapphires, bearing in his right hand the scepter of royal power. In her mind she heard the trumpets ringing and the people shouting their acclaim, and her eyes filled with tears of pride. But that was still far off. A fresh gust of rain brought her back to reality. She wondered at Mother's refusal to let Rendil ride with Lord Gendol. Still, did not Mother always know best? She sensed his angry rejection of her decision and stood aghast at his temerity.

Her mind turned to Lady Palissa, still asleep in the other bed. Had Dol really sent her to help them in their hour of need? She herself had been the one to think so that very first day – Palissa with her hair like the light of fire or the leaves on the Gelfin Tree. "I discovered it," she reminded herself proudly, "and Rendil and Condin both agreed and Mother too." But Palissa did not believe in Dol; she had not even heard of him. This worried Rilya. True, she had heard Mother speak of the Great One, whose messenger Dol was, but he was a strange, remote figure, beyond her imagination. And to think that Lady Palissa had actually come from him! She shuddered with mingled horror and fascination.

The voice of Galna interrupted her reverie. "Wake up, your Highness, wake up, my lady!" she called, bustling about cheerfully, lighting the lamps and setting out their fresh clothing. Rilya popped out from behind the bed curtains.

"Good morning, Galna. Is it so far past dawn already?"

"Past dawn? Why, it's almost to the morning watch. But I can't blame you for not knowing. The day is hardly a day at all, for the grayness and wet. What's this?" She paused by the window, examined the drape, and then flung it aside. "Oh dear, dear," she moaned, "the casement has blown open and rain has ruined the drapes."

Instantly Rilya recalled her adventure of the night before. "No, Galna, it wasn't the rain. The Dark Ones were walking last night. I saw one myself and drove him away by invoking Dol."

"Dark Ones? But the Dark Ones are spirits. They have no need to open windows. Wait!" She examined the window again. "Look!" she cried, pointing to the deep stone ledge. "A boot print! And here on the floor another! That was no spirit you frightened with your prayers. That was a flesh and blood man!"

Rilya leaped out of bed and ran to join her. "Oh Galna, you're right. And they go straight toward Lady Palissa's bed! Palissa, Palissa, wake up! Are you safe?" She tore open the bed curtains and stared open-mouthed, speechless with disbelief.

"Dol preserve us," whispered Galna, "she's gone!" For a moment she too simply stared, but she recovered herself quickly. "They can't have taken her; you would have seen or heard. And besides, there are her bedclothes and her slippers. She must have just gotten up early. Help me look!"

Galna darted for the door with Rilya following. Together they searched the whole second level of the tower: the bedchamber, the privy chamber, the wardrobe, the main hall. But Lady Palissa was nowhere to be found. Rilya was sobbing with grief by the time they returned to the bedside.

"Oh, Galna, it's all my fault. I should have checked last night to see if she was all right."

"Now, now, your Highness," Galna soothed, putting her arms around her, "what could you have done against grown men? They might have taken you too."

"But I failed in my duty of royal hospitality. What will Mother ever say?" Rilya stifled a fresh sob and wiped her reddened eyes.

"Well," said Galna grimly, "we shall certainly have to tell her, and the sooner the better."

But when they arrived at the royal chambers, they found a small crowd already gathered, with Landon at the throne clinging to his mother's knee, and most of her bodyguard and several gentlemen-in-waiting milling about them in high consternation.

"Helfon," whispered Galna to the nervous little scribe who stood by the open door wringing his hands, "what has happened?"

"Terrible, just terrible," he answered hoarsely, shaking his head.

"What is?" she demanded, but at that moment Landon spied them and came running up.

"Rilya, Rilya," he cried, "guess what!" His face was deathly white, his great blue eyes as big as saucers. "Rendil and Condin are gone!"

"Rendil and Condin too!" she gasped. "Oh, Mother!" She pushed her way through the bodyguard and flung herself onto the dais at the Queen's side. Galna, following close at her heels, halted before the throne.

"Your Majesty." The old nurse curtsied deeply, then, forgetting her manners, rushed ahead without having leave to speak. "Your Majesty, Lady Palissa is also missing. When we got up this morning, she was gone. We searched for her all over, but we couldn't find her." Suddenly she recalled herself and blushed with confusion. "Begging your Majesty's pardon."

The Queen made a gesture of indulgence but before she could speak, Rilya broke in. "The Dark Ones took her, Mother! I saw them. We saw their footprints. I scared them away, but…"

"Hush, my child." The Queen gently laid a hand on Rilya's shoulder, causing her to break off in mid-sentence. "Galna," she addressed the flustered woman, "what were you saying? What is this about Dark Ones?"

"Your Majesty," Galna continued, reassured, "Princess Rilya tells me she saw a man or some men in her room last night, but she chased them away by making noise. We found boot prints this morning near Lady Palissa's bed, but no sign that she had been carried off by force."

"Thank you, Galna." The Queen nodded to her kindly. "Radin!"

"Yes, your Majesty!" The guardsman snapped to attention.

"You have heard what Galna said. I wish you to go back to the tower and investigate."

"Yes, your Majesty." He thumped his fist to his breastplate in salute and stomped out.

"It's my fault, Mother," Rilya broke in once more, urgently. She could not let poor Galna be blamed for this. "I should have sounded the alarm, I should have at least called Galna, I should never have gone to sleep without seeing if Palissa was all right. Please, Mother, punish me, please don't punish Galna." She stopped for breath, tears of desperation brimming in her eyes.

"My child." The Queen reached out to clasp her small hands tightly, encompassing her with a look of affection and gratitude. "You are not at fault, nor, I think is Galna. No dark

112

spirits have snatched away Lady Palissa, unless they be the dark spirits lurking in the hearts of your two brothers." She said this flatly and with such an air of finality that Rilya was shocked.

"Mother! Whatever could you mean?"

"I mean that against my explicit will Rendil and Condin have gone to join Lord Gendol and his troops and have taken Lady Palissa with them. I assume that she went of her own free will."

"They climbed down a rope from the tower window," interrupted Landon who had been listening quietly all this time. Now his eyes were aglow with excitement at his brothers' feat. "And they took their horses out under the wall through the old tunnel."

"Landon!" His mother flashed him a look so severe that he backed away and hid his face from her. But she melted again instantly. "No, little one, come here to me. It will not do to be angry with you." He returned hesitantly and she tousled his silvery curls. "You are only a small boy and you admire their adventure, foolhardy though it is. But hear me, and hear me well. You must not admire their disobedience. Do you understand?"

"Yes, Mother," he answered, greatly subdued.

The Queen said nothing, but a brief smile crossed her face. Behind the smile, Rilya thought that she detected weariness. "Mother," she asked, "then was it Rendil in our room last night?"

"No, dear, I think not. The guards who searched for him earlier found a rope dangling from one of the narrow apertures in the tower wall that cast light onto the stairs. On the ground near the rope they found this..." she held up a

113

small girl's white stocking…"which I presume belongs to Lady Palissa."

Rilya nodded dumbly.

"Begging Your Majesty's pardon." Galna curtsied again.

"Yes, Galna?"

"Then I am at fault, Your Majesty. Two days ago, Prince Rendil called Lady Palissa to a private conference in his chambers. Although I went with her, as is proper, he dismissed me at once. She was upset when she came out, I could tell, even though she tried not to let me see it. I thought I should mind my own business. But," she added grimly, "I was wrong. I should have reported to you instead."

"Perhaps you should have, Galna," the Queen answered, "but it would not have helped much. That evening when I spoke with her, I sensed the change in her attitude and the unhappiness, which you had noticed. I tried to reach her, but I am afraid I failed. As for Rendil and Condin, they have both long since closed themselves to me."

This was too much for Rilya. She could not bear to hear that her adored eldest brother had deliberately incurred the displeasure of their Mother, had, moreover, seriously disobeyed a royal command, and, worst of all, had absconded with her new friend without either of them letting her in on the secret. "Mother!" she burst out, "he can't, he wouldn't, not Rendil, would he?" Her tears spilled over and she began to sob. "And they didn't even tell me!"

"Oh, my dear child!" Rilya felt her mother's arms about her and she sagged against her gratefully, pouring out her hurt and disappointment on the regal shoulder. "You do not understand either," she heard her add, "but how can I blame you?" The Queen lapsed into silence for a moment, until Galna asked, "Your Majesty, will you send the troops after them to bring them back?"

"No, Galna," she replied, "I have ordered them not to leave the fortress. In one sense, Rendil is correct. He is old enough to be responsible for his actions without having to be forced like a child. As for the other two, I entrust them to the care of Dol." She paused and, suddenly, all the sadness and weariness within her rose to the surface in overwhelming waves. "It is hard," she whispered, "so hard." For once, no melody at all could be heard in her voice. "My royal Husband is dead, my most trusted advisor has ridden forth, perhaps to his own death, and now my sons, on whom I wished to rely, have cut themselves off from me. Even the light of Dol, which has burned for me as a sure and steady guide, seems dim and dead within."

"Don't worry Mother," Landon spoke up earnestly. "Rilya and I will take care of you. Won't we, Rilya?"

She nodded solemnly. "Yes, Mother. Don't worry, Dol will protect us."

The Queen looked from one of them to the other, a strange expression on her face. Then she began to laugh and her laughter swelled, low and sweet, as she clasped them to herself. One or two of the nearby guards stared at her, startled, but no one noticed the great tears that darkened her midnight eyes.

Patsy had no time that day to miss her silk stocking. The boys woke her late in the afternoon and, after a quick supper, they set out again, amid thick fog and drizzle. This time, Condin elected to walk, leaving Patsy to occupy the saddle alone. She was beginning to get used to the height and motion of a horse, but still could not feel quite secure, even though Condin held the reins and led Burdil himself. The trail was somewhat easier now and he and Rendil swung along freely, Condin even humming to himself in a clear and pleasing voice. Patsy began to realize, with a fresh surge of resentment, that, in spite of everything, they were actually enjoying themselves. She wondered how they could be so callous as not to feel as she felt: stiff and sore and still damp from their previous night's soaking. But they did not. They even seemed to have made up their differences, at least for the moment, in the common excitement and effort of their adventure. Patsy sighed and set herself for another long night, as darkness fell and they still moved on, ever upstream.

Rilya stared moodily out of the tower window in the direction of the setting sun, although gray clouds still hung low and no sun was visible. Landon stood next to her, his elbows on the stone ledge, his chin in his hands. He had scarcely left her side all day, nor did she wish him to.

"Maybe I should stay with you tonight," he said, "in case the Dark Ones come again."

"No," Rilya replied, "I heard Galna telling Sir Pandil that she would stay in the room with me from now on, and there will be a gentleman-in-waiting for you. She still acts as if she thought it wasn't Dark Ones at all. She lowered her voice just then, but I heard her say something about soldiers."

"Soldiers!" exclaimed Landon. "Are there enemies so near then? They haven't sounded any alarm!"

"No, there are only the men of the Guard and the squad left behind by Lord Gendol. And which of them would ever dare to break into the rooms of the royal family and search through their personal things? No, I still think it was the Dark Ones. Mother will surely bless us tonight and that is the best protection."

"If it is soldiers, I'll run them through with my sword!" Landon thumped his wooden weapon fiercely upon the ledge, then stopped, his attention riveted on something outside the window. "Rilya, look! There's a soldier now!"

"Where?"

"There, riding northward on the Great Road. Do you see?"

"Yes, but he is one of our own men." She peered intently after him as he disappeared over the brow of a hill. "I wonder where he is going. Mother said she had ordered the soldiers not to leave the fortress, but maybe she has changed her mind and is sending someone to bring Rendil back after all. I wish he hadn't gone," she added bitterly. "Mother is so unhappy.'

"I'm unhappy too," Landon agreed morosely as he turned away from the thickening gloom into the light and warmth of the tower. Rilya gave a last long look northward, then followed him.

CHAPTER 14
THE FORDS OF HELDOR

Their second night of travel had started out well for the three runaways, but this good fortune did not last long. The rain, which had somewhat abated, began pouring steadily again. Their path became more and more muddy and veered perilously close to the river's edge. Although Burdil was sure-footed, Patsy felt increasingly nervous about riding him alone and began to beg the boys to let her dismount and walk with them.

"No!" Rendil rejoined sternly. "The path is too dangerous. You are safer by far on horseback."

Patsy swallowed this rebuff along with her injured pride, although she felt that he was treating her like a child. However, she soon had occasion to be grateful for his refusal. Rounding the trunk of a large tree, Rendil tripped, lost his footing, and began to slide down the steep bank into the river.

"Help!" he cried. "Dol save me!" Patsy screamed as Fendal reared in panic and Burdil began to snort and shy away. Condin grabbed the horses' reins, calling "Whoa, whoa, steady there," and, in the next breath, "Rendil, are you all right?"

For a sickening instant, no sound could be heard but the steady dropping of rain and the roar of angry waters. Then they heard a faint voice far below on their right, "Condin, Condin!"

"Rendil," he called back, "are you all right?"

"I have caught hold of a tree root," came the reply, somewhat louder. "But I am neck-deep in water and cannot hold on for long."

"Wait!" Condin cried. "I'll throw down a rope." Quickly he pulled a stout coil out of Rendil's saddlebag and, casting about for a moment, found a rock around which he tied the end of it. Then he crouched down, inching toward the edge of the embankment. "Rendil, where are you? Call out again, so I'll know where to throw this."

"Here I am." The voice sounded faint again. "Please hurry."

Condin dropped the rope down the slope, aiming blindly in the dark. "Can you see it?" he called. "Have you got it?"

"No. Yes. I cannot reach it. More to the right. More. Yes, now I have it. Hurry!"

"Hold on!" Condin shouted. Scrambling to his feet, he wound the rope around the pommel of Fendal's saddle, then slapped him on the rump. "Ho, there! Pull, boy!" Fendal neighed and began to pull, stumbling and hesitating, backward into the woods. Patsy screwed her eyes shut and bit her lip as leaves crunched and branches cracked and Condin urged the horse on for what seemed an eternity of effort.

Finally, the rope went slack as Rendil heaved himself up onto the trail and collapsed in a gasping, sodden heap. "Is he there, is he all right?" Condin yelled from back in the woods.

Patsy flung her eyes open and stared hard at the exhausted prince. "Yes," she called, "he's here!"

A moment later, Condin came crashing out of the underbrush with Fendal in tow. He stopped short when he saw Rendil. "Are you all right? How did it happen?"

"Tripped over a root," Rendil gasped, "lost my footing."

"Well, you're in no condition to travel now. We'll have to stop and rest for the night."

"Cannot stop here. Must reach Fords by morning." As if to emphasize his sense of urgency, Rendil tried to stand up, but his legs would not hold him and he fell back to his knees. "Must go on," he repeated, shaking his head in an effort to clear it.

"Well, then, mount up and let me lead." Condin grasped the bigger boy by the shoulders and helped him to his feet, propping him up while he pulled himself onto Fendal's back. Rendil slumped low on the horse's neck, burying his face in its silky mane. Since he made no effort to take the reins from Condin, Condin kept them and tossed the reins of his own mount up to Patsy. "Here," he said, "you'll have to guide him yourself."

Patsy froze. "But...but...I can't. I don't know how."

"Then you'll just have to let them hang loose," Condin snapped, "and hope he follows me." With that he stalked off down the trail, leading Fendal and not deigning even a backward glance to Patsy.

The rest of that night was pure agony. Well-trained Burdil followed his master with sure instinct, but Patsy had no confidence either in him or herself. Rendil, on the other hand, recovered himself quickly, but even though he asked Condin to stop while he dismounted, then insisted that he was strong enough to lead, and finally commanded him to hand over the reins, the younger boy ignored him and pushed stubbornly on. He was slower and more cautious than Rendil, but as the older boy chafed and fumed, he became increasingly angry and reckless. The ensuing tension only added to Patsy's nervousness, until she began to tremble uncontrollably at the

120

slightest sign of danger. Several times Condin slipped, but he righted himself immediately and went on, refusing to halt or to show any sign of weariness.

By the time the first rustlings of dawn could be heard overhead, Patsy felt she could stand it no longer. She was just on the verge of screaming, "Stop! Please!" when, to her astonishment, they did, before she could utter a sound. "Wha...what?" she stammered, caught off balance. "Where are we?"

"The Fords of Heldor," answered Condin shortly. "Can't you hear?"

Patsy listened, puzzled, but all she could hear, besides the dripping of rain, was a few birds beginning to chirp in the treetops. "I don't understand." She shivered once more, miserably.

Condin ground his teeth, while Rendil explained with weary impatience, "The river is shallow here and its bed smooth and easily forded. The Great North Road passes this way only a short distance hence."

"Oh." Patsy suddenly realized that for some time now the river had sounded only faintly in her ears. "Is this the place we were in such a hurry to get to?"

"Yes."

"Why?"

"That's what I would like to know," Condin interposed sourly. "First you nearly kill yourself, then you insist we have to get to the Fords by morning, then you won't trust me to lead you safely. Well, I did, no thanks to you, and here we are. Now, would you mind telling me why?"

For a moment, Rendil did not answer. Although Patsy could not see his face in the dim light, she knew well enough by this time that he was trying to control his anger. When he spoke, the unsteadiness of his voice confirmed her guess.

"Because," he said, forcing the words through tight lips, "we must travel by daylight from now on and I wish to pass this place and make sure of our route, before anyone happens along and sees us."

"Why must we travel by daylight," Condin asked sharply, "if we are going to continue to follow the river? Were you that frightened by what happened last night?"

"No!" Rendil shot back. "Of course not! We are not going to follow the river any more. I plan to travel parallel with the road from now on."

"You fool! There are too many farms and villages along the road. We'll surely get caught!"

"That is a risk we shall have to take. We will skirt around the edges of the inhabited places as far as possible, keeping mostly to the forest. But if we wish to reach Moldan Gorge ahead of Gendol, we must move and move quickly."

"You're out of your mind! Even if we galloped down the Great Road in broad daylight, we wouldn't reach Moldan Gorge ahead of Lord Gendol. He has a three days' lead on us. Besides, why do you want to get there before him? Isn't it enough that we join him there? Or have you got some stupid idea of trying to wrest command from him?"

"I do not trust him," Rendil answered icily. "He may be a traitor."

"He may well think that you are the traitor, from the way you're acting," was the caustic reply.

"Well, why don't we just take the road?" Patsy should have known better than to interrupt, but it seemed the obvious solution and she was sick and tired of traveling on slippery and dangerous paths by night. "After all, who's going to catch us?"

"Mother," said Condin.

"Lord Gendol," said Rendil in the same breath. They both paused, startled. Then Condin added, "Never mind. She's only a girl, she doesn't know anything."

"I assume then that you agree to my plan?"

"No, I don't! It's the most stupid idea you've ever had. All we have to do is keep on following the river and we'll arrive in plenty of time."

"Very well, you follow the river, if you so desire. We are going this way. Come." He turned and beckoned imperiously to Patsy. Then, with a flick of Fendal's reins, he rode off in the direction of Heldor.

Patsy remained where she was, stung to the quick by Condin's insult, and too exhausted to think of a reply. Besides, she did not know how to make Burdil move and was not sure that she wanted to go on with Rendil anyway. But after a short while, she realized that he was not coming back and that she had no choice but to follow him. Helplessly, she looked down at Condin who stood motionless beside her on the ground. "What do we do now?"

For answer, Condin savagely kicked into the muddy ground, then gave Burdil a vicious slap on the rump. "Move!" he cried in a voice thick with tears. Obediently, Burdil began to canter off through the woods, with Patsy clinging to the saddle for dear life. A few minutes of perilous travel brought her up with Rendil, who reached out and grabbed the horse's bridle, bringing him to a halt.

"Well, I see you still wish to accompany me," he remarked sarcastically. "Is that wretched brother of mine anywhere behind you?"

"I don't know," Patsy gulped. All of a sudden she began to cry. "Please, let's stop. Please!" she sobbed. "I can't go any further. Do we have to travel all day too?"

"We cannot stop here," he replied grimly. "We are within sight and hearing of the Fords. Now if Condin would only come, we could leave this place." Presently, Condin did come, sullen and disheveled. "Good," Rendil grunted. "Mount up and let us be off." Without a word Condin vaulted up behind Patsy and, reaching around her waist, took the reins from her. Together, the three of them moved out of the woods, heading toward the road and the Fords.

As they gained the road, Patsy noticed to her surprise how light it was. Rendil noticed it too and spurred Fendal on to a gallop. With the dawn wind in their faces, they thundered toward the Fords, splashed across without a pause, and veered off into the fields just short of the scattering of houses and inns that was Heldor. Dogs barked and a rooster crowed as they bolted past, but they made straight for the woods and reached them in safety. Patsy could hear behind them in the town the shouts of men now mingled with the barking. Her heart beat wildly and she could feel Condin trembling and Burdil heaving with exertion, but they did not stop until they had penetrated once more deep into the forest.

At last they halted at the edge of a small clearing. Rendil listened carefully before dismounting, but no sound could be heard except the twittering of a few birds. It was raining again, very gently. "We have not much shelter here," he said, looking around him, "but I think it is safe to rest awhile."

Condin dismounted in silence and helped Patsy down. They had nowhere to sit but on the wet ground, and nothing but cold food to eat. After eating, the two brothers slept, sitting up with their heads on their knees. Patsy lay pillowed against their saddlebags, with Rendil's leather cape under her and a blanket over her. For a long time she cried silently, the hot, miserable tears streaming down her face. When finally they subsided, she still could not sleep. "Why did I ever give in?" she thought. "Why did I ever leave Celdondol?" She recalled the events of the past few days and the memory burned in her soul. "I would order you to hand over the Sign and I would go without you." "You can't have my cross. It's mine!"

"I should have let him have it," she concluded bitterly. "Stupid old cross!" She had nearly forgotten about it, but now it dug into her chest as she lay against it. "Hasn't done any good anyhow," she grumbled aloud, yanking it from under her clothes and gripping it savagely in her fist. She was on the verge of tearing it from around her neck and throwing it away, when suddenly there leaped into her mind the kindly face of Mrs. Denton, followed by the deeply searching, yet loving gaze of the Queen. "You have been given a great mission, little one," the low voice echoed in Patsy's mind, "and you are free to accept or refuse it." And she had accepted; she had said she was willing to try.

"All right," Patsy said, again aloud, "I'll go on trying." Her grip loosened on the crucifix and she stuffed it back inside her blouse. "But, God," she added, "you'd better help me like the Queen said you would, because I can't go on this way much longer." It was the second prayer of her life, but this time, deep down in her heart, she felt she had an answer. Closing her eyes, she slept.

Rendil awakened her around noon and the three of them ate without speaking. Then they mounted up with Patsy in front of Condin, a decidedly more comfortable position. Rendil took the lead, without any explanation of where he thought he was going. As he rode, he hummed the familiar droning tune of the enchantment song, and once Patsy thought she heard him sing: *Clouds command now: break and fly! Rain: do cease thy wayward fall!* But the clouds did not break and the rain continued to fall.

They traveled a long time through the forest, over thick carpets of fallen leaves and under trees of such great height that, even though Patsy craned her neck and stared upward, she could not see the tops. "What kind of trees are they?" she asked Condin, who had, up to now, maintained his sullen silence.

"Fangolfin trees," he answered, and added after a moment's hesitation, "they are the pride of the forests of Arendolin."

"We don't have anything like them in our world. Or at least not where I live."

"Nor do they grow anywhere else in our world, but only in the land blessed by Dol." His voice echoed pride and even a certain affection.

"Oh!" answered Patsy, impressed. She looked up toward the treetops again and a drop of rain splashed in her eye. Condin chuckled at her exclamation of annoyance.

"I hope he knows where he's going," she grumbled, nodding in the direction of Rendil who was a little way ahead of them.

"Humph!" Condin snorted. "He thinks he's so great!"

"Well, isn't he? I mean, isn't he going to be king?"

"Maybe someday, but he isn't yet. It's only because he's Mother's favorite that he gets all sorts of privileges and thinks he can lord it over everybody." Condin's voice was edged with bitterness.

"Well, I..." Patsy hesitated, feeling this to be rather unfair and not knowing how to answer him.

"Father always preferred me," he added, to her surprise.

"You mean, if your Father had lived, he would have made you king after him?"

"I don't know." He sounded surprised in his turn. "I never thought of it. I really don't care about that anyway. It's just that..." Patsy heard his voice tighten up. "It's just that I wish Father were still alive," he ended miserably.

"Well, I guess your Mother and Rendil and everybody else wishes that too."

"Not like I do. You don't understand." He choked and swallowed. "Why am I even talking to you? You're just a girl."

Patsy ground her teeth in anger, but said nothing. "I'll show them," she thought, "someday I'll show them!" But meanwhile she really did not understand, and could only let his words turn over and over in her mind.

By this time it was late afternoon and the gray, shadowy forest was becoming dark and forbidding. Rendil began to slacken his pace and finally halted altogether as the

127

other two came abreast of him. "I think," he said, "we had better return within sight of the road before nightfall, so as not to lose our bearings."

Condin nodded wordlessly and they started off again, veering toward the left. Rendil led confidently for some time, but the thickets only grew more impenetrable and there was no sign of either road or trail. "We should stumble upon some farmer's field any moment now," he reassured them, but no such field came into sight. Presently the trees began to thin and it grew lighter ahead. "Yes, here at last!" he exclaimed with satisfaction, urging Fendal forward. But as they broke through into the open, they realized that it was only a forest clearing. An involuntary expression of dismay escaped Rendil's lips.

"Lost, aren't you?" Condin gibed acidly. "What are you going to do now?"

Rendil drew himself up with dignity. "Now," he said, "we must make use of the aid so generously afforded us by Dol. My Lady Palissa," he inclined his head to her, "will you invoke your God, by the power of his Sign, to guide us?"

Patsy stared at him, flabbergasted. "I…" She began to protest, but caught herself. Now she wasn't just a girl, now she was important, and she had to show them that she was. "But I don't know what to do!" she wailed interiorly as she fumbled for the cross. Two sets of eyes focused intently upon her as her own eyes blurred nervously and, for a moment, refused to focus on their object. "Think," she told herself fiercely, "think!" But no thought would come, except the rather incongruous one that love is more powerful than any enchantment. "I don't need love right now," her heart cried out, "I need help!" She could feel Condin's restless shifting and Rendil's gaze boring through her and her own perspiration trickling down. She clutched the Sign tightly in her fist and strained with all her might, but no light would come. Finally she cried aloud in desperation, "O God, do something!"

To her amazement, a gruff voice replied, "I'd say he might, with three fine young'uns like you lost out here in these woods at nightfall."

Chapter 15

Gifil

Patsy froze in horror. "Who goes there?" Rendil shouted as he grabbed for his sword.

"Now, now lad, put that thing up. I'll not be hurtin' you." The owner of the voice moved into the clearing, a weather-beaten, scraggly-bearded man of uncertain age.

"Who are you?" Rendil demanded his hand still on the sword hilt.

"And I might ask the same of you, seein's how you're trespassin' on my property."

"Your property?" Rendil sounded slightly incredulous.

"Aye. And my father's afore me and his father's afore him." He paused for a moment, but the children only stared at him warily. "Well," he said at length, "too bad you ain't minded to be sociable, 'cause I was fixin' to offer you a roof and beds for the night."

"Oh, please, let's go with him!" Patsy burst out.

Rendil showed signs of wavering. "What did you say your name was?" he asked uncertainly.

"Folks hereabouts call me Gifil," he replied. "And what'd you say your name was?"

"I would rather not discuss that," Rendil answered coldly, "but we will accept your kind offer of hospitality for the night."

"Humph!" Gifil commented to no one in particular, "mighty uppity, ain't he, for bein' but a lad." He looked round at the three of them. "Well, I don't like takin' in

130

strangers what won't give their names, but seein's how you younguns might be lost and might be in danger too, for onc't I'll do it. Come along then and be swift about it." Without another word, he turned and strode off rapidly into the forest.

Patsy's heart pounded with fear lest Rendil hesitate again and lose sight of him. But he seemed to have made up his mind and quickly urged Fendal on after the man. Even so, they found it difficult to follow him as he made his way swiftly among the glades and thickets. Patsy wondered what he meant about their being in danger. Were there wild animals in these woods? She glanced around nervously, but it was too dark to see anything. Presently she thought she spied a glimmer of light in the distance. Her heart leaped into her mouth. "What's that?" she whispered to Condin.

"Where?"

"Over there. A light. It's gone behind the trees now." She peered anxiously ahead, but for several moments nothing could be seen.

Then Condin whispered, "Yes, there, I see it. It looks like a lantern or something."

"It's much closer now, but where is Gifil?"

Indeed, they had lost sight of him among the trees. But Rendil moved boldly ahead, aiming for the steadily growing light. The other two followed and, before long, they burst out of the forest into a clearing. There before them stood a small cottage, through whose windows firelight gleamed, warm and inviting. Gifil was leaning against the door of the cottage, talking in his funny, dry way to someone inside.

"Ah, there they be," he cried as he spotted them. "Step right up, don't be shy. I was just tellin' my missus how

131

we'd be havin' three guests for the night and she'd best put extra bread on."

The children rode forward slowly into the circle of light and dismounted. Patsy did feel acutely shy. She hung back in Rendil's shadow as he stood silently by Fendal's side and waited.

"This is my missus," Gifil gestured by way of introduction to the long, lean-faced, work-hardened woman poised firmly in the doorway. "Melna, these here are the young'uns I was tellin' you about."

"How do." She inclined her head gravely in their direction. Her voice was rough in texture, but surprisingly gentle in tone, and Patsy did not know whether to be frightened or relieved by this, the first woman she had seen in several days.

"Step on in," she beckoned to them as she moved back into the cottage, "it might be cold and wet out there."

Rendil started forward, then checked himself suddenly. "What about our mounts?" he asked Gifil.

"I'll bed 'em down for you. There's a shed over yonder." He reached for Fendal's reins but Rendil clenched them firmly in his fist.

"No, thank you, we will bed them down ourselves if you will show us where. Lady Palissa…" He turned around to find her and nearly stepped on her, she was so close behind him. "Lady Palissa, I think it is safe for you to accompany this woman. We will join you presently."

Patsy stared at him for a moment stupidly, while fear of these strange people battled within her against the desire for warmth and shelter. But when Rendil asked in surprise, "Would you rather come with us?" the desire for warmth and shelter won out. "No!" she squeaked, and pushing past him, she darted into the cottage. Once inside the door, she halted abruptly, breathless at her own temerity.

"You needn't be bashful," the woman called Melna said, "we ain't fixin' to hurt you. My man and me, we been livin' here for many a season now, and folks round about all know us, how good we be to everybody."

"Thank you," said Patsy inanely, as she came a step closer.

"Here, have yourself a seat by the fire and get warm whilst I put on the supper." Melna indicated a low wooden stool by the hearth.

"Thank you," Patsy said again, this time with genuine gratitude. She took the proffered seat, huddling as close to the blaze as possible. Melna smiled and the smile erased all harshness from her face.

"Reckon that's a sight better than ridin' round all night in the rain. And such a little lass too. What might be your name?"

"Patsy," Patsy blurted out, without thinking.

"Passy?" the woman echoed, puzzled. Then she shrugged her shoulders and murmured to herself, "Well, these fine folks do give their young'uns queer names." She busied herself silently, setting the table with wooden trenchers and spoons and intricately carved wooden cups. Patsy watched her, fascinated. For a moment she had frightened herself, giving out her name when Rendil had been so reticent. But the woman had seen no significance in it and, besides, it was not the same name as the others called her by. So Patsy relaxed, leaning her head upon her knees, and had nearly nodded off to sleep when the door burst open and the boys strode in.

"Here we be," rumbled Gifil, "and hungry as bears." He hung his leather cap and short vest on a peg and sat down at the table. "Set yourselves," he motioned to the boys, "I do believe supper's ready."

"Aye," Melna affirmed, "and you can come too, little gal. But first, why'nt you take off your cloaks?"

"Yes, thank you, we will." Rendil threw back the hood of his cape and began to undo the clasp at the neck. Condin and Patsy were gratefully following suit, when they were arrested by a loud gasp from Melna.

"Might of Dol!" she shrieked. "Gif, what've you done! These young'uns be royalty! Go away," she began to retreat from them defensively. "Why've you come here? To spy on us?"

The three young people looked at her and at one another in astonishment and alarm. "I do not know…" Rendil began, but Gifil interrupted him.

"Hesh, Melna," he ordered sternly. "I brung these young'uns here purpose-like, knowin' they might be royalty, and I'll tell you why. I was takin' the trail upriver from Heldor this mornin' and just a mite after sun-up, I runned smack into a troop of King's men in their scarlet and gray. They was combin' the woods up and down either side of the river and the leader, he says to me, all business-like, ' Have you seen three youths of noble blood, two boys and a girl, riding horses from the royal stables? They ran away from Celdondol two days ago and the Queen urgently desires their return.' And I says I hadn't. And he says if I do, please bring'em down to Heldor and don't let'em get away. So they went on down for

134

the Fords and I headed up for home. Long about sunset, I runned into these here youn'uns and thinks I to myself, these must be the ones they was lookin' for.

"But what reason have you," Rendil interrupted, "for thinking us of royal blood?" He seemed determined to brazen his way through at any cost.

"Our hair, stupid," Condin drawled, before either Gifil or his wife could answer. "Do any but the children of Rendol have 'locks of star-shine'?"

"'And eyes like the night sky'?" added Melna nervously, completing the old saying.

"Aye," Gifil said, "and that one be like the fire on the Gelfin Tree." He looked wonderingly at Patsy. "I ain't seen it but once, when I was a lad, but I'll never forget."

There was a moment of silence during which Patsy and Condin looked at Rendil and he looked intently at the floor. "Very well," he said at last with a sigh, "yes, we are the ones they were looking for. What do you intend to do with us?"

"Told you what we're fixin' to do," rejoined Gifil, feigning indignation. "We're fixin' to give you bread and a roof for the night."

"And in the morning?" Rendil eyed the man suspiciously.

"Reckon you be three against two and armed. Not much we can do but let you go your way."

"Gif, be you meanin' that?" his wife gasped.

"Aye." He turned to her earnestly. "Reckon I can't let no soldiers lay hands on him what will be king."

Patsy could not help but believe him and noticed that Rendil too seemed to be relaxing. She wished they would sit down and eat.

"May I ask a question?" It was Condin who spoke.

"Aye. Go ahead."

"These soldiers in the king's livery: were they coming downstream from the mountains or upstream from Celdondol?"

"Told you. They was comin' downriver toward the Fords. And I heard one of 'em say to another, 'I wonder what Gendol will do if we can't find them?'"

The two boys looked at one another in genuine horror. "Mother must have sent word to him," Condin concluded.

"Or else he has left spies at Celdondol," Rendil rejoined grimly. "The company left to guard the fortress was hand-picked by him."

"In any case, what do we do now?"

"Well, why don't we eat while we're talking about it?" Patsy interrupted petulantly. "I'm hungry."

"Aye, lads," agreed Gifil, "the little gal is right. Hang up your cloaks and set down. Thinkin's always easier on a full stomach."

So they did as they were bidden and Melna passed around a loaf of rich brown bread, a pot of honey and a pitcher of what looked like beer. Patsy tasted it and made a face. It was as bitter as the honey was sweet. "Oh," Melna clucked, "I mighta knowed it would be too strong for you. Here." She leaped up from the table and came back in a moment with another pitcher, this time of water. "Sorry it ain't milk," she apologized. "It will be in the mornin'."

For awhile no one spoke and the only sounds that could be heard in the little cabin were the crackling of logs on the fire and the faint scraping of wooden utensils on wooden plates. At last, when they had eaten their fill and the bread was nearly gone, Gifil leaned back in his chair, folded his arms on his chest and said, "Well now, you might start by tellin' me your names."

Rendil raised his head proudly. "I am Rendil, son of Rendol Clarendil, and heir to the throne of Arendolin."

"Your Highness." Gifil and his wife both rose to their feet and bowed, much to Patsy's surprise. "We be honored to have you under our roof," Gifil added.

Rendil acknowledged their homage graciously and motioned them to sit down again. "This is my brother-in-blood, Condin, son of Rendol." They inclined their heads in grave recognition. "And this is Lady Palissa, emissary of the high gods, bearer of the Sign."

Patsy was embarrassed but she tried to act as dignified as possible. "And you told me your name was Passy," Melna commented reproachfully, "as if you was nobody."

"Passy?" Condin echoed incredulously.

"I…" Patsy stammered. She could feel her face burning neon red. It was Gifil who came to her rescue with a sudden chuckle.

"And the three of you runned away from Celdondol the day afore yesterday!" He went on chuckling, as if delighted by the incongruity of their situation.

Now Rendil flushed in his turn, but, annoyed as he was, he could no longer evade the issue. "Yes, after a manner of speaking, that is true."

Gifil suddenly turned serious. "Why, and where be you bound?"

Rendil hesitated, taken aback by his directness, and Patsy wondered what he would say. After a long pause, he began slowly, "I am on a quest to recover my father's lost enchantment and assume my rightful place as King of Arendolin. The Lady Palissa is my helper appointed by the Great One, and…" he swallowed, "and my brother too has come to assist me."

"Well," Gifil nodded consideringly, "you be a mite young for all that, but I reckon it'll have to do. How come you runned away then, instead of goin' with ceremonies and such like? And how come they're all out after you?"

"Because," Condin interposed smugly, "our Lady Mother had forbidden him to leave the fortress."

Rendil flushed again and compressed his lips with anger but, unexpectedly, Gifil rose to his defense. "Well, I reckon she might be just tryin' to protect you, mother-like. Ain't no harm in it, but ain't always good either." He paused and added, half to himself, "Also ain't much good for a young'un not to mind." Aloud he said, "What about Lord Gendol?"

"We suspect that he is a traitor," Rendil replied flatly.

"A traitor!" Gifil seemed genuinely dismayed. "What proof be you havin' for that?"

"None whatever." This was Condin again.

"Yes, we do!" Patsy blurted out indignantly. "He refuses to accept the Sign and he doesn't believe in Dol!"

"How do you know?" Condin shot back.

"Because…" Patsy was groping furiously for words when Gifil intervened.

"Hold on, hold on. Ain't *no* good for you young'uns to be fightin'. Now supposin' we says we don't know about Gendol, one way or t'other."

"We do so," Patsy asserted sulkily.

"No," Rendil answered, "he is correct. We really do not know—one way or the other," he added with a sidelong glance at Condin's self-satisfied smirk.

"Well, then, that still leaves me askin' where you're bound. Where do you hope to find this here enchantment you be lookin' for?"

"I hope to reach Moldan Gorge before the night of the dark moon, when the enemy will launch their attack. I hope to ride forth to battle at the head of the troops, with or without Lord Gendol, and, in the presence of the Sign, I am confident that we shall conquer." Rendil lifted up his head proudly and his eyes shone with excitement.

Gifil looked sympathetic but not too impressed. "And will the enchantment be there a-waitin' for you?"

For a moment Rendil did not even hear him, but eventually he realized that they were all looking at him, waiting for an answer. "I beg your pardon?"

"I says, you still ain't told me where this here enchantment might be found."

Rendil seemed angry at first, then entirely deflated. "I do not know," he admitted at last. "But if I do not have it by the time we reach Moldan, all will be in vain."

"If we keep on getting lost," Condin interposed, "we'll never even get to Moldan."

Rendil looked as if he were about to throttle his younger brother when suddenly Patsy burst out with, "Why can't Gifil show us the way?" It was a flash of inspiration. She was beginning to feel warm and comfortable in the company of this man and dreaded having to say goodbye to him. At least he could referee their quarrels.

Rendil took up the idea at once. "Yes, please, would you consent to guide us? We need someone to lead us by the safest, shortest route to Moldan Gorge."

Gifil was completely taken aback. "Well, I don't rightly…"

"Oh, please say yes!" To Patsy's surprise, Condin also joined in the pleading.

"Well, now," Gifil gazed consideringly at the three eager faces. "Seein's how you all want it, reckon I can't rightly say no."

"Hooray!" They all applauded enthusiastically as his face relaxed into a grin.

"Then should we get on with discussin' the route?"

"Yes, do," urged Rendil.

At that point, Patsy lost the thread of the conversation. She felt so relieved by Gifil's agreeing to her proposal that she slumped back into her chair and closed her eyes. "Thank you, God," she breathed silently. At last he seemed to be doing something for them.

Once her eyes were closed, it became impossible to reopen them. Although she tried to listen as the boys and Gifil formulated their plans, the steady drone of voices faded further and further into the distance until it finally disappeared altogether.

Patsy awoke with a start some time later and did not know where she was. Something crackly and fragrant was beneath her and a strange red glow filled her eyes. For a moment she lay still in silent terror, trying to remember. The

140

castle? No. The forest? No. A cave? No. Gifil? Yes! The last thing she knew, they were in Gifil's cottage. Then she recognized the strange red glow as the fire burning low on the hearth and she realized that she was lying in front of it on a pallet of straw. She had been dreaming that she was at home, in her own house, and her father was saying to her, "The Sign is all right, honey. Do whatever Mrs. Denton tells you."

"I wish it were true," she thought to herself, with a pang of regret. She was about to close her eyes again, when she heard whispering behind her. By straining her ears, she could just make out Melna's voice.

"Gif, I ain't likin' it, I tell you. All this here rain – it's a bad omen."

"Hesh, Melna," he replied softly, "don't take on so. With him what will be king right here, under our roof, it's bound to come all right."

Patsy smiled to herself and slept.

CHAPTER 16
COMMAND THE CLOUDS

They left early the next morning, after a breakfast of wild rice, milk and honey. Melna loaded their saddlebags with fresh provisions and extra blankets, and helped Patsy repack her bundle.

"Oh dear," she moaned as she pawed through the small mound of wrinkled and damp clothing, "I've lost a stocking!"

"It's a wonder you didn't lose everything, the way you was carryin' it," Melna observed wryly. "Here, I reckon I might be havin' just what you need." She opened a polished wooden chest and, after a moment's searching, produced a pair of thick white woolen stockings, close to Patsy's size.

"Oh," Patsy cried, "they're lovely and they look so warm! Where did you get them?"

"Had a little gal myself once, just about like you."

"What happened to her? Did she get married?"

Melna laughed softly. "No, fever runned through here one fine summer, carried her off in three days' time. Buried in yonder meadow, she is." She broke off and began to stare vacantly out the window into the gray morning mist.

Patsy was embarrassed, not knowing what to say. After a moment's reflection, she decided to say nothing, and began pulling the stockings on her feet instead. They fit well and felt warm and snug inside her boots. All at once, a new thought struck her. "Why don't you come with us?" she asked. "Won't you get lonesome here by yourself, without Gifil?"

Melna looked as if she had been called back from another world. "Huh? Oh!" She shook herself and laughed again. "No, honey, now don't be mindin' me. There's many a neighbor hereabouts, to keep me company. Besides, we got four fine lads, my man and me, each with his own missus and young'uns. They all be up north now, a-fightin' for the King. I reckon Gif will bring back word of them, when he comes."

"I hope so," Patsy said, grinning with relief.

A thick, dingy fog smothered everything, as they set out across the meadow and into the forest. Gifil led the way on foot, with the young people riding, Patsy this time in front of Rendil. They could scarcely see one another, so heavy was the mist, and Patsy wondered how even Gifil could keep from getting lost. But he continued to move ahead, as if by some unerring instinct, and they followed blindly in his train.

For a long while they traveled in unbroken silence, until they lost all sense of time as well as direction. At first Patsy did not mind; she felt as if she were in some sort of dream world and let her thoughts roam freely. But as the hours wore on, she began to get very tired and increasingly nervous. Were they never going to stop? Where were they? Suppose Gifil were really lost? These were questions she dared not ask aloud, but she decided to break the silence anyway. Strangely, it took a great deal of effort.

"Melna says she and Gifil have four sons in the army," she declared, much too loudly.

There was no response. Rendil shifted slightly in the saddle and they kept on riding.

"How many days until we get to Moldan?" she tried again. Again there was no response. Still they rode on until, finally, she could stand it no longer.

143

"Oh, won't the sun ever shine?" she wailed.

"If I had my enchantment," Rendil replied grimly, "I could make the sun shine."

"But when are you going to get your enchantment?" By now she had lost all patience.

"I do not know." For the first time, he too sounded depressed and hopeless. They rode on for a few more minutes in silence. Gifil, only a few feet ahead, seemed to pay no attention to their conversation. Then Rendil spoke again. "Condin?"

"Yes?"

"I…" He swallowed and Patsy could almost feel the effort he had to make to say what he wanted to say. "I am sorry for my behavior the other night. I never thanked you for rescuing me and for leading us safely to the Fords."

For a moment there was silence and Patsy wondered if Condin would refuse the apology. His face could not be clearly seen but when he did speak, surprise and confusion were mingled in his voice.

"Oh, that. It wasn't really much." He hesitated. "I guess I shouldn't have argued with you. You were right about not following the river. We would have run straight into that search party."

Rendil sighed. "Yes, but we did lose our way, thanks to my over confidence. If Gifil had not found us, we would still be wandering aimlessly."

Patsy perked up at this, expecting them to make some acknowledgment of the power of her Sign and its efficacy in bringing help. Instead, Condin giggled suddenly. "Say, what was it Gifil called you? Passy? I like that!"

144

"It's Patsy!" she shot back. "And it was his wife, not him."

"Passy!" Condin laughed again, ignoring her. "I do like that, don't you?" He jabbed at Rendil.

Patsy felt her face getting very red as Rendil joined in the laughter and even Gifil glanced back over his shoulder to see what the joke was.

"Yes," the older boy agreed, "I think it quite a suitable name." He tweaked playfully at the back of her hood, exposing her tousled curls. "Say, Firehead, you would make a fine sister!"

At this, Patsy exploded. "Don't call me firehead!" she began furiously. But before she could go on, another thought shoved its way into her mind and struggled so imperiously to the fore that she nearly choked on it. "Call fire your sister!" she shouted, whirling about in the saddle to face Rendil.

The boys roared with laughter and Gifil joined them. "Ho!" cried Rendil. "I might as well call fire my sister! Why, Lady Palissa, I thought you were so mild."

Patsy was nearly in tears now, not so much from humiliation, as from the force of the idea, which had taken hold of her. "The song, stupid, the song!" She clenched her fist in desperation. "That's what the song says."

"The song? Do you mean the enchantment song?" Rendil was beginning to take her seriously.

"Yes, don't you see? Sing it!"

Rendil looked at her as if he might start laughing again, but instead he obligingly began the song:

'Neath the silver bow thee down;

Fire thy sister, friend thou call.

Clouds command now: break and fly!

145

Rain: do cease thy errant fall!

He paused, frowning. "Is that what you meant? I do not understand."

"I think I do," said Condin.

All eyes turned to his thoughtful face, swimming as if disembodied in the mist. "You apologized to me just now. Wasn't that sort of like bowing beneath the silver? I'm talking about hair, of course. And," his mouth twitched in a grin, "you certainly called fire your sister."

"Yes," Rendil answered impatiently, "but you cannot be suggesting that this fulfills the conditions of the riddle."

"Why not?" Patsy demanded, but he did not answer because Condin was staring at him intently.

"Rendil," he said in a queer voice, "your hair. I think it's turning."

"Turning?" Rendil sounded puzzled.

"Yes. It's growing darker." Condin's eyes shone with excitement. "Rendil, command the clouds!"

Rendil looked at him helplessly. Then, all of a sudden, he seemed to feel the change deep within himself. Patsy, close by him, felt it too, strong and sweeping. For a moment, she was back in the presence of the Queen, as she had been that dark, moonlit night. But this was somehow different. She gazed at Rendil's face and saw that it had become man-like and stern. He threw back his head and cried aloud in the tongue of the ancient ones and, as he did so, the mist vanished and through the rain-bejeweled treetops sunlight glistened down.

CHAPTER 17
THE RIDER RETURNS

Rilya and Landon stood on the battlements, basking in the warm afternoon sun and gazing out over the fields toward the forest and the North.

"Did Mother make the sun shine after all?" asked Landon.

"She told you, silly. Didn't you listen?" Rilya answered. "She said it was raining because of what Rendil did and only he could undo it."

"Does that mean he's coming home then?"

"I don't know. I wish it did. I miss him so much. And Lady Palissa."

"And Condin," her brother added wistfully, but she went on without hearing him.

"Has it been nine days already since she came to us? Or ten? She must really be an emissary of Dol, for Rendil to include her in his plans like this."

"Then why did they leave without Mother knowing?"

"I don't know. I wish I did." Her eyes traveled longingly up the Great Road until they reached the horizon. Suddenly a speck materialized on the Road, which, as she watched it, became a figure on horseback, growing ever larger and nearer. "Landon!" she cried, gripping his arm. "Look! Is that the soldier coming back again? The one Mother sent out?"

"Where?" Landon boosted himself up on the battlement in order to see better. "Yes!" he shouted, staring wide-eyed in the direction of her pointing finger.

"Oh!" She clapped her hands with excitement. "He must have news about Rendil."

"Come on, let's find out!" Landon jumped down and began running for the guard tower. "Wait!" Rilya cried as she picked up her skirts and plunged after him. But by the time they had descended the battlements and dashed around to the main courtyard, the rider had already entered the fortress and was nowhere to be seen. Landon accosted one of the sentries at the gate. "You there! Did a rider come through here just now?"

The soldier looked startled at first, but then collected himself and saluted smartly. "Yes, your Highness, he did."

"Well, which way did he go?" Landon demanded.

"I didn't notice, your Highness," the sentry replied in a somewhat vague manner.

"Oh, bother!" Rilya exclaimed, but Landon was undaunted. "I bet he went to Mother, first thing. Let's find out!" And off he ran for the castle, as fast as his chubby legs would carry him. After a moment's hesitation, Rilya followed suit and quickly outdistanced him, so that she arrived first, breathless and panting, outside the Queen's audience chamber. Helfon, the scribe, sat at his desk in the anteroom, squinting myopically at a lengthy scroll from the files.

"Helfon!" Rilya gasped. "Has the rider been to Mother yet?"

He looked up slowly from his reading, as if resenting the interruption. "I beg your pardon?"

"Helfon, is the rider here?" cried Landon as he came clattering in.

The scribe peered from one to the other in ill-concealed annoyance. "And what rider might you be speaking of?"

"Why, the soldier," Rilya answered in surprise. "He just now returned with news of Rendil and we felt sure he would report to Mother first."

"Your Highness," he replied, "her majesty the Queen has not received anyone in audience this afternoon, nor did she have any appointments scheduled. And she did not leave word of any urgent matters upon which you should be informed." And with that, Helfon returned to his reading.

The two children looked at one another in dismay. "I suppose we'll just have to wait until Mother comes tonight for the blessing," Rilya concluded dolefully.

"Why don't we see if she's in her privy chambers," Landon suggested.

"But she would never receive a soldier there!"

"I don't care. I want to see Mother."

"Well, all right." So the two of them trudged off to the Queen's apartments where they found Radin standing guard at the entrance. He saluted when he saw them and smiled broadly.

"Radin, is Mother in?" Rilya asked.

"Yes, your Highness, she is," he replied.

"May we enter?"

"Yes, of course." He opened the door and held it for them as they paraded through. But they had not gone three paces before they crashed into Lady Calya, who had leaped up from her seat when she heard the door open and was advancing full-tilt to meet the intruders.

"Oh, pardon me!" Rilya exclaimed as she and Landon trod on each other in their haste to back away.

"Where do you think you are going?" Lady Calya snapped in reply.

"We wish to see Mother." Rilya steadied herself and held her ground. She had long since made up her mind not to be cowed by this woman's unpleasantness.

"Her majesty is resting and will not be disturbed."

"Oh, please," Rilya begged, "this is important."

"We want to know if the rider had any news about Rendil," Landon piped up from behind Rilya's back, where he was hiding because he was very much cowed.

"What rider? Is this one of your infantile games?"

"No," Rilya answered firmly. "A soldier just rode into the fortress, coming from the North and we thought maybe he had been with Rendil." She glanced wistfully at the closed door of the Queen's bedchamber. "I guess we were wrong."

"Yes, indeed, your Highness, I am sure you were," Lady Calya replied in abrasively soothing tones. "Now I would suggest that you return to your quarters like good children before your royal Mother awakens and becomes angry with you."

"Mother would never become angry!" Landon shouted, but Rilya grabbed him by the hand and dragged him out before they could be expelled forcibly. She herself was trembling with humiliation and fury. "Good children" indeed! Yes, she told herself grimly, Mother would have been annoyed, but not with them. So upset was she that they had nearly reached the tower entrance before she heard Landon crying, "Let go of me! You're hurting me!"

Rilya came to herself and dropped his hand. "I'm so sorry," she exclaimed. "I was thinking about Lady Calya."

"I hate her!" he proclaimed as he rubbed his sore fingers. "Why does Mother keep her around?"

"She says she is an excellent hairdresser, a seamstress without rival, and we should learn to put up with people who are disagreeable," Rilya recited tonelessly, as if repeating a lesson for Sir Pandil. "Anyway, never mind. Galna must have supper ready by now. We'll talk to Mother tonight."

But the Queen was so late in arriving that Rilya began to wonder if she would come at all. Landon was all fidgety with excitement and kept running to the door to look for her, until Galna threatened to send him to bed. "Look at the moon and stars instead," she offered by way of diversion. "We haven't seen them in several nights. Do you notice how the moon has waned already?"

Rilya and Landon both looked and Rilya, with a thrill of fear, saw that it was true. "The night of the Dark Moon is coming," she whispered half to herself.

"No it isn't, silly," Landon countered, having heard her. "There's still plenty of moon left. Besides, Mother will protect us when the moon is dark. Doesn't she always?"

"I will do my best," a gentle voice replied.

"Mother!" they cried, whirling around to face her.

"Mother, what did the rider say?" Landon blurted at once.

"Yes, Mother, please," Rilya chimed in, "did he have news from Rendil?"

"I hope his Highness is safe?" Even Galna could not contain herself.

"Wait, wait," the Queen called laughingly as she warded off their questions with a wave of her hand. "One at a time, please! Now, to which rider are you referring?"

"The soldier," shouted Landon, who was too wound up to be either polite or coherent.

"What soldier?" The Queen was beginning to sound puzzled.

"The one whom you sent out after Rendil the day he left," Rilya explained. "He returned this afternoon and we were sure he would report to you at once. Haven't you seen him yet?" She ended rather lamely, with a sinking feeling that her mother hadn't.

"My dear children," the Queen sounded not only puzzled but also dismayed, "I did not send out any soldier in pursuit of your brothers. In fact, I gave the order that none of the garrison was to leave the fortress. Are you sure you have not imagined this?"

"We saw him," Landon asserted, "going and coming."

Rilya nodded in confirmation. She was surprised that her mother knew nothing about the messenger and not a little hurt that even she had doubted their seriousness of purpose. "Don't you really have any news about Rendil?" she asked forlornly.

The Queen smiled a gentle, tranquil smile. "Yes, dear child, but not of that sort. What I know, I have seen by the light of Dol." Her smile broadened into great waves of happiness. "I have seen that Rendil's enchantment has begun to gather to him and that he has won it in a manly and honorable way."

152

"Oh, Mother!" Rilya exclaimed, and with a spontaneous rush of joy, she flung her arms around the Queen and kissed her. "Everything is going to be all right then?"

"The darkness of his disobedience is slowly being mended," the Queen replied. Then her smile died away. "But there is another, a greater darkness. I have felt it for some time, weighing heavily on my heart, yet, up until now, I could not understand. Perhaps now," she added slowly, "I begin to do so." Her words were solemn and Rilya felt chill fear growing in her as she listened.

"I do not want to alarm you," the Queen continued, sensing her reaction, "but I must warn you: from now on, be very careful to whom you speak and what you say. Did you tell anyone else about this messenger you saw?"

"Only Helfon and Lady Calya," Rilya replied, "but they didn't believe us."

"And the sentry at the gate," added Landon. "Why can't we tell anyone? Is it a secret?"

"In a way, yes. Or you might call it a game – a game of pretending that you know nothing about Rendil. Can you play this game for me?"

"Yes!" Landon cried at once. "I like pretending games."

"Good. And you, Rilya?"

"Yes, Mother, of course," Rilya answered more quietly. She was not deceived by the light words; her mother's face was serious and urgent. "Is Rendil in danger?"

"No, dear," the Queen replied, "I do not think so yet. Galna," she turned to the old nurse standing silently by the window, "have you understood my words?"

"Yes, your majesty." Galna nodded without leaving her place.

"Very well, then. Come," she beckoned to the children, "and let me bless you."

Landon ran to her side and knelt expectantly. For a moment the Queen said nothing, but looked down at him with an expression of deep tenderness and sorrow. Finally she laid her had on his brow and whispered, "May Dol protect you, my dear little son."

"May it truly be so," he answered, wide-eyed and trusting. Then he broke into an impish grin. "You're my favorite lady," he announced. "I'm going to kiss both your hands like they do in the story books!"

"My lord!" Galna gasped, but the Queen threw back her head and laughed until her laughter filled the room.

"Why, my lord prince," she exclaimed gaily as she extended her hands to him, "I am honored by your predilection." He seized her proffered hands and kissed them with such a serious, comical bow that Rilya giggled and even Galna had to smile. Then, in a transport of unabashed delight, he bounded for the door, cried "Good night!" and dashed for the stairs. They could hear him whooping and clattering all the way up to the top.

When he was quite gone and silence had fallen, the Queen turned back to Rilya. She was still smiling, but with a smile of haunting sadness. "My child," she beckoned to the girl.

"Yes, Mother," Rilya replied, but she hung back, afraid of what was coming.

"Dear daughter," the Queen's expression changed and became very grave. "I had thought perhaps to spare you, but I see that I cannot. You are old enough now to be aware of evil and to face it. Therefore I must be honest with you."

Rilya wished acutely that she could have run out with Landon. But Mother was right; she was too old for that now. She tried to swallow, but her mouth was dry. "What is it, Mother?" she whispered at last.

"We are in great danger. I am not sure yet from what quarter, but I know that treachery lies in our midst. The intruder in your room the other night was one of our own soldiers. The messenger you saw – and I do believe that you saw him – left the fortress and returned without my knowledge or consent. Someone must have dispatched these men and must have given them a definite mission to accomplish. Our task now is to find out who and what before it is too late."

"How can I help?" Rilya felt herself trembling with anxiety, yet she was proud that her mother was confiding in her and wanted desperately not to let her down.

"You must go about your duties as if nothing were wrong," the Queen replied, "and at the same time be very cautious and circumspect. I am not sure whom we can trust."

"You can trust me, your majesty!" Galna blurted out with unaccustomed vehemence. "I mean, begging your pardon for interrupting, but I would never betray you, any of you, never." She burst into tears of mingled hurt and distress.

"Dear Galna." The Queen stepped instantly to the old woman's side, took her hand and squeezed it lovingly. "I am sorry. I did not mean to intimate that you were disloyal. How could you be? You who cared for my royal husband when he was in the cradle, and now for his children until this day. No, if I had not trusted you completely, I would never have spoken this way in your presence."

155

"Thank you, your majesty." Galna fished out a large white handkerchief and wiped her eyes with it. "If you'll excuse me, your majesty, I don't know why I said that. I don't even know why I stayed. I should be turning down her Highness's bed, so I'll just go now, if you don't mind."

"Of course, Galna," the Queen answered, as the flustered woman backed away, curtsied, and stumbled in confusion from the room.

For a long time after she had left, Rilya and her mother stood and looked at one another, neither of them saying a word. Rilya, princess of Arendolin and heiress of enchantment, was long accustomed to rest and play in the depth of her mother's gaze. But though she now searched her mother's face, she found there neither rest nor play, but only somber sorrow. "Mother," Rilya gulped, "will you bless me?"

The Queen extended her hands and placed them lightly on her daughter's silver head. "May Dol protect you, my dear child," she intoned. "May he give you courage and wisdom for this night and for many days and nights to come."

"May it truly be so," Rilya answered as she took her mother's hand in the ritual gesture and kissed it. In return, she received a strong embrace, brief but invigorating. The Queen turned to leave and Rilya watched her go in silence, but at the door she paused and came back.

"One last thing," she said, with the curious shadow of a smile on her lips. "You must take good care of your little brother. He too will learn the truth eventually, but it is not time yet. And..." she drew a breath and the shadow-smile died. "You must realize that my own enchantment, strong as it is, is only partial and incomplete without that of the King. And on the night of the Dark Moon, it is quite powerless."

Rilya did not know what to answer. She felt numb inside, overwhelmed by the import of her mother's words. But the Queen did not seem to expect a reply. Instead, she murmured, "Do not be afraid, little one. Dol will protect us." And with that she was gone.

For a long time that night, Rilya tossed and turned on her bed, unable to relax or to repress the anxious and fearful thoughts that filled her head. It seemed as if all consolation and security had been withdrawn from her and she was lost in a forest of ravening wolves and fierce wild beasts. "Dol, help!" her heart cried out over and over, but Dol was far away, as far away and powerless as her mother's enchantment. "Quite powerless," the words mocked her, "quite powerless."

A soft, nearby thud set her bolt upright, staring wide-eyed in the dark. What was it? She listened intently, her heart pounding, expecting the Dark Ones to burst in on her at any moment. But then she recognized the soft, slightly uneven tread. It was only Galna after all, just coming to bed. With a loud sigh, she flopped back on the pillow again. "I am not sure whom we can trust." "You can trust me, your majesty!" Rilya smiled to herself. Yes, Galna was there and they could trust her. She would not let anything happen to them. The thought was comforting; Dol himself seemed almost near again.

But what else had Mother said? "My own enchantment is partial and incomplete without that of the King." Rilya had not thought much about her parents' enchantment, but had always taken it for granted. Now she tried to remember her father in the full exercise of his power. Spontaneously, her mind returned to the morning of his last departure: the invocation of Dol, the flaming of the Gelfin Tree, how her father had passed unscathed through the fire

157

and returned to his place in radiant glory. Then another scene presented itself to her: the evening before, when they had all gone to the King's privy chambers, Rendil, Condin, Landon and herself. Mother had stood near, her face aglow with love and joy, and Father himself had blessed them. She remembered the pressure of his hands, strong and firm, upon her head. And she remembered the depths of his gaze, overwhelming with majesty and strength and tenderness. Rilya strained to hold the memory, but it faded quickly from her grasp. Tears flooded her eyes and, turning her face into the pillow, she wept.

CHAPTER 18
REBELS AND TRAITORS

The next morning, Rilya and Landon were taking a short cut through the castle gardens on their way to the stables, when they spied Lady Calya coming toward them in the distance. She was strolling arm in arm with Captain Fandol, the commander of the garrison, and obviously enjoying his company. "Oh, no!" Landon groaned when he saw her.

"Quick!" Rilya gasped, "hide behind the fountain. Maybe she hasn't seen us." The two of them turned and scooted back down the path, but too late.

"Your Highnesses, good morning!" the unwelcome voice rang out behind them.

"Maybe she means some other Highnesses," Landon mumbled under his breath as they ducked behind the fountain's base. Rilya lifted herself up and peered cautiously through the cascade of splashing waters.

"No, I'm afraid not." Calya and Fandol were coming toward them quickly, waving and calling. "We'll have to go back and meet them."

"You go," Landon quavered as he crouched into his hiding place.

"We'll go together," Rilya answered as she grabbed his hand and pulled him out. "The royal children of Celdondol are not cowards!" With that, she stepped out from behind the fountain, square into the path, and confronted their pursuers. "Good morning, my lady, good morning lord captain," she said cheerfully as she curtsied before them. "Were you calling us?" She jerked her head at Landon, who was still hanging back, and mouthed fiercely, "Come on!"

Landon stumbled out and bowed mutely. To Rilya's surprise, Fandol bowed in return and Calya curtsied. "Good morning, my lord prince and lady princess," Fandol began, "what an agreeable coincidence this is. We were just speaking of you and now you appear."

"Oh?" Rilya replied. She could see Landon grinning with foolish relief, but her own reserve was in no danger of melting. She knew the captain only by sight: a handsome young man, wounded in the battle when Father was killed, but recovered fully now. Lord Gendol had personally chosen him to command the garrison in his absence. "He'll like that well enough," Galna had commented with a sly smile. "He's sweet on Lady Calya, you know, and this will give them plenty of time to pursue the matter."

It was Lady Calya now who endeavored to explain. "You see, when I first heard that a messenger had arrived with news from his Highness Prince Rendil, I did not believe it, since Her Majesty the Queen would surely have been the first to know and as yet no one had reported to her. However, I thought perhaps I had better inform Lord Fandol here, in case there had been some neglect in the matter. He assured me that he knows nothing of any such messenger, but he finds your story very interesting and would like to hear it again from your own lips."

"We were mistaken," Rilya replied coldly.

"What?" Calya answered with surprise, "you seemed very certain yesterday."

"There was no messenger," Rilya repeated.

160

"Yes, there was!" Landon contradicted. "Why did you say that? We saw him, going and coming!" Rilya could have kicked him. She felt her cheeks becoming very pink, but could think of no way to repair the damage.

Fandol's eyes had narrowed with interest at this outburst. "You say you saw him both leaving the fortress and coming back? Did you tell your royal Mother this?"

"Yes," Rilya shot back before Landon could open his mouth. "But she didn't believe us. She said no messenger had brought her word of Rendil."

"I see." Suddenly the captain stooped until he could look Landon straight in the eye. "And what do you say?" he asked the little boy. "Do you think your Mother believed your story about the soldier who came yesterday from the north?"

Rilya caught her breath with surprise and anger. The nerve of him! What would Landon say? Her own mind was racing wildly but she could do nothing whatever to alert or caution her younger brother. "Dol, help!" she prayed.

But Landon was not the least bit intimidated by the handsome, personable young warrior facing him. He grinned a big, impish grin and announced loudly, "Mother says we don't know anything about Rendil."

Rilya released her breath with an audible puff of relief and wondered what Fandol would do now. But he merely smiled and clapped Landon reassuringly on the shoulder. "Well, little prince," he said, "I guess if your Mother says you don't know anything, then you really don't." He straightened to his full height and turned to Lady Calya. "I see no need to detain the royal children further. They obviously were mistaken after all."

"Yes, quite," Calya answered, although she looked disappointed and annoyed. "We are very sorry to have disturbed you," she said, with a curtsy to Landon and Rilya. "Good day."

"Good day," the children responded politely. They passed around the two grown-ups on the path and proceeded slowly in the direction of the stables. However, once they had rounded a corner and their interrogators were out of sight, Rilya gave way to panic.

"Come on," she gasped, grabbing Landon's hand, "let's get out of here!" With that, the two of them took to their heels and ran. They did not stop until they had reached the safety of the exercise yards.

All the rest of that day Rilya sat on pins and needles, starting nervously when any servant or guard so much as approached them. But no one questioned them further about Rendil or the mysterious rider. That evening when the Queen came to bless them, they recounted for her the whole conversation.

"Landon gave everything away!" Rilya exclaimed petulantly.

"No, I didn't! I just said what Mother told me to! Didn't I?" he turned to the Queen for confirmation.

She smiled at the two of them. "I think you both did the best you could under the circumstances. Yes, Landon did say too much, but you must be careful, my daughter, not to phrase your denials so strongly. For you to have said there was no messenger was very nearly a lie, and as such could only have invited a reaction from your hearers."

"But Mother," Rilya protested, stung to tears by her mild rebuke. A night and a day of nervous tension had begun to take their toll.

The Queen eyed her with concern. "You are tired," she said. "Did you sleep well last night?"

"No," Rilya gulped.

"Oh, dear child," the Queen put her arm about her reassuringly. "You must not worry. The great God and Dol his servant have never yet failed us. Have they not sent us Lady Palissa with the Sign? Has not Rendil already begun to recover his enchantment?"

"Do we still have to pretend we don't know about Rendil?" Landon interrupted, wide-eyed.

"Yes, dear, I think that is for the better, although I doubt if anyone will question you further. Now that they know I am aware of the messenger, they will be much more on their guard."

"Mother," Rilya interrupted this time. "Did you say that Lady Palissa has the Sign? I never saw her with anything special."

"Why, of course dear. It is the silver pendant which she wears about her neck, the Sign of the Great One."

"Oh! Did Rendil know that? Is that why he took her with him?"

"Yes, and I am sure now that the Great One has not abandoned them."

Rilya smiled happily, although she still felt very tired inside. Her mother blessed her then, and Landon, and took her leave of them. When she had gone, Landon turned to his sister and asked, "Why did Mother say they wouldn't ask any

163

more questions? I like Captain Fandol. Why can't we talk to him any more?"

"I'm not sure why," Rilya answered truthfully. But in the back of her mind she wondered if Calya and Fandol really were the traitors after all, or if Mother had someone else in mind.

The children passed that night in blissful slumber and the next day in uneventful routine. However, late in the afternoon, as Sir Pandil droned on about the intricacies of Arendolese grammar and Landon fiddled idly with a loose button on his shirt, Rilya thought she heard the sound of an alarm coming from the town. Pricking up her ears, she listened more intently. A fire perhaps? Then she heard it again, a trumpet blaring insistently, and with it, shouting. She glanced surreptitiously at Landon, but he was too absorbed in his own distractions to notice. The shouting was growing nearer and louder, and Rilya was becoming more and more fidgety, when all of a sudden the great gong in the castle courtyard began to boom.

"What's that?" Landon cried in alarm, as he jumped up and ran to the window. Rilya followed him, her heart pounding wildly.

"Children, children!" Sir Pandil exclaimed, tapping his cane on the floor. "Sit down please. The lesson is not terminated."

But the children were deaf to his orders. By opening the casement and hanging as far out the window as possible, they could just see what was happening at the gate. A man in tattered garments and riding a mule had now entered the fortress, surrounded by a crowd of clamoring townspeople. Soldiers and guards were pouring into the courtyard from all directions in answer to the gong. Captain Fandol and his escort, in uniform, were pushing their way through the melee, trying to reach the strangely clad man. Having accomplished this, Fandol conferred with him a few moments. Then one of his escort grabbed the mule by its bridle and began to clear a path back through the crowd to the castle. "Make way, make way!" Voices floated up to the children in their tower perch. "To the Queen! To the Queen!"

"They're going to Mother!" Rilya exclaimed.

"Come on!" Landon shouted. "Let's go see what it's all about!" They pulled themselves in from the window and were about to make a dash for the tower stairs when Sir Pandil confronted them in the doorway, cane in hand.

"Sit down, please," he intoned sternly. "The lesson is not terminated."

The children looked at each other and groaned. But one glance at Old Wirebeard's face told them that they had no choice. So they took their seats and squirmed in anguish while the determined tutor finished his lecture. "He's deaf," Rilya thought miserably. "He probably doesn't even know anything is happening." All the while, the sound of horns and shouting and people converging on the fortress could be heard filtering up from the courtyard. Rilya strained her ears with all her might, but she could not catch any articulate meaning. So absorbed was she in her effort that she did not notice that the droning of Sir Pandil's voice had ceased, until he banged his cane on the floor directly in front of her. Startled, she turned her attention away from the window.

"My dear children," the old man said, peering at them over the top of his spectacles, "I am well aware that something of unusual import is transpiring in the fortress. However, you

165

who are of the royal blood of Celdondol must learn to discipline yourselves and attend to duty first. Now you may go and…"

Neither Rilya nor Landon heard him finish the sentence, because they were already out the door and pounding down the tower stairs. They reached the Queen's audience chamber in record time, only to find it deserted.

"Where are they?" Landon wailed, dumbfounded.

"The Great Hall!" Rilya gasped. "Mother must have received them in the Great Hall." She hesitated, but Landon grabbed her hand and began tugging her down the corridor.

"Come on," he urged impatiently, "we've got to find out what's happening."

So Rilya swallowed her scruples and off they ran again. When they arrived at the entrance to the Hall, they found its massive bronze doors tightly shut and closely guarded. A low and excited hum of voices emanated from within. Landon in his eagerness walked right up to the door, but one of the guards moved to bar his way.

"Your Highness, you mustn't go in there," he exclaimed. "Her majesty is receiving the bearer of very urgent news."

"Oh," Rilya moaned, "do we always have to be the last ones to know anything?"

The other guard looked down at her sympathetically. "You may not want to know about this, your Highness. From what I gathered in the courtyard, some dissatisfied scoundrels whom the King, your Father, drummed out of the army have stirred up the people of Galgor, one of our vassals to the south. They are taking advantage of our present weakness to march on our Kingdom and destroy it. Their troops are already

166

advancing up the river, burning and pillaging as they go. They are expected to arrive in Celdondol by tomorrow."

The two children looked at one another. "Don't worry," Landon affirmed, "they won't conquer us. We can fight them off, can't we?"

The first guard smiled. "We'll certainly do our best, your Highness."

"There, see!" Landon turned to his sister. "We men will make sure that you women have nothing to worry about."

But Rilya did not smile nor was she reassured. Once again her world lay in ruins. Was this the darkness that Mother felt, or was it only the beginning of something even worse? At the moment she had no way of knowing.

CHAPTER 19

THE SPELL OF THE DARK ONES

Rendil's hair had indeed begun to turn. It showed black now, not only at the temples, but across the whole crown of his head as well. Only in the back and at the nape of his neck were streaks of silver still to be been. His face too, had changed: his jaw had become more square and firm, and Patsy noticed the beginnings of a dark moustache and beard.

He seemed to have changed interiorly also, in a way that she found annoying and difficult to understand. He would lapse into moody silence for hours on end, and no effort at conversation could evoke a response. Then again, he would be gay and witty, with a new ease and confidence that were entirely unstilted.

Patsy did not quite know what to make of it, but neither did she waste too much time in trying. Now that the sun was shining, she had so much else to feel and see and hear. The air had grown warm and balmy, and all the travelers had shed their cloaks. Wisps of Patsy's curls fluttered gently in the breeze. The birds were visible now and her eyes followed with delight as they circled and wheeled and darted among the towering fangolfin trees. Their varied and brilliant colors fascinated her: scarlet and blue, black and gold; while their fiercely sweet melodies made her heart leap and soar.

They traveled on by day beneath the flimsy canopy of newly leafed forest and paused before sunset in grassy clearings dotted with the sweet fragrance of wild flowers. Patsy loved flowers. Once, on a sudden impulse, she gathered a large bouquet of delicate pink and white ones and began to weave them into a garland. But her fingers were clumsy and the wreath kept falling apart as soon as she put it together. At last she became aware that the others were watching her, and her cheeks burned with humiliation.

"Here," said Rendil, reaching over to take the flowers from her lap, "do it like this and they will hold together firmly." As she watched in amazement, he proceeded to twine them together deftly until, in a moment, he held in his hands a thick woven crown. Patsy was so satisfied with the result that she did not even ask him how he did it.

"Now, for whom did you wish this laurel wreath of honor?" he asked playfully.

She hadn't thought about it. "For Fendal?" she squeaked. She had gotten rather fond of the beast in the past few days.

"For Fendal! Ho! Won't he look splendid in his new bonnet!" Rendil leaped up from his place by the campfire, dashed over to where their horses were tethered at the edge of the clearing and plunked the garland at a rakish angle over Fendal's ears. Gifil and Condin hooted with delight.

"Don't know of no self-respectin' horse what would stand for a hat like that," the old woodsman remarked dryly.

"Well," Condin replied with a grin, "as I have often told my brother, Fendal never was a self-respecting horse anyway."

"At least he is a gentleman," Rendil shot back, not at all offended. "See how graciously he accepts the gift of a lady."

Indeed, Fendal did seem pleased. He lifted his head and whinnied appreciatively. Patsy, on the other hand, did not quite know how to respond to all this. She looked from one to the other and smiled uncertainly.

"Reckon you ain't used to bein' chaffed like this," Gifil observed.

"I haven't any brothers, that's why," Patsy answered, with a sudden burst of self-insight.

"You have now," Rendil spoke up, and Condin nodded in affirmation. "That is, if you will forgive our teasing."

Patsy felt a warm glow inside her that spread clear to her toes and radiated in her face. "Oh, thank you," she replied. "I'll try not to mind any more." She grinned broadly. "Fendal really does look nice in his new hat."

They went on this way for three days, in idyllic bliss, neither hastening nor lingering. But by the fourth day, Rendil began to show signs of impatience. "How much longer must we travel before we reach Moldan?" he asked Gifil as they were setting out in the morning.

"'Bout four more days at this pace," he answered. "Less if we walk faster and don't stop 'til nightfall."

Rendil groaned. "I had hoped to arrive in time to consolidate my position and survey the situation before we join battle. The night of the Dark Moon is only five days away. We had better hurry, as you suggest."

So, to Patsy's chagrin, they increased their pace and pushed on all that day without a break. She had secretly been hoping that they would forget all about their destination and the battle that awaited them there. But, alas, they had not forgotten at all. As the day wore on and Rendil's anxiety mounted, her own grew also in proportion. It seemed to her that they were rushing headlong into certain disaster, while it clearly seemed to him that they were standing still.

Late in the afternoon, they found themselves struggling through a dense and nearly impenetrable thicket. Gifil had slowed almost to a crawl in his efforts to clear a path before them, when Rendil, in his impatience, leaped from his horse and began hacking at the underbrush with his sword.

"Reckon you'll ruin your sword and wear yourself out afore you get anywhere that-a-way," Gifil cautioned.

Rendil accosted him, red faced and panting. "Couldn't we have avoided this?" he demanded.

"You wanted the shortest, directest way to Moldan, and this here is it. If'n you recollect, I warned you afore we left home that it warn't all so easy." Gifil folded his arms and rested easily on the balls of his feet. He seemed to feel no strain, although he had been driven all day at nearly a run.

Rendil, however, was tired and ill-tempered besides. "How dare you speak to me like that?" he flared. "Do you not remember that I am your sovereign, the rightful heir to the throne of Celdondol?"

"Yes, your Highness," Gifil answered mildly, "I recollect that, but I reckon it ain't goin' to get us out of this hole we're in."

"Then what do you suggest?" Condin interposed, lest Rendil lose control of himself completely and drive the old man away.

"Well," Gifil answered slowly, "might be best if'n you young'uns kind of clear yourselves a place and bed down here for the night, whilst I go on a mite further and try to see my way through. Might be I could climb a tree even."

"That sounds good to me," Condin replied quickly.

"Me too," Patsy added.

Rendil's face was working strangely, and when he spoke his voice was thick. "I will go with you."

"If'n you want, but you'll only hold me back."

Patsy was thinking fast. "You're the only one of us with a sword," she said to Rendil. "Suppose some wild animal attacks us. What would we do without you?"

He looked at her stupidly.

"Please," she begged, fingering her cross as if for moral support.

"Very well," Rendil agreed at last, "I will remain behind. But see to it," he glowered at Gifil, "that you are back here and able to lead us out by morning."

The old man accepted this command with an expressionless nod and left at once. Patsy stared after him as he went, with a half-panicky feeling of abandonment. Suppose, out of spite, that he didn't come back? She could hardly blame him, Rendil was treating him so shamefully. But Gifil did not seem put out at all, and Patsy knew that he was worthy of their trust. He had disappeared already in the tangle of underbrush, so she turned her eyes back to her two companions. Condin had meanwhile dismounted, leaving her alone on Burdil's back. "Well," he said to Rendil, "are we just going to stand here, or are we going to make camp for the night?"

Rendil clenched his sword in his fist, then gradually loosened his grip until the weapon fell from his hand to the ground. "I have behaved badly again, have I not," he asked tonelessly.

"Yes, rather," Condin replied. For once he did not gibe.

"Oh," Rendil moaned, "all the gods must be against me. But we might as well make camp for the night."

So they did. Patsy slid down from her mount and helped as best she could to clear a spot big enough to build a fire and lay down their bedrolls. As they worked, she wondered why Rendil had not asked her once more to invoke the power of the Sign. After all, it had brought Gifil to their rescue the first time she tried it, and she herself felt more confidence now as a result. But something inside her made her decide not to remind him of it.

Quite a bit of strenuous labor was necessary to produce a habitable campsite, but by nightfall they had managed. They had just finished supper when, out of nowhere and with ghastly suddenness, Gifil reappeared.

"Who goes there?" Rendil shouted, as he had the first night the old man had come to them.

"Hesh now," he answered, "it's only me. You'll be disturbin' the whole forest with your ballyhoo."

"Oh, well then, why do you not give some warning of your approach?"

Gifil dismissed the question with a wave of his hand. "Ain't got no time for talkin' nonsense. "We've got to move on. Found some folks up ahead what need help a sight worse'n what we do and need it now."

"Who and where?" Rendil asked suspiciously.

"Now look here, your Highness," Gifil answered tartly, "I know you're a prince and all like that, but don't be always a-standin' on your dignity. It ain't wise. Even royalty has sometimes got to listen and I know that's what the King, your father, would've did."

Rendil blushed scarlet with humiliation at this rebuke, but said nothing. Condin had already begun to break camp and Patsy was reluctantly helping him, goaded on by the undertone of anxiety in Gifil's voice. They finished quickly, while the old man and the young prince stood facing one another in silence. Finally Condin said, "We're ready."

The old man grunted in acknowledgment. "Mount up then, and I'll tell you where we're goin' while we're goin'."

Condin swung into the saddle and pulled Patsy up after him. Rendil knew he was defeated. "All right," he sighed wearily, as he gathered up Fendal's reins and lifted himself onto his back. Immediately Gifil plunged into the dense thicket, so that the others, even on horseback, had to hurry to follow him. He forged ahead swiftly in the darkness, following the path he had cut for himself earlier, and his voice floated back to them as he went.

"Seems that I comed on this here cabin a ways up ahead, and thinks I to myself, 'Aha, the folks what live here might be knowin' a path that'll lead us north.' So I goes up and halloos but no one answers. So I tries the door, opens it and goes in. And here's the most sad sight what I ever did see. The man 'most dead with a big hole festerin' in his side and his missus there tendin' him, all swelled up with the young'un inside her. 'Mister,' she says, all tearful, 'can you help us? We ain't had no victuals in a week.' Well, I hadn't brought none with me, and I know'd you had plenty, so I comed right on back after you, fast as I could. And here we be."

Patsy was horror-struck when she heard his story, and tingled with anger and shame at Rendil's behavior. She had no way of seeing his face, but she self-righteously hoped that he was sorry now. They continued on in silence, arriving more quickly than she had expected at a dilapidated cabin nestled in a tiny hollow of the forest. Through its window a single dim light burned.

Gifil strode right up to the door and knocked, then opened it and went in. The others dismounted slowly and followed, bringing what food they had with them. In the doorway they paused to look around. By the flickering lantern light, Patsy could see Gifil already bending over the figure of a man lying on a cot in front of the cold fireplace. Nearby stood a young woman, scarcely older than Rendil, but big with child and awkward.

"Come on in," Gifil called to them without turning his head. They entered wordlessly, their boots thudding on the bare wooden floor. They all wore their hooded cloaks and Patsy knew that this time they would not take them off.

"Food's cold I'm afeared," Gifil said to the woman, "but you're welcome to it." However, she made no response and did not move, so Rendil took some bread and dried meat from his pouch, walked over and held it out to her. She looked at him with wide and frightened eyes, then snatched the food from his hands and began to eat ravenously.

"Whoa there," Gifil cautioned, "slow down or you'll get yourself sick." As she obeyed, he added, "Got any water to drink?"

She swallowed a mouthful of dry bread and shook her head. "Well's out back," she said. "Ain't got strength enough to draw from it." Her voice was soft and hoarse.

"We will get some for you," Rendil said before Gifil could give the order, "but we will need a lantern. Do you have another?"

175

"Ain't got no wick in it," she answered dully. "You'll have to take this one."

Rendil hesitated and looked at Gifil, who nodded. "Might as well. Bring back some firewood too."

"Ain't got none of that," the woman interposed.

"We'll gather some if we can," Condin offered.

No one said anything more, so Rendil picked up the lantern and the two of them headed for the door. Patsy, who did not relish staying alone in the dark with these strange people, quickly moved to join them. Gifil's voice caught her in mid-flight. "You might be less underfoot if'n you stayed in here."

She felt like protesting that she would not be at all underfoot, but she obeyed nonetheless. The boys went out and closed the door behind them, plunging the room into darkness.

For awhile no one moved or spoke. Then Patsy heard the woman inching her way slowly and unsteadily toward the fireplace. She seemed to be groping for something. With a sudden scrape and crash, she kicked it with her foot and knocked it over. A stool, Patsy judged by the sound. Gifil reached out quietly, righted it, and helped her sit down.

"What's your name?" he asked.

"Talya," she replied, "and my man is Cafil."

"Pleased to meet you," Gifil said, and Patsy could imagine him bowing in the dark. "My name's Gifil and this here is Passy. Now, how'd you come to be in such a fix as this?"

"Well," she began with a sigh, "my Caf, he thought it were right nice last spring, when they asked him, would he like joinin' up with the King's army. He said, 'Tally, I'll make some

176

money and buy you purty things and we can get married when I come back.' Well, I didn't like it none, but what could I do? So he said yes and off he went. And I waited for him and worried and fretted until he finally comed back. But when he did, it were all wrong. He had got this here hole in his side and he said the King were dead and the army near beat and there weren't hardly no money to go around. Well, we got married any ways and moved into this here cabin of his and did it up best we could. But mister," her voice rose to a sort of hoarse wail, "that hole in his side, it never healed! We'd think it was closin' up and then it would open again and it kept on doin' that. My Caf, he can't work, he can't plow or hunt or chop wood or draw water and now I'm too far along to do anything. It's an evil spell, I know'd it. The Dark Ones have cursed him. Help us!" She burst into loud sobs, just as the door flung open and the boys tramped in. The glow of their lantern fell directly on the woman's grief-contorted face, giving it a terrifying aspect.

They paused in alarm when they saw her, while Patsy began sidling toward the suddenly preferable darkness outside. Once more Gifil's voice caught her in mid-flight. "Did you fetch the wood and water?"

"Yes," Rendil answered, recovering himself and stepping forward with a pail brim-full. He set it down next to Gifil and stood hesitantly for a moment. Then, seeing a cup on the shelf over the fireplace, he took it, dipped it in the bucket and offered it to the young woman. She mopped her face with her apron and began to drink in convulsive gulps. Meanwhile Condin brought an armload of wood over and arranged it on the hearth.

Gifil waited until Tally had drunk her fill before he asked, "Might there be some folks hereabouts who would come and help you out? We can't stay and you'll be needin' a gal with you right soon, I reckon."

"Nearest folks is half a mornin's walk that a way," she gestured with her hand. "Used to be I could go there for things, but not of late. They be afeared to come here, on account of the curse on my man."

"Curse?" asked Rendil.

"An evil spell from the Dark Ones," Gifil explained. "He was with the King at Moldan." He looked piercingly at Rendil as he said this, but Rendil was staring with wonder and alarm at the figure lying so still upon his cot.

"I can't get the fire to start!" Condin burst out suddenly.

"Oh, you young'uns," Gifil sighed. "Here, let me do it." He moved toward the fireplace, but Tally interrupted him.

"It ain't no use, Mister," she stated flatly. "When the moon's on the wane, no fire burns in this here house. It's part of the spell. It were pure luck I could get the lantern goin'."

"What manner of curse is this?" Rendil asked sharply.

"We might be findin' out as we go along." Gifil's voice was grim. "Meantime, we'll sleep here for tonight. In the mornin', if you'll tell me the way, I'll go and fetch those folks for you. They can't refuse to come."

"No." It was Rendil who spoke, too quietly. Patsy could sense the anger in his voice.

"No?" Gifil echoed. "What might you mean by that?"

"I will explain outside," he answered through tight lips.

Gifil stood up slowly. "We'll all bed down out there," he said to Tally. "You get some sleep if'n you're able, and we'll see what's what in the mornin'." With that he strode out through the still open door and the others followed. Patsy suspected that this time he too was really angry.

CHAPTER 20

WARM THE WEAK

Condin was the last one out. He closed the door firmly and joined the others with their horses at the edge of the clearing. When everyone was there, Gifil turned to Rendil and said, "Now, your Highness, would you mind tellin' us what you mean?"

"It ought to be obvious," Rendil answered coldly. "We have only four more days left for our journey to Moldan, and on the evening of that fourth day, battle will be joined. If we wish to arrive on time, we cannot possibly wait an entire morning while you go hunting for someone to help these people. Therefore, we will not do so. We will break camp immediately at dawn and you will lead us on to Moldan as you promised."

"Your Highness." Gifil's voice was as quiet as Rendil's, but brittle with rage. "Ain't no king worth the name what would abandon poor folks like this in distress. And I don't feel no call to obey a king what would give a command like you just gived. Go on to Moldan yourself, if'n you dare, but I ain't walkin' with you one step further."

"We cannot go on to Moldan alone and you know that," Rendil retorted. "You must come with us and you will, at sword's point if necessary. We will commend these unfortunate people to the care of Dol, who is more powerful than we are, in any case."

"You be Dol's representative in this here Kingdom, for the doin' of good," Gifil drawled bitterly, "but it's a mighty powerful evil you be a-doin'. Maybe the Dark Ones' spell has lit on you too."

"Enough of this!" Rendil snapped, drawing his sword. "Condin, get the rope and bind him hand and foot, lest he slip away from us during the night."

"Rendil," Condin answered slowly, "don't you think he's right? We do seem to have some responsibility for these people."

Rendil gave a sardonic sneer. "So you have turned traitor also, have you? Lady Palissa, speak up, what is your opinion on the matter?"

Patsy stared at him in shock and confusion. Her opinion, insofar as she had one, was that he, Rendil, was utterly detestable. Unfortunately, he was also correct. If they wished to reach Moldan on time, they could not afford to lose another day, waiting for someone to come and help Caf and Tally. Up to this point, she had not cared if they reached Moldan on time. But now she felt torn between loyalty to Rendil and his mission and anger at his high-handed behavior. However, before she could decide what to say, he interrupted her thoughts.

"I have another idea," she heard him saying, as if from a great distance. "If the power of Dol is not strong enough to suit my lord Gifil, perhaps the power of the Great One will be. Lady Palissa, I wish you once more to invoke your God through his Sign that you bear."

Patsy continued to stare at him in the darkness, wondering if she had heard him rightly. But she had, and bitter resentment welled up within her at the realization. Three or four hours earlier she would have willingly offered her services, but for him to command her, and under such impossible circumstances, was almost more than she could endure. Yet

181

she was afraid of him, afraid of his anger and his sword. It was the same old struggle all over again and she could have wept with frustration.

"Well," his voice goaded her, "would you also refuse me? May I remind you that you at least have an obligation to your God?"

Yes, she did. "All right!" she gulped furiously as she jerked the cross from under her cloak. She could not see it in the dark and tears stung and blinded her eyes anyway, but she gripped it convulsively in her fist. "O God," she prayed, "do something!" The formula had worked before. She waited for something unexpected to happen, but nothing did. "O God, do something," she prayed again, this time aloud. Again she waited and the others waited too, tense, motionless. No sound could be heard, except the sound of her own sobbing breath.

But a thought was working its way up within her, a question: what did she think God would do? "I don't know," she answered the thought impatiently. "Who cares what he does?" But the question had fully surfaced in her consciousness now and it was demanding an answer. What would he do? Patsy loosened her grip on the crucifix and ran her finger over it as a blind person might. The figure on the cross was twisted, contorted, like Tally's grief-stricken face.

"He died to save all men." They were her own words, coming back to her out of some unfathomable abyss. "He did it because he cared." Jesus, he whom they called the Great One, cared. Did he care for these poor people too? And if he did, then why didn't they? Other words came back to her, those of the Queen: "By pride and rashness Rendil will never win the enchantment, nor will you succeed in helping him. It is by love, humility and compassion that your quest will be completed."

For several moments Patsy stood very still, until her breathing grew calm and even. She had her answer and lacked only the courage to give it. But that was swift in coming. Suddenly she lifted her head and announced in clear, confident tones, "God won't do anything this time. He wants us to wait while Gifil goes for help like he planned. And I, for one, will wait."

Dead silence greeted her words and once more her heart began to quail. But then she heard Condin speak up. "I too will wait. I don't know who this 'Great One' is, but I'm sure he'll provide for us if we do what he wants."

Patsy heaved a great sigh of relief. It was now three against one; Rendil surely would have to give in. But no.

"Very well," his voice trembled with repressed violence. "I shall be forced to go on alone, and Dol shall be my guide." He drew a long, rasping breath then fairly shouted at them, "Go to bed, all of you! Traitors is what you are! Traitors!" And with that, he flung down his sword and trampled off into the underbrush.

There was nothing else for them to do but obey. Wordlessly they rolled out their bedding on the cold, bare ground and lay down for the night. Patsy closed her eyes and held herself quite still, pretending to sleep. She wondered if the others were doing the same, but Gifil's familiar, rumbling snore soon told her that his slumber, at least, was genuine. She could only shake her head in fond amazement and go on pretending.

Hours seemed to pass. Where was Rendil? She hoped that he had not already tried to start off alone. But Fendal was

183

still there; he would not leave without his mount. Fendal. She heard him snort softly, his low snort of recognition.

"Ho, boy, quiet now." In the deep stillness, Rendil's murmur was clearly audible. "At least you have not abandoned me." A gentle whinny, as if in answer. Burdil too shifted uneasily. "Shh! Be still." A short pause, then: "What have I done wrong? How have I failed? I have only tried to accomplish my mission. Is this part of the testing, or was Lady Palissa right and I am only reaping the fruits of disobedience?" Another low snort. "Oh, I know you cannot tell me. Perhaps the song can. One verse has already been fulfilled. What is the next?" He began to chant softly: 'Broken branch then succor, soothe; Listen! Silent ones shall speak. Flame command now...' His voice broke, but he tried to force himself. "If only I could, if only I could! 'Flame command now...'" It was no use, and with a short, wretched moan, his song died away into sobs.

Patsy heard him weeping and, as she listened, her heart was torn with anguish. She longed to go to him, to try to comfort him, but what could she possibly say or do? At the same time, she felt more shy and awkward than ever. Never had she seen a young man cry. And if he were really guilty of disobedience, then she was also, and all the more insofar as she had seen the issues more clearly. In the end, Patsy did the only thing she felt capable of doing: she closed her eyes, lay quite still, and pretended to sleep.

Morning dawned at last, clear and chill. Patsy, waking out of an uneasy doze, became conscious of birds chirping and of movement near her. She started up and saw Gifil already rolling up his bedding and extracting some dry bread from his knapsack for breakfast. He paused when he noticed her staring

184

at him, then silently offered her a hunk of bread, which she accepted with a nod. Rendil! She began to look around for him anxiously, but, to her relief, he was right there, lying next to Condin, sound asleep. She turned her gaze back to Gifil.

"Thank'ee, lass," he said in an undertone.

"Are you going to leave us now?" she whispered, trembling at the thought.

"No," he replied, "'taint fair. I'll wake him first and ask him again." With that, he picked up a small stone and flipped it in such a way that it landed with a plop very close to Rendil's ear. Rendil stirred and turned over, murmuring something, then sat up and rubbed his eyes. Even in the pale dawn light they looked sunken and red.

For a moment, the crown prince of Arendolin seemed not to know where he was. He turned his head stupidly from one side to the other, as if trying to remember. At last he focussed on Gifil and his face cleared. He stood up unsteadily, a motion that inadvertently awakened Condin, and began to approach the old woodsman. Patsy swallowed her breath and waited.

When Rendil had come quite near him, he stopped, held out his hand and said to Gifil, "I am sorry. Will you please forgive me?"

Gifil remained expressionless. "Will you let me fetch these folks what'll help Caf and Tally?" he asked.

"Yes. I realize now that you were right. My first duty as King is to succor the poor and afflicted, and this takes precedence over everything else."

A slow, glad smile began to spread across Gifil's countenance. "One more thing," he said.

"Yes?"

"Will you take a hard, crotchety old fool back into your service?"

"Oh, most willingly!" Rendil exclaimed in a voice shaking between laughter and tears. And the two of them fell on each other's necks in a strong, manly embrace.

Patsy felt that she would simply burst with joy and relief. She looked at Condin, who was still fisting the sleep from his eyes. "What's going on?" he asked with an uncomprehending yawn.

"Rendil says we're going to wait for Gifil after all."

"Oh? Good!" Condin grinned mischievously. "That means I can go back to sleep. I'm tired of getting up at the crack of dawn and riding off into who knows what horizon." And he promptly rolled over again and pulled the covers up around his ears.

But Gifil had seen him. "Ho, there!" he chuckled, "Playin' possum are you? Get up! You young'uns will have to look after our new friends as best what you can while I'm on my way. And we'll have to hurry. It's near to sun-up now."

So they packed up their bedding and ate in haste, while Gifil went to the cabin to get his directions from Tally. She stood with him in the doorway, pointing to the east and making a few listless gestures. Then Gifil beckoned to them to join him. As they approached, Patsy heard him saying, "These young'uns will stay with you. They's fine folk, but ain't nothin' to be afeard of. This here's Rendil..."

Rendil drew breath sharply at the sound of his own royal name, and Gifil bit his lip in regret, but the woman only nodded dully without recognition.

"And this here's Condin," the old man went on quickly, "and Passy you met last night. They'll see to your needs while I'm gone."

Tally nodded dully again, but said nothing, so Gifil turned and clasped hands with Rendil. "Might take less time'n we think, if'n I can get them to hurry."

"Be on your way, then," Rendil answered, "and may Dol protect you."

They watched him set off, following him with heavy hearts as he vanished into the forest, heading toward the sunrise. But after a few moments, Tally went back into the cabin and sat down. She seemed even more weak and enervated now than she had the night before, in spite of the food she had taken. Eventually the others entered also and stood there looking at her in uneasy silence. The whole atmosphere was chill and oppressive, just like it would be in a haunted house, Patsy decided. But what a tiny house to be haunted! In the thin gray light she could make out the cold hearth, a cupboard above it with a few cups and plates, and the cot in front of it with its mysterious occupant. Near the only window stood a bare table with a couple of stools, and opposite that, another cot, where Tally must have spent the night. And that was all. Patsy remembered Gifil's cabin, not much larger, but infinitely more homey and cheerful, with its crackling fire, its rugs and cushions, and its benched all hand-carved and brightly polished. The contrast between it and this bleak and miserable place made her shiver.

"Would you care to break your fast?" Patsy jumped at the sound of Rendil's voice, but Tally's only response was a blank stare. "Would you like to eat something?" he tried again, holding out some dried meat to her.

187

"No," she managed finally in a hoarse whisper. "I just feel too poorly. There ain't nothin' no man can do. You might as well not try." She buried her face in her hands, but even the effort of tears was too great for her to make.

Rendil and Condin looked at one another helplessly, paralyzed in the face of her despair. Patsy, however, felt curiously alert and rested. If God wanted this, there had to be something they could do. She shivered again and wished she had a blanket over her cape. Then she realized that Tally had not even a cape. Without a word, she darted out the door, ran to their horses and returned a moment later with her bedroll under her arm.

"She must be cold," she declared to Rendil.

"Yes, she must." He looked startled at first, then appreciative of the observation. Taking the proffered blankets, he wrapped them carefully around Tally's shoulders. Slowly the young woman lifted her head and stared at him, then grasped the covers and pulled them about herself.

"The water bucket is empty," Condin remarked, suddenly coming to life. He picked it up and clattered out to fill it.

"What about the man?" Patsy asked. "Is he warm enough?"

Rendil stepped over to the cot and she followed curiously. Together they gazed down at the figure of Cafil, as still and pale as death. He appeared to be in his early twenties, with a splendid chestnut beard, but woefully thin in the face. A pile of ragged blankets covered him. "Probably all they have in the house," Patsy thought to herself. Rendil reached carefully under the covers and placed his hand over the man's heart.

"He is still alive," he muttered, "but barely."

At that moment, Condin returned with the pail full of water. He dipped some into a cup and offered it to Tally, who took it and drank slowly. "Thank'ee," she said after a minute or two. Her face looked a very little brighter.

"How long has your husband been in this condition? I mean, unconscious?" Rendil asked her.

"Since nigh on to four days ago. Ev'ry time the moon's on the wane, he gets all weak and clammy-like, but never as bad as this. The Night of Dark Moon is comin' and I'm afeard..." She broke off with a faint choking sound.

Rendil shook his head grimly. "I am also afraid," he said under his breath. "Victory is our only hope." Aloud he said to Tally, "So your husband is accursed because he was with the King at Moldan?"

"That's what we reckon."

"But not all those with the King were so afflicted, not even among the wounded. Why then this man?"

"Listen, Mister." Tally drew a long, shaky breath. "I'll tell you all what my Caf told me, if'n you swears not to repeat it."

"I give you my word," Rendil answered at once.

"And them?" She gestured at Patsy and Condin.

"I promise," Patsy said.

"And I," Condin echoed.

She gazed from one to the other, hesitating, suspicious. At last, something in Rendil's face seemed to reassure her. "You've got eyes like the King," she remarked. "I only seen him onc't, but I'll never forget. Such dark eyes, all light inside."

Rendil smiled briefly, but Patsy could tell he was pleased. He walked over to the table and sat down. The first thin streaks of sunshine had begun to filter through the window.

"All right," she drew breath again, "it's like this. When my Caf joined up with the King's army, they marched on up to Moldan Gorge, the whole big bunch of 'em, along the main road. And at the end of the road, there was an old fort and a bridge acrost the gorge. There was a few soldiers there too, a-holdin' the bridge as best they could agin' the enemy. So the rest of 'em, they camped there and they could see that, t'other side of the gorge, the enemy was a-campin' too. My Caf, he said it were an awful fearsome thing. They would look by day and see nothin' but shadows, and by night there weren't nothin' to see at all. No fires, no light, no nothin'. But they knew the enemy was there and they would get cold and bumpy all over for knowin' it. The men wondered how they was ever goin' to fight agin shadows. And when they heard tell how the battle was goin' to be on the Night of Dark Moon, they was more afeard than ever.

"Well, two days afore that, word went 'round the camp that they was a-lookin' for a man what knew the country there-abouts. So my Caf, what used to go huntin' up there with his old man, said he did. They took him to this here tent where the King was with all his captains, and the gen'ral, the one they calls Gendol. And this here Gendol says, 'Can you lead us around to a place where the gorge be narrow enough for horses to leap acrost? We want to surprise the enemy and drive into the heart of 'em.' And my Caf says he reckoned he could. Then they started talkin' amongst themselves and the King said, 'Gendol, you'll be the one to take the men around
190

the side and I'll ride in front of the main army.' But Gendol said, 'Wouldn't there be more glory in it for you, if'n you led the small bunch? Besides, you can use your magic to git yourself out if'n you git into a fix.' And the King answered, 'I don't know that my magic'll do any good. We ain't got the Sign, you know.' But after awhile Gendol talked him into doin' it and the meetin' broke up. Wish I knew what that there Sign was, but I don't and my Caf didn't either. It would of come in handy."

Tally paused wearily and rested her face in her hands. Meanwhile Rendil and Condin had been looking at one another in astonishment. "That's not what Gendol told you and Mother, is it?" Condin asked.

"No," Rendil replied, "there was no mention of a surprise flanking maneuver, and I had supposed that Father and Gendol were together. I wonder whose idea it was. Perhaps it was Father's after all. He and Gendol were both much esteemed for their imagination and daring."

"It doesn't matter much now, does it?" Condin remarked dryly.

"No, I suppose not. In any event, we know that Gendol had lied to us." Rendil glanced at Tally who had raised her head and was eyeing him curiously. "Do you feel strong enough to continue?" he asked her.

"Might I have some of them victuals now?" she requested in turn.

Rendil stood up and handed her some of the dried meat he had offered her earlier, while Condin refilled her water cup. She ate and drank slowly and in silence. Watching her, Patsy wondered if the boys were as much on pins and needles as she was. But Rendil had seated himself again and, for once,

191

looked patient and reflective. Condin, too, merely settled himself cross-legged on the floor by the hearth and waited. So Patsy also sat down, opposite Rendil at the table. It was warm there; she would not have thought that the pale sunlight could be so warm. By the time Tally had finished her meal, she was actually dozing. But the soft, hoarse voice awakened her at once.

"Reckon I can go on with what I was sayin' now."

"Yes, please do!" Rendil seemed to leap into life.

"Well," she said, "it were like this, near as I can recollect what my Caf told me. They started out at daybreak on the day afore Dark Moon, the King and two comp'nies of the best soldiers, and my man a-leadin' them. They rode a long ways down the gorge to a place where the rocks stick out on both sides, makin' a kind of nat'ral bridge, and they crossed over there and rode back up the other side. It were dark afore they got near the enemy camp, which was what the King wanted. My Caf, he were powerful afeared and so were all the others, but not the King. He said, 'Stick close behind me, men, and we'll git through this together.' Now he and Gendol had agreed betwixt themselves that when Gendol's men blew the trumpet, they would both attack at the same time, and cut down the enemy back and front. Well, they waited and waited in the dark, until finally they heard the trumpet blow. Then the King drew his sword and rode hard and all the men rode after him, a-swingin' their swords as they went. My Caf said he could feel his sword bitin' into things and he could feel other swords fightin' his off, and he could hear the most awful screechin' and hollerin', but he couldn't see nothin' at all. It were all darkness, except for this pale sort of light round about the King. Then he heard the King shout, 'Men, men! They are all turning on us! Why isn't Gendol attacking?' And one of his captains yelled back, 'But we can't see nothin'! How can we fight?' And the King hollered, 'I can see! What is this? I thought you could see too!' Then he shouted in a voice like a trumpet some words my Caf couldn't understand, and all of a sudden, this terrible light shone all around them, and my Caf could see everything. What he saw, mister, he didn't want even to tell, it were so bad."

Tally faltered and stopped. "But you must go on," Rendil broke in at once. He was excited now, his fist clenched on the tabletop. "I command you...that is, I urge you in the name of Dol, please go on." Patsy fingered the Sign nervously. She was beginning to be uncomfortably warm at her place in the sun, and wondered if something strange were not happening. Rendil's eyes glittered with interior fire as he fastened them on the wretched young woman, who seemed scarcely strong enough to breathe. But she summoned her courage and spoke again, in a barely audible whisper.

"What he saw, Mister, were their own men fallin' and dyin' all around, and fierce black shapes pressin' in hard on 'em, and acrost the gorge, Gendol and his men sittin' there and not attackin' at all."

"Treason!" shouted Rendil, leaping to his feet and pounding his fist on the table.

"That be what the King hollered too," Tally answered, "and he started thrashin' about with his sword harder than ever. But it were no use. The enemy just kept on a-comin' and more of our men fell in the light than fell in the darkness. My Caf, he was right next the King now and he heard him, all choked kind of, say, "I was a fool. I betrayed my own men for the sake of greater glory." Then the bright light dimmed down

193

and disappeared. At that very moment, my Caf felt the sword a-piercin' his side and everything went black and he heard no more."

"Treason," Rendil whispered fiercely, "treason." He lowered his head for a moment, then raised it again. "I will heal your husband, have no fear. And I will avenge my father's death."

"Your father?"

"Yes. I am the son of Rendol Clarendil and I will avenge my father's death!" With that, he threw back his hood to reveal a shock of hair no longer silver at all, but black as the raven's wing. The tongue of the ancient ones burst forth from his lips like a clap of thunder, and as it did so, fire blazed up on the cold and barren hearth. The heat of it seared Patsy to the bone.

CHAPTER 21
CELDONDOL UNDER SIEGE

Relative silence had descended at last upon the fortress of Celdondol, but, even so, Rilya could not sleep. After three days of alarm and excitement and danger, the very stillness was nerve-wracking.

"Midnight and all's well!" The voice of a sentry drifted in to her from the ramparts.

Midnight already. With a sigh she climbed out of bed and tiptoed to the window. It was open and the night air was clear and warm, redolent with the odor of hundreds of campfires. Rilya looked down into the castle yard and saw some of them, burning low now, with the men of the town clustered in their bedrolls around them. Then she looked up and out, beyond the soldiers on the ramparts, to the fields and the river. There, other campfires glowed, the fires of the enemy. Although from her vantage point she could see very few of them, she knew that they surrounded the fortress entirely and extended down every street of the town as well. Celdondol was under siege.

Next she looked toward the great court of the castle where, although she could not see it, she knew the Gelfin Tree stood, blazing yet unburned, sending out its brilliant glow by day and by night as a sign of the protection of Dol. The Queen had made the tree to flame by her enchantment, "to strengthen the people and give them hope." Rilya too felt reassured.

Last of all, she glanced up to the sky, hardly daring to look, because she knew what she would see: the moon on the wane, a small, cold sliver, growing smaller every night. She

195

shuddered and looked away. Three more days until the dark moon, and what would happen then? She shuddered again and tiptoed back to bed. Sleep was long in coming.

Next morning at breakfast, Landon announced that he wanted to try to find the Queen. "You might just be in her way," Galna suggested as she set his portion in front of him.

"I don't care," he pouted. "We can't go out to the garden, we can't go up to the ramparts, and I'm tired of sitting in this silly old tower and missing all the excitement! At least Mother can tell us what's happening. She hasn't even been here since the soldiers from Galgor came!"

"Your royal Mother has enough to occupy her mind without you two yapping at her heels. Now eat your porridge and be still!" Nervous anxiety was making Galna very cross.

"Do we have to eat this awful stuff every day?" Landon made a face at his bowl.

"It's because of the siege," Rilya explained patiently, repeating what Galna had told her. "We're surrounded by the enemy on all sides, so we can't leave to buy any more food. And since all the people from the town have crowded in here for protection, we have more mouths to feed with the little food we do have, so it has to be portioned out bit by bit to make it last longer. It's called 'rationing'."

"Oh." Landon did not sound impressed. "Well, if I were Mother, I would just send the soldiers out to drive all those bad old Galgorians away and then we could have plenty to eat."

"Well, would you listen to him talk!" Galna exclaimed.

"And I'm just going to find Mother and tell her so!" he concluded obstinately.

That was why after breakfast an odd little procession could be seen threading its way down the northeast tower of Celdondol. It consisted of one small but determined soldier equipped with scarlet cape - the birthday gift of a doting older brother – heavy boots, and wooden sword; and one reluctant female companion in velvet dress and dainty shoes. "You might as well go with him," Galna had said, "to keep him out of trouble," but Rilya didn't think anyone could accomplish that, not even Mother. She comforted herself with the hope that they would reach the audience chamber safely and that mother would merely laugh at him and send him back to their quarters. But the minute they reached the tower entrance, she realized that the affair would never be as simple as that.

The massive wooden door of the tower was closed and it took the combined strength of both of them to push it open. As they did so, Rilya gasped with astonishment at the sight and sound that greeted them. The long corridors were filled with people. Old folks, women and children were everywhere, chattering, playing, scolding, gossiping, running here and there, the entire non-combatant population of Celdondol jammed into the halls of the castle. The vaulted ceilings re-echoed with the hubbub of their voices, creating a sense of presence that was overwhelming, especially to one who had, all her life, been sheltered from the common people. Rilya's first instinct was to withdraw back to the privacy of the tower. Even Landon hesitated for a moment, startled at the throng confronting him. But then he squared his shoulders and plunged right in, shouting, "Make way! Make wa-a-ay!" Rilya followed him, cheeks burning with self-conscious embarrassment as people began stepping aside for them, some out of automatic respect, others with grins of amusement or

197

even chuckles. She could hear some of them whispering, "Look, the royal children;" and "Look at the silver hair, the mark of enchantment for sure." The comments only added to her humiliation.

At last, to her relief, they turned into the corridor leading to the Queen's audience chamber. But here there were more people than ever, mostly women and children, all milling around in a tight mass and talking excitedly.

"Oh, bother!" Landon exclaimed. "Why can't we get through?"

"I can't see," Rilya replied, standing on tiptoe and craning her neck.

So the enterprising Landon accosted a woman standing on the fringe of the vortex. "I say," he shouted, "what's going on?"

"The Queen's holding audience, lad," she shouted back enthusiastically. "She's blessing everyone in sight and all their children too. A fine woman, she is, the Queen!"

The Queen! Rilya felt she should have known. "Come on," Landon cried, "we've got to reach her!" And with that he plunged into the crowd again, pushing and shoving and darting between people with all the determination a small boy could muster. Rilya followed more slowly and politely, with a litany of "excuse me's" constantly reiterated, until finally she stood at the inner edge of the crowd, directly in front of the Queen's audience chamber. The scene that presented itself astounded even her.

Her mother was standing, without pomp or ceremony, at the entrance to the antechamber, while the people came up, one by one, or in clusters of two or three, to receive her blessing. Some knelt, others bowed, but all showed her the utmost deference. Rilya watched, fascinated, as one very old man tottered to his knees before her. The Queen clasped his head in her two hands and bowed low over him, deep tenderness shining in her eyes. She tried then to help him up but he was so stiff that he could not rise and two women in the crowd sprang forward to assist him. He was followed by two tiny children, twins, shepherded by their flustered young mother. The Queen laughed with delight as she swept up each of them in turn, squeezed and kissed them, and set them back again on their unsteady feet. She flashed a warm, reassuring smile at their mother and, leaning forward, said something to her in a whisper which Rilya strained her ears to hear.

However, what Rilya heard was not the Queen's words but her own name being called. Looking all about herself in perplexity, she finally recognized Landon's voice, and simultaneously caught sight of him, standing just behind the Queen, peering out from around her skirts. Near him, flanking the Queen on either side, were Radin, the faithful bodyguard, and Calya, the lady-in-waiting. Landon beckoned to her to join them. Rilya hesitated at first, but then the Queen also spied her and made a glad gesture of welcome. So she took a deep breath, leapt across the small open space in front of the crowd and caught the outstretched hand of her mother.

"Have you come also to receive my blessing?" the Queen asked gaily, looking not in the least surprised.

"I…" Rilya hedged. But she had to be truthful in the face of her mother's loving gaze. "Landon insisted on coming, so I followed him. I didn't think you would want us. Galna didn't think so either," she added, somewhat defensively.

The Queen frowned at her with mock severity. "Well, my too sensible daughter, I hope you realize now that such is not the case."

"Yes, Mother."

"Good! Let us go inside." She stepped forward and held up her hands to the people. Instantly the babble of voices was stilled, except for a lone infant's cooing. "My dear people," she called out, "we must leave each other for now, but this evening we shall meet again and I promise that I shall not be late."

A loud cheer greeted this announcement. The Queen waited for it to die down, then cried, "Until tonight!" as, with a wave, she turned and disappeared into her chambers. Rilya caught a glimpse of the sea of answering waves as she and Landon bounced after their mother, followed by Calya, while Radin closed the door and took up his post outside it. As the noise of the townspeople faded away behind them, Rilya sighed with contentment. The Queen's ease with her subjects, the love and devotion that passed between them in almost visible currents, the trust they had in their ruler—these things deeply reassured her. Somehow all would be well yet.

The Queen betook herself through the anteroom into the audience chamber and motioned for the children to join her. Calya started to follow as well, but the Queen stopped her with a look. "I should like to see my children privately for a few moments, please."

"Yes, your Majesty." Calya curtsied and retired, her face assuming its usual expressionless mask. As soon as she had closed the door, Landon, whose face was scarlet with impatience, burst out, "Why can't you send out the soldiers and drive all those Galgorians away? I'll lead them myself, since Rendil isn't here!"

His mother looked startled then amused. Laughingly, she said, "Is that what you have come to tell me, my little son?"

"Yes!" he cried. "Just give me the word and we'll ride immediately."

"Thank you for your valiant offer," she replied, "but I am afraid that such an action would merely cost you your life and the lives of your men as well."

"Why?" he demanded. "Surely we're stronger than they are."

"No, my son." She shook her head sadly. "We are outnumbered at least twenty to one. The only resources we have with which to defend the fortress are the enchantment of Dol and a brave show of strength."

"But Mother," Rilya put in, "how are we going to hold out then? Have we got any hope?"

"Yes." The Queen smiled again, the same smile Rilya had seen a few nights earlier, bespeaking now unfathomable depths of confidence and strength. "I know by the light of Dol that Rendil has fulfilled the second sign and that his enchantment gathers ever more powerfully to him."

"Hooray!" both children cried, clapping their hands.

The Queen's smile grew even broader and deeper. "I have every hope now that he will win the victory, even though the most dangerous trial is yet to come. And when he has regained his enchantment in all its fullness, then I shall be able to draw upon its strength to supplement my own."

"Oh!" Rilya's eyes widened. "Do the people know that?"

"No, and I still do not wish them to know."

201

"Why?" Landon asked. "I'm tired of pretending that we don't know about Rendil."

"Yes," Rilya added, "wouldn't it make everyone, or at least the soldiers, feel better if they were sure that help was coming? And the other darkness you were worried about has manifested itself now, hasn't it, with the coming of the Galgorians?"

"I am not so sure." The Queen's expression became somber now. "I have no light from Dol on this subject, but I cannot help feeling, and feeling strongly, that there is still treachery in our midst."

"Treachery!" Landon cried. "How dare anyone be a traitor to Dol and the Queen? I'll run them through with my sword!" He banged his wooden weapon emphatically on the floor.

The Queen could not help smiling once more, but weariness and sorrow showed clearly in her eyes. "I think that the best thing you could do, both of you, would be to go back to the tower and stay there. At least you will be safe there."

"But how can we protect you then?" Landon's face crumpled with disappointment. "We can't let anything happen to you."

"Oh, dear child." The Queen reached out and clasped him to herself. "You must not worry about me. I would love to have you with me, and would personally feel much safer with such a strong young warrior at my side, but…" Her words were interrupted by shouting and trumpet blasts from the direction of the ramparts. "Do you hear? Even now they are beginning to attack us. Be off with you, quickly, while I ascertain what is happening." She rose and made for the door, as a loud crash resounded from without the castle. But before

202

she could even get the door open, Calya burst in, wide-eyed and pale.

"Your Majesty," she gasped, "what is happening?"

"That is what I wish to know," the Queen replied. "Please send Radin to get a report."

"But, your Majesty, then who will guard us?"

"I will," Landon shouted before his mother could find an answer.

"You?" Calya stared at him. "If I were not so upset, I would laugh."

"Nevertheless," the Queen interposed coldly, "under the circumstances, he shall have to do. Now, please dispatch Radin as I have ordered."

"Yes, your Majesty." Calya looked as if she would say something more, but then thought better of it, curtsied and turned to go. As she did so, another crash could be heard, along with the splintering of wood and the shattering of glass. At this, Calya fairly flew to the outer door of the antechamber. "Radin!" she screeched as she flung the door open, "Radin! Her Majesty orders you to find out what is happening."

"Yes, my lady," they could hear his calm answering rumble from without. "I'll do my best, but with all these people, it won't be easy. No, wait! One of the draftees is coming." Then they heard two other sounds simultaneously: the anxious and frightened clamor of the townspeople and a man's voice crying over the top of it, "Make way! Make way!"

The voice grew nearer and nearer until finally the owner of it struggled through the crowd and into the antechamber. He was a man of late middle age, a merchant from the town, pressed into military service by the present crisis. His face was etched with fear and concern, but he bore himself well. Noticing the Queen standing in the inner doorway, he brushed past Radin and Calya, approached her and bowed courteously. "Your Majesty," he said, "I have a report from Captain Fandol on the ramparts."

"Very good," she replied, "what is it?"

"Your Majesty, the enemy has built a catapult and moved it up into attack position. The soldiers on the ramparts are fighting hard to drive them back but one of their missiles has struck the northwest tower. I don't know the extent of the damage."

"Very well, then. You and Radin are to go and investigate the damage and evacuate to safety the occupants of the tower."

"Yes, your Majesty."

"Mother!" Rilya's voice came in an odd little squeak. "Galna is still up there. Do you suppose she's hurt?"

"I do not know. Soldier!"

"Yes, your Majesty?" The man had already bowed and turned to go.

"Bring the nursemaid Galna here to me. And see to it that she is treated gently."

"Yes, your Majesty." The man bowed once again and left.

Thus, to the children's relief, they were allowed to remain with their Mother after all. Galna joined them later on, shaken and indignant, but unhurt. The huge boulder had smashed through their window in the main hall of the second level and had rolled right into the fireplace, thoroughly spoiling Galna's dinner. "It wasn't much," she fumed, "but they had no call to ruin it!"

All that day, fighting went on intermittently, now at one point of the wall, now at another. The Queen with her little entourage remained in the audience chamber, while messengers came and went with reports of the action. They had managed to drive back the catapult, but not before several more missiles had been hurled, one of which knocked two men off the ramparts and killed them. A lookout thought he could spot another machine in the making, down at the river's edge. The enemy was ripping up the boat docks for wood. Finally, at dusk, a list of casualties: two men dead, ten wounded, one of them a member of the Queen's Guard.

The Queen listened to the report in silence, then dismissed the messenger. When he had gone, she shook her head sadly. "And this is only the first day of actual fighting. We shall need every ounce of strength and courage that Dol can afford us."

After this, she and her entourage – the two children, Galna, Lady Calya and Radin – removed themselves to her privy chambers for the night. As they passed through the corridors, with Radin and Landon marching side by side at the head, people gathered round the Queen from all over, asking anxiously how long the siege would last, how long they could expect to hold out, how many were wounded, when help would come to them and from where. The Queen did her best to console them, saying that Dol had never abandoned their forefathers and would not abandon them now, that surely they were strong enough to hold out for a fortnight, and that by then Lord Gendol would have returned in force with the main army.

Rilya had forgotten about Lord Gendol, but she was confident that not he, but Rendil, would return victorious at

205

the head of their troops. She still wondered why Mother could not say so and why she continued to feel that someone in the fortress was against them.

At last they reached the privy chambers and went to bed for the night, the Queen and her children in the inner chamber and Calya and Galna in the attendant's quarters adjoining the sitting room. Radin they dismissed to the barracks for the night, although he was reluctant to go. "You must save your strength for now," the Queen told him, with a kindly smile. "Later, I may be needing you at night as well."

Much to her own surprise, Rilya fell asleep immediately, but awakened with a start, she knew not how much later. For some reason or other she thought she had heard a noise, and for a few moments simply lay there, tense and listening. Were those strange sounds coming from the sitting room? She got up quietly, so as not to disturb Mother and Landon, tiptoed to the door and put her eye to the keyhole.

What she saw was the faint glow of a very small lamp, and in the half-circle of its radiance two shadowy figures, one male, the other female. "Oh!" she thought with disgust, "it's only Calya and that Captain Fandol who is courting her." But they didn't look as if they were courting; they were conversing intently in a low, excited tone of voice. Rilya shifted her ear to the keyhole and concentrated with all her might. Conscience objected that this was very impolite, but impulse brushed away the objection impatiently.

"It would be insane to go ahead now," Calya was saying, "no matter what Uncle Gendol had planned. He never foresaw this pestilential insurrection."

"True," Fandol replied, "but I am quite confident that he will have no difficulty in dispersing the Galgorians once he returns in force. They do not seem to have skilled leadership or a coherent plan of attack."

"But what shall we do until then? We need the Queen to control this rabble from the town. If anything happens to her, there will be a riot or a panic at the very least, and all will be lost."

"Not necessarily. Since the Queen is powerless on the night of the Dark Moon, the flame of the Gelfin Tree may die out anyway, as it certainly will if anything happens to her. We will simply spread rumors to this effect, then encourage the people by telling them that they must rely on their own strength."

"Do you think they will believe that?" Calya herself did not sound convinced.

"They will not have much choice under the circumstances," Fandol rejoined grimly. "I only wish I knew where the young prince is." At this point his voice faded out. Rilya hastily put her eye back to the keyhole and saw that he was taking his leave. She watched, her heart pounding with excitement and frustration, as Calya shut the door softly behind him, extinguished the light and tiptoed back to her room.

Rilya too went back to bed. For a long time she lay there, wondering if this were the treason that Mother had so long suspected. She would have to tell her everything, right away in the morning. In the meantime, she hoped she would not be scolded for eavesdropping.

CHAPTER 22
THE FADING OF THE GELFIN TREE

The next morning Rilya found that, try as she might, she could not tell the Queen what she had seen and heard because Lady Calya hovered over them constantly with unusually subservient attention. Wherever they were – breakfast, the royal progress to the audience chamber, the blessing of the people, the receiving of messengers from the ramparts – Calya was ubiquitous, in a way that soon began to grate on Rilya's already frazzled nerves. Landon too was constantly at his mother's side, and she did not want him to hear either. Finally, about midday, she could bear it no longer. She suddenly ran up to the Queen, threw her arms around her neck, and whispered in her ear, "Mother, I have to talk to you alone, at once."

"Why certainly dear," the Queen answered, somewhat puzzled. "Is something the matter?" She drew her aside to a far corner of the room; not far enough to suit Rilya, but there was no other place to go.

"Mother!" Rilya gulped a huge breath, then poured out the whole tale in disjointed murmurings, with many nervous glances over her shoulder. "Is this the treason that you suspected?" she asked anxiously in conclusion, noticing the pallor of her mother's face.

"Yes, dear," she answered tonelessly, "I fear that it is."

"But what do you think they are planning to do?"

"I suspect that they are planning to kill me."

Rilya stared at her mother, speechless with horror. The very matter-of-factness of the statement made it all the more incomprehensible.

"If I die," the Queen went on, ignoring her daughter's expression, "the Gelfin Tree will surely be extinguished. They must prepare the people for this eventuality."

"But why?" Rilya found her voice at last, a hoarse, dry whisper.

"So that Gendol may claim the enchantment and take over the Kingdom. They did not plan on the disappearance of Rendil. That is why I did not wish anyone to know of his success and possible victory. He is our only human hope now, but we must act ourselves and act quickly."

But she had no sooner spoken than Lady Calya approached them from across the room. Rilya stiffened. "Yes, my lady?" said the Queen coldly.

"Your Majesty," she said with a curtsy, "I beg your pardon, but there is an orderly here from Captain Fandol."

"Very well, send him in." Without a backward glance, the Queen repaired to her throne and seated herself to receive him. Rilya hesitated, then came up and stood beside her mother. Landon, as if by some instinct, was already there.

The orderly, like so many others in the past two days, strode forward, saluted, and made his report. "Your Majesty, the Galgorians have launched an offensive against the main gate, with catapult and battering ram and massed troops. We have concentrated all our forces at that point and the flame throwers are striving valiantly to disable the catapult, but already six of our men have been killed."

"Thank you, soldier," the Queen replied gravely. "Is that all?"

"Well, yes, Your Majesty, that is officially, but…"

"But what, soldier? You may speak freely."

"Thank you, Your Majesty." He shifted uneasily. "It's the Gelfin Tree, Your Majesty. The sacred flame seems to be getting lower and begging Your Majesty's pardon, but there are rumors going about that this is happening because your enchantment is on the wane and that you will become powerless on the night of the Dark Moon." Rilya felt nauseous and faint as she heard this, but she forced herself to remain standing upright. The Queen's expression did not change; she seemed to have recovered herself fully, and was at once both grave and serene.

"Your Majesty, now don't take me wrong," the orderly continued, "I don't believe any of this myself and I don't mean to be advising you, but maybe you could say a few words to reassure everyone that it isn't true. Some of the people are getting mighty uneasy. A couple of us asked Captain Fandol about it and he said he hadn't heard any rumors, but if it were true, we'd simply have to rely on our own strength of arms to get us through."

Now he was really finished. "Thank you, soldier, for this intelligence," the Queen answered him. "Yes, I will speak to the people. In fact, I wish you to find four heralds and send them here to me at once. And report back here yourself."

"Yes, Your Majesty." The soldier saluted and withdrew in haste.

"Mother!" Landon wailed, almost before he was gone. "It isn't true, it can't be true! How could anyone think such things?"

"But it is true, my little son," the Queen answered sadly. "I am powerless on the night of the Dark Moon, even if only for a night."

Landon stared at her, uncomprehending, while tears trickled forlornly down his cheeks.

"But Mother," Rilya quavered. She still felt faint and leaned her head against the back of the throne. "What good will it do to speak to the people? What can you possibly tell them?"

"I will tell them," the Queen replied with deep serenity, "that the Gelfin Tree flames by the power of Dol, of whom I am but a poor servant. They must call upon him for the sign of his continued protection and rely upon his strength rather than their own."

"But…" Rilya began again, but could not go on. She wanted to protest that saying this would not stop anyone from killing her, but Calya was too near and she had to keep still.

"We have nothing to fear from the Galgorians, at any rate," the Queen went on. "They will not dare a night attack, unless…" Her voice trailed off, but Rilya could hear her murmur to herself, "unless they also get wind of the rumors."

At that moment the orderly returned with four heralds in tow. They bowed to the Queen and stood in a line awaiting her orders. "Very good," she said. "I wish you to issue a proclamation to all the people within the castle, that they are to assemble at sunset in the great courtyard around the Gelfin Tree. At that time the Queen will address them. And you, soldier, I wish you to convey this same message to Captain Fandol, so that the troops may also be present as far as possible. Do you understand me? Then go now, and quickly."

211

They bowed and left, but as they did so, Rilya could not help feeling that all was lost.

Somehow the rest of that day dragged on: the muted cacophony of battle, the messengers from the ramparts, the return of the heralds with their proclamation delivered, and, at last, the final list of casualties, and sunset. The Queen's entourage waited until the castle was empty of people, then proceeded in state to the Great Hall, first the heralds as escorts, then the children, followed by Galna and Lady Calya, then the Queen, robed in midnight blue. Radin, henceforth officially designated as the Queen's private bodyguard, brought up the rear.

As they entered the Great Hall, now darkened except for a single torch at either end, Galna whispered, *sotto voce*, to no one in particular, "Might of Dol! What excitement! And to think, after all these years, that I should be a part of it!" Rilya could not help smiling to herself. Galna had never been included in the royal party before; too bad it had to be under such circumstances as these. Her own stomach was churning with fear as they marched through the Hall toward the bronze doors at the main entrance. It gave a near-disastrous lurch when the doors swung open and she saw, on the other side, Captain Fandol waiting to greet the Queen.

Rilya could not even bear to look at him. Instead, with head bent, she hurried to her place, then turned to watch her mother. As the Queen appeared between the great doors, a loud murmur of approval went up from the crowd. Captain Fandol stepped forward and bowed ceremoniously. "Your Royal Majesty," he said, "good evening."

The Queen inclined her head gravely in acknowledgment, her face showing neither agitation nor disgust. "Thank you, Lord Captain," she said. "You have done well these past days in conducting the defense of the fortress."

"I have done my best, Your Majesty, for the glory of Arendolin." With that he abruptly stepped aside. Rilya could not help seeing him now. His face was utterly impassive, a tightly controlled mask; only the slight trembling of his lips betrayed strong inner emotion.

The Queen moved forward to the top of the steps and surveyed the people briefly. The Royal Guard was deployed in parade formation down one side of the steps, while the regular troops lined the other side. At the foot of the stairs stood the draftees, a motley crew of townsmen, outfitted and equipped as best as could be under the circumstances. Beyond them massed the rest of the people, surrounding the Gelfin Tree.

Rilya followed her mother's gaze and, summoning her courage, looked beyond all the people to the sacred Tree itself. To her dismay, she realized that the rumors were true; its flame had grown noticeably smaller and dimmer. She shuddered and glanced up at the sky, but the moon had not yet risen. She knew that it would be but a tiny, pale sliver and she was glad not to see it.

Silence had fallen now among the people. The Queen stepped back a pace or two from the top of the stairs, lifted her arms momentarily in prayer, and then began to speak. "My beloved people," she said. "Five days ago we gathered in this courtyard to beseech the protection of Dol in our extremity of need and to ask that, by means of the royal enchantment, he might bestow on us the sign of his benevolence, the flame of the Gelfin Tree. Graciously he heard our request and flame did burst forth upon the sacred Tree. Now, however, you see

213

that the flame is dying out and you are perplexed, wondering if Dol has abandoned us or if the royal enchantment has failed."

She paused, and Rilya held her breath. Captain Fandol, like the good soldier he was, stood at attention, not moving a muscle, while Lady Calya nervously examined her fingernails.

"I must tell you the truth then," the Queen continued, in deeper and more ringing tones. "Yes, my enchantment is on the wane and on the Night of the Dark Moon I shall be powerless indeed."

An expression of consternation burst forth from the crowd, but the Queen held up her hands immediately for silence. "My people," she called out, "you must not fear. Do not be afraid! The power of Dol and his benevolence do not depend on the Queen's enchantment, although they are ordinarily expressed through it. Dol will not abandon you, his people, nor will he withdraw the sign of his protection, if you beseech him earnestly to continue it. Therefore, I am asking you, the people, to keep vigil, tonight and tomorrow night, before the Gelfin Tree. You will be divided into watches for the purpose; I have appointed commissioners to see to it. In the meantime, for tonight I shall keep vigil with you, here, before the royal doors. Tomorrow night, I shall retire into seclusion. And I beg you, my dear people, to pray for me."

With that the Queen stepped back toward the doors. For a moment, she stood quite still, head bowed. Then she motioned to the four heralds, who proceeded down to the courtyard and began their task of organizing the people for the coming vigil. After standing there a moment longer, she turned to Captain Fandol. "Lord Captain," she said, "I wish the soldiers of the garrison to keep watch for the first round, both tonight and tomorrow."

"Yes, your Majesty." Captain Fandol looked surprised, but quickly recovered himself. "Very good." He saluted, then swung about and descended the steps to issue orders to his men, leaving the royal party to stand alone before the main doors of Celdondol. Rilya waited eagerly, expecting that they also would be asked to remain for the night, and glad for the opportunity to do something, anything, however futile. But her hopes were speedily dashed.

"Children," their mother said, "I wish you and Galna to return to my privy chambers for the night. Lady Calya and Radin will remain here with me."

"Oh, Mother!" Landon moaned.

"But Mother…" Rilya gulped, as her eyes filled with tears.

"I wish no 'ohs' or 'buts' this time," the Queen rejoined firmly. "I wish to be obeyed. Let me bless you and then you may go."

"Yes, Mother," they both sighed in unison. Together they knelt before her, as she placed one hand on each silver head.

"May Dol surround you with his strong arms," she intoned, "and preserve you safe and whole."

"May it truly be so," Landon answered as he kissed her hand. Rilya did the same, but choked on the words and nearly sobbed. She wished painfully that she had her Mother's serenity, her faith, the interior vision that sustained her. But she had none of these. All that remained to her was a dull sense of foreboding, an aching fear of the morrow.

CHAPTER 23
MOLDAN GORGE

Far to the north, that fateful morrow began in a dreary pewter dawn, scarcely perceptible to the eyes of the four weary travelers. They had been on the trail for nearly an hour already, and Patsy yawned and burrowed deeper into her cape, wishing desperately that she were back in bed. Ever since they had left Caf and Tally two and a half days ago, they had pushed steadily on, with hardly a pause for rest, along narrow and rocky paths that wound upwards toward the mountains. Once, from a clearing on a hillock, they had caught a glimpse of those mountains, gray slabs of barren granite, forbidding access to the horizon. Patsy had shivered and asked Rendil if he would please make the sun shine hotter. But he had laughed grimly and replied that so great was the spell of the Dark Ones in these parts that it took the fullest exertion of his powers to make the sun shine at all.

Indeed, even now, seated as she was in front of Rendil in the saddle, she could feel the struggle going on within and around him. He exuded a preternatural warmth that seemed to assail the atmosphere and be driven back by it, over and over again. Patsy returned in her mind to the cabin of Caf and Tally where she had first felt this warmth. She remembered the fire blazing up on the cold hearth, Tally bursting into tears of hope and gratitude, Caf growing increasingly more ruddy and life-like. He had still not regained consciousness when they left that noon, but Gifil was confident that he would. She remembered the neighbors he had brought with him, a simple, humble couple, wide-eyed and tongue-tied in the presence of

216

the king's son. Patsy smiled to herself; looking back on the scene gave her great comfort.

Looking forward gave her none at all. This very night, the Night of the Dark Moon, they would engage in battle an unseen horde of unthinkably evil creatures. Before that, they must face and unmask the traitorous Lord Gendol, wresting the allegiance of the troops away from him and transferring it to Rendil. As the necessary prerequisite for victory, Rendil had yet to fulfill the third test and regain his full enchantment. And in all of this, she, Patsy, was irrevocably involved.

She felt all the old fears welling up in her once more. "They're going to make me ride into battle after all," she thought, "even though the Queen promised it would never happen."

"Well, you disobeyed the Queen," her conscience reminded her.

"But if I hadn't," she argued, "Rendil would have forced me."

Bitter resentment mingled with her fear and overpowered it. Yes, Rendil had forced her, but she would not let him do so again. "I will not ride into battle," she resolved grimly. "And I will not give up my cross!" She clutched at it underneath her cloak and it bit into her hand like something alive.

"But won't you fulfill your mission?" her conscience goaded.

"No!" she shouted silently, as fear regained the upper hand. "Not if it means getting killed." Her mission: she was beginning to loathe it, and everything and everyone connected with it. "I never should have taken the cross from Mrs. Denton, never. It's all your fault, God," she stormed. "I never

217

should have trusted you. I don't believe in you any more. Do you hear me? I don't!" But only silence greeted this pronouncement and the cross remained, burning like fire, against her chest.

They traveled on like this, hour after dismal hour, Rendil in conflict with the evil without, Patsy in conflict with the evil within, the other two thinking their own incommunicable thoughts. The sun was edging its way toward noon amid a thick and dingy haze, when they emerged unexpectedly from the forest to find themselves on the brink of a wide chasm that plunged steeply into gray rock, cleaving the wilderness neatly in two. Patsy was about to ask what it was when Gifil answered her unspoken question.

"Moldan Gorge," he said flatly.

Patsy froze, petrified, and she felt Rendil stiffen behind her. Moldan Gorge, the northern border, the land of the enemy! Frantically she stared across the chasm into the impenetrable forests beyond, but nothing could be seen, nor could any sound be heard except the angry murmur of the river far below. She recalled Tally's tale of the invisible foe and shuddered.

It was Condin who broke the silence. "Where do we go from here?"

"Well," answered Gifil, "there be several ways we could go. Reckon we might rest a spell whilst we discuss it."

"Very well," Rendil agreed at once, much to Patsy's relief. She was in no hurry to go anywhere, although the idea of resting on the edge of the ill-fabled Gorge filled her with apprehension. However, they turned back into the forest a few paces to a clump of rocks they had just passed, dismounted there and sat down.

Patsy immediately leaned back against a good sized boulder and closed her eyes, but Rendil and Condin crouched eagerly in front of Gifil. "What have you in mind?" Rendil asked.

"Looks to me like we might be doin' one of three things," Gifil replied. "We might try to find the place where the King crossed over and cross over ourselves."

"That seems foolish to me, under the circumstances," Condin remarked.

"Yes," agreed Rendil, "if even Father and his men were cut to pieces, we certainly would not fare any better."

Patsy was glad they had at least that much sense, but she kept her eyes shut and said nothing.

"Well, then," Gifil went on, "we might go on over to the road, which ain't too far from here, and ride into the camp open-like, and you can have it out with Gendol now, afore the battle commences." He paused, waiting for a reaction to this proposal.

The two boys looked at one another and Condin shrugged his shoulders. "That's a possibility," Rendil said slowly, "although such an open confrontation might be dangerous. We might easily be taken prisoner, or our presence be otherwise rendered totally ineffective."

Patsy opened her eyes and sighed audibly. She would have been glad to get away from the Gorge and back into the company of other people, but, as usual, no one was paying attention to her.

"Continue," Rendil said to Gifil.

"The third thing we might be doin' is we might go on up the Gorge this way, until we run into the outposts of the army. Most of the ordinary folk, I reckon, would be loyal to

219

you, and we could sort of feel our way from there. Might I remind you," he added, "that you ain't got no armor."

"Yes," Rendil acknowledged ruefully, "you are right. I think your third idea is the best one, and very much like what I had in mind myself. What do you think?" He turned to Condin.

"I agree," Condin answered.

Patsy opened her eyes and sat forward, expecting Rendil to ask her opinion also. But he did not. "Very well," he said as he rose and brushed the crumbs of leaves from his leather breeches, "let us be off. We have not much more time."

"With that, they all stood up and remounted. Patsy trembled with rage and disappointment as Rendil heaved her into the saddle. She did not care if he noticed. Would he never stop ignoring her? Would he never stop ordering her about as if she were a child or worse? Granted that never before had he been thoughtful enough to consult the others and really listen to them. But couldn't he have consulted her too? Not that she disagreed with the plan as finally formulated, but he might at least have given her the opportunity to say so. She bit her lips savagely to keep back the tears, but two of them splashed down all the same. "I don't care," she thought, "I just don't care!"

Her bitter, self-pitying reverie continued unabated as they wound their way up the Gorge, keeping out of sight just behind the trees. However, they had not traveled for more than half an hour when suddenly they were brought up short by a voice out of nowhere: "Stop! Who are you and where be you goin'?"

Patsy screamed.

"Hush!" Rendil hissed.

But Gifil gave a soft crow of delight. "Fal, my lad, is that you?"

And to their amazement, a tall, dark bearded young man in Arendolese armor leaped out of the underbrush and flung his arms around Gifil, crying, "Pa! What be you doin' here?"

Patsy was still staring, wild-eyed, but she could hear Rendil chuckling behind her, while Condin too grinned with relief. Then she realized: it was one of Gifil's four sons, all of whom were in the service of the King. With a huge sigh, she relaxed. The day seemed almost bright again.

"Who be these young'uns, Pa?" Fal asked as Gifil disentangled himself from his embrace.

Gifil looked warily around him. "Be there any soldiers with you or any folks nearby what might be hearin' us?"

"No, Pa. I'm s'posed to blow my horn if'n anything turns up."

"Good. First off, then" – he turned to address Rendil – "this here's my youngest lad, Falil."

"I am happy to meet you," responded Rendil with the utmost sincerity.

"And this," said Gifil to Fal, with what was meant to be a grand flourish, "is his Highness, Prince Rendil, him what will be King."

Fal gaped in astonishment, then, coming to himself, pulled off his helmet and bowed low.

"And this here's Condin, his brother, and this is Lady Passy," Gifil added, finishing the introductions. "Now, as to why we're here…" He explained the situation as briefly as possible, while Fal listened consideringly. "And I think what we might be needin' first of all," he concluded, "is a set of armor for his Highness here."

"I can get that," Fal nodded slowly, "and for his brother too. But I don't know about this little gal," he added. "She's a mite small."

Patsy felt her cheeks burning, but within her the resolution reiterated itself: " I will not ride into battle!"

Since no one made any audible comment, Fal went on, "Now if'n I reckon right, what you want is to get to the head of the army just afore the battle without Gendol knowin' that it's you."

"That is correct," Rendil affirmed.

Fal thought for a moment, then nodded again. "Aye, that's easy enough. But what will you be doin' then?"

"I am not sure. That depends upon how Gendol reacts when I confront him." Rendil's lips were tight and his voice grim.

"Well, Dol be helpin' you!" Fal ejaculated. "But we'd best get busy." With that, he hid the little party a short way up the Gorge until his relief arrived, then led them on foot to a point within earshot of the noisy, bustling camp. There he left them while they waited for what seemed an eternity—Gifil peaceful and reflective, Rendil and Condin silent and withdrawn, Patsy nervous and fidgety, certain that someone would discover them.

"If'n you keep jumpin' up and movin' around, for sure they will," Gifil admonished her, but she could not sit still.

At last Fal returned, flushed and triumphant, with a large bundle under his arm. "They was askin' me what I wanted with two more sets of armor," he explained as he undid the bundle on the ground, "and I had some purty tall tale-tellin' to do, but here it is."

Patsy looked curiously: helmets and breastplates, scarlet cloaks and gray tunics – the uniform of Arendolin. Rendil grinned his appreciation. "Well done, soldier," he said and immediately began to remove his own cloak and tunic and don the new clothing. Within minutes both he and Condin were transformed from stripling princes to soldiers of Arendolin. Rendil's own sword and shield completed the picture.

"That'll do," Fal grunted. "That way you can walk through the camp with no one noticin' you. I brung some things for the little gal too," he added.

Patsy glanced at the ground, surprised to realize that there was another, smaller bundle of clothing left.

"A page's outfit," he explained as he picked it up and handed it to her.

She took the proffered items and examined them uncertainly: leather breeches, gray tunic and scarlet cape, all about her size, and a close-fitting, round scarlet cap.

"Sorry, little lady," Fal apologized, "but you'll never get through if'n you ain't got a uniform of some kind."

Patsy didn't really want to get through, but she didn't want to be left behind either, so she reluctantly retired a short distance away and climbed into the new clothes. They fit well enough, except for the cap, which remained perched precariously atop her mop of orange curls, despite every effort to push it down. Finally, in desperation, she seized her own hooded leather cape, tied it tightly under her chin, and jammed the scarlet cap firmly on top of it.

As she emerged from the underbrush, Condin hooted softly, "Well if it isn't Passy the Page!"

"Shut up!" she rounded on him fiercely, as Rendil snickered and Fal guffawed.

Condin looked surprised and somewhat hurt, but Gifil clamped a kindly hand on her shoulder. "It's only for a short spell," he consoled. "Now we'd best be goin'."

"Right," Fal said. "This is the way we'll proceed. If'n you approve," he added, nodding to Rendil.

"Whatever you say," Rendil answered.

"Pa and me'll go first, with Passy here, and I'll lead one of the horses. You two wait until you can just barely see us, then follow after. If'n anybody asks about Pa, I'll tell'em it's my old man what can't keep away from a good scrap."

"Right enough!" Gifil chuckled.

"Where are you leading us?" Rendil asked.

"To my captain's tent," Fal replied. "Seein's how he's already at the front with Gendol, you'll be safe enough there for the afternoon. At sundown, they'll blow the trumpet and we'll all get ready for battle. That's when, I reckon, you'll be wantin' to show yourself."

"Very good," said Rendil. "Lead on."

So Fal seized the reins of Condin's mount, motioned to his father and Patsy to follow him, and plunged through the curtain of trees into the camp. Patsy's heart pounded wildly as they moved among the soldiers, but no one took a second look at them. She could feel Gifil's steadying hand again on her shoulder, and tried to act relaxed and nonchalant, but her feet somehow would not pick themselves up and she kept stumbling.

"Easy, lass, easy," Gifil mumbled without bending his head. "I think we're almost there."

But just at that moment, the one thing they had least expected happened. "Hey, Fal!" a rough voice hailed them. "Who's the old man?"

"Uh, Captain Diril!" Fal gulped as he stopped short and saluted the burly, middle-aged officer coming toward them. "This here's my Pa. He comed around to see how his young'uns are getting on."

"Well, well," the captain exclaimed, "pleased to know you!" He thrust out his hand to Gifil, who pumped it warmly.

"Same here," the old man rumbled.

"Come a long way?" the captain asked cheerfully as he fell into step with them.

Gifil made some reply, but Patsy didn't hear it. She was shrinking as close against Burdil's flank as she possibly could and hoping that this surprisingly friendly officer would not notice her. To her amazement, he did not, until they came to his tent. There, they paused for a moment uncertainly. Then Diril said to Gifil, "I'm sure you realize that we'll be mustering for battle in a short while. In fact, I'll be leaving immediately for headquarters. Would you care to stay in my tent until the fighting is over? You'll be safe here, and you can tether your horse as well."

"Thank 'ee," said Gifil. "Don't mind if I take you up on that." He moved to enter the tent as the captain held the flap for him, while Patsy unthinkingly followed. It was a fatal mistake.

"Hey lad!" Diril growled. "Where do you think you're going? Get out of there!"

"He's with me, Captain," Fal interposed quickly. "I got a job for him to do."

"Well, errand or no errand, he stays out of my tent, do you hear?"

"Yes, sir!"

So the three of them went inside and left Patsy standing there, shaking so badly that she had to cling to Burdil's stirrup in order to stay on her feet. She felt like throwing up, but could not because she had not eaten in hours. Her mind was too numb to think, or even to wonder what was happening, when, a few minutes later, Fal and the captain emerged together and headed in opposite directions.

Diril strode off without a backward glance, but Fal shot her a sympathetic look as he passed by. Patsy did not notice where he was going, nor was she surprised when he returned shortly with Rendil and Condin in tow. "Come," he said to her, "it'll be safe now, I reckon."

Without a word, Patsy stumbled after them into the tent and collapsed in a forlorn heap on the captain's cot.

"By the gods," Condin was saying, "I thought we were finished when that officer turned up."

"Sure 'nuff," Fal answered, 'I did too. But it comed out all right – he invited Pa to stay here durin' the battle."

"Excellent," remarked Rendil, "but we do not have much more time to waste. Perhaps you could tell us how to reach the front lines."

"That'll be easy," said Fal. "Fact is, I can draw it for you."

Patsy then heard scratching on the dirt floor and accompanying explanations, but they were meaningless to her and she did not stir herself to listen.

Finally Fal said, "You know, I been thinkin' somethin' else."

"Yes?" Rendil queried.

"How are the men s'posed to know what's goin' on or who you are unless someone be a-tellin' them?"

"What do you propose?"

"Well, this here's the idea. You ain't goin' to show yourself to Gendol until dusk, when the troops are all mustered. But when you step forward and all the men are askin' themselves what's what, then I'll start flappin' my jaw that it's the King's son. Never mind if'n they don't believe me – the word'll spread like wildfire anyways, and they'll be ready for when you'll be takin' over."

"Good enough," Rendil approved. "What do you think?"

"I agree," answered Condin. Again, no one asked Patsy, but by this time she really did not care. She sat up on the cot and stared listlessly at nothing while Fal and his father settled into a family conversation: how his three brothers were, how his wife and children were getting on. At long last, in the distance, then nearer and nearer, they could hear the trumpets sounding.

"That's it," said Fal as he stood up and began to buckle on his sword. Patsy felt the nervous knot in her stomach, which had begun to loosen slightly, tighten once more. When Fal had finished, he turned first to Gifil. "Well, Pa," he said quietly.

"Good luck to you, lad," Gifil answered, taking both his hands and clasping them strongly.

Next he bowed to Rendil. "May Dol be lookin' after Your Highness and givin' you victory."

"And may Dol protect you and restore you safely to your family," Rendil responded. He too reached out and clasped Fal's hands. Then the young man wheeled abruptly and left.

For a moment after his departure everyone was silent. Then Condin asked, "Now what?"

"In a very short while," Rendil answered, "I must ride. As for the rest of you…" he paused. "Condin, you have a mount and armor, but no weapons."

"I will ride with you anyway." Condin's face glowed with pride and courage.

"Thank you," Rendil said gladly. "And you, Lady Palissa?"

"No!" Patsy exploded. "I will not ride into battle!"

Rendil recoiled as if struck, but he answered gently. "No, my lady, I did not intend that you should. I am only asking…"

"No!" she shouted again, trembling. "You can't have my cross, it's mine!"

"But, I wished only that you would invoke…"

"No! You can't force me anymore! I'm sick and tired of being forced, of being…" She could not go on. Her voice broke and she burst into hysterical sobs.

"Reckon the little lass is just afeared," Gifil said quietly as he moved to put a soothing arm about her. But she pulled away from him and huddled by herself on a corner of the cot, weeping uncontrollably.

For a while, the echo of her own sobs filled her ears, admitting no other sound. But then she heard, far, far away, the voice of Condin. "It is growing dark."

And she heard Rendil answering heavily, "Yes, and we must ride and trust in Dol. Peace be with you, Gifil, and thank you for everything."

"Good luck to you, Your Highness, and you, lad. May Dol ride with you." Gifil's voice was husky.

"If there is any way in which you can soothe her and persuade her to invoke the power of the Great One this one last time..."

"I'll try."

"Thank you."

Then silence. They were gone.

For a while Patsy continued to weep, until she was too drained to go on. She felt within herself a dull realization that the conflict was over and, this time at least, she had won. But why did the victory bring her no peace? A kind of hollowness tore at her heart and lungs, so that her breath still came in sobs, long after the tears had dried.

She heard Gifil moving softly about the tent and turned to look at him. He had lit a small lantern, and by its glow she could verify what she knew and did not wish to know: that they were alone. "I will not ride into battle!" she gulped.

"Reckon you won't have to," he answered gently.

She eyed him warily. "You're not going to try and talk me into it?"

"No." That was all. The single word made her feel emptier than ever.

"I'm too tired. God will just have to understand." The words sounded defensive, even in her own ears.

"Reckon so. Whyn't you lay yourself down and rest?"

This seemed like a good idea, so she tried it. But she could do no more than lay there. The all-obliterating, all-forgiving sleep she so desired would not come.

Gifil sat down on a low stool near the entrance to the tent and rested his hands on his knees, but he too seemed tense and restless, though still. After awhile, she heard him murmur, "O Dol, how can I be sittin' here like this?" And yet he went on sitting there for some time longer, and Patsy went on lying quite still.

Suddenly he leaped up from his stool. "No!" he cried softly. "I can't be sittin' here like this!" He hesitated for a moment longer, and Patsy knew he was looking at her, but she did not move. He whispered something else, which she could not catch. Then, with firm, determined tread, he turned and left the tent. Now he too was gone and Patsy was left alone.

Alone. What an exhilarating thought! Alone, for the first time in weeks! No more strange people making incessant demands, offering impossible choices, bullying, pleading, threatening. She felt light-headed, exultant. But her thoughts went on without pause: No more Queen with her beautiful eyes, her consoling benedictions of strength and peace, her challenging words of love and fidelity. No more Mrs. Denton, no more Daddy, no more God. Only Patsy, all alone.

She sat up quickly, listening. Was that Gifil returning? No, it was only her imagination. There was no sound, none at all. Panic choked her. Thoughtlessly, instinctively, she groped for the Cross and clutched it in her hand. It seemed to twist and writhe like something alive. So, she was not quite alone; one Presence remained and from that Presence she wished only to flee.

"Gifil!" she cried, "where are you? Don't go away! Wait for me!" She seized the lantern and stumbled out of the tent. Night had nearly fallen and though she cast her gaze frantically about, she could see nothing and no one. "Gifil!" she cried again. Far off in the distance a black shape paused, then stopped. It was he. "Gifil, wait for me!" Patsy sobbed as she plunged headfirst into the darkness.

CHAPTER 24
NIGHT OF THE DARK MOON I

Rilya sat tensely on the edge of her cot and gazed across the room at her mother's empty bed. "Only this one last night," she told herself, "and it will be all over." The Night of the Dark Moon. Tonight. Last night the Queen's bed was empty too, but last night was only the vigil. Tonight she was in seclusion, in her throne room, alone. At nightfall she had sent the children away to her privy chambers, with Calya and Galna, to rest. Two of the Queen's Men were dispatched to stand guard outside their door, while two others remained with Radin at his post by the Queen.

Rilya churned with anxiety. Why was Mother not hiding herself? Why did she not put that hateful Calya under arrest and Fandol with her? Why did she not at least surround herself with guards? But such questions could not be asked aloud.

She looked over at Landon, but he was not sleeping either. He lay flat on his cot, dangling his wooden sword up over his head and contemplating it morosely.

"Mother's in danger, isn't she?" he asked, too loudly.

"Shh!" she hissed. "Keep your voice down!"

"Why?" he asked, in the same tone.

"Because," she whispered fiercely, "Calya's one of the traitors."

"Calya?" Landon's eyes grew very round, then narrowed with sudden anger. "I'll run her through with my sword!"

"Shh!" Rilya felt that she would burst with exasperation. "You can't, silly. Your sword's only made of wood."

"Well, it's sharp enough." He looked hurt. "And besides, we've got to protect Mother."

"How? She refused to let us stay with her, and she forbade us to leave here." Rilya gestured hopelessly.

"We'll have to go to her anyway. The good of the kingdom demands it!" With that, he sat up and began to pull on his boots.

"But we can't," Rilya protested as she too began to grope for her shoes. "Calya and Galna are both out there. They'll never let us by."

"Maybe they're both asleep." He listened for a moment. "I think I hear Galna snoring. Come on, let's see!" Hastily he threw his scarlet cape over his nightshirt and started for the door.

"Wait!" Rilya grabbed her own cloak and dashed after him.

The door was tightly shut, but Landon put his ear to the keyhole. "Yes," he declared triumphantly, "she's asleep!"

"Let me listen too." Rilya didn't trust him. But when she bent down to the keyhole, Galna's rumbling breath clearly reached her ears. "All right," she conceded, "but what about Calya?"

"Do you see her out there?" he asked.

She shifted her eye to the hole. "It's too dark, I can't see anything."

"Well why don't we just try it then? If she attacks us, I still say my sword's sharp enough. Besides," he added by way of compromise, "we can always call for the guards."

Rilya's face brightened at the thought, then fell again. "I forgot about them. They'll never let us pass."

"Why not? We'll just explain to them our mission. They're not traitors or nursemaids, they're soldiers!"

"Yes, but..."

"Oh, come on!" he exclaimed impatiently. "We've talked long enough." With that, he shoved up the latch and pushed open the door, making no effort to do it silently.

Rilya drew breath sharply at his temerity, but Galna's snoring continued without a break, and no other sound could be heard.

Landon motioned her to follow him and began to tiptoe across the sitting room. Her heart in her mouth, Rilya trailed behind, expecting that at any moment Calya would step out of the shadows and accost them. What she expected did not happen, but something else totally unexpected did. They were nearly to the outer door, when they heard footsteps approaching from without. Rilya froze with dread. Landon too stopped momentarily, but then, to her dismay, continued his course right up to the door. He and the footsteps arrived simultaneously.

The sound of a deep voice penetrated through the door, followed by two other voices, one of them a clipped tenor that Rilya recognized as belonging to one of the guards. But she could not make out what they were saying. After a brief conversation, the three men marched off down the corridor together, their heavy tread fading gradually from the children's hearing. Neither of them moved a muscle until the sound had died away. Then they came to life again like reanimated statues.

"Did you hear what he said?" Landon whispered as Rilya joined him at the door.

"No, did you?"

"Yes, he said it looked like the enemy was preparing a night attack and the Queen had ordered all guards to the ramparts."

"So that's why they left! Do you suppose…" Rilya's heart gave a somersault and she could not go on. In her imagination she saw Radin and his companions leaving too, and realized that the Queen was doubly in danger now. "We must go to Mother, quickly!" she hissed, grabbing Landon's arm.

"All right," he answered, "let's go!"

He swung open the door and tiptoed out. No one was in sight. Hand in hand, they began their perilous journey to the Queen. "Quickly, quickly," Rilya urged again, but in spite of herself, her feet seemed made of lead. Ordinarily they would have skipped along, or even run, but now the very daring of their enterprise made them creep at a snail's pace, stopping every few moments to listen and to stare wide-eyed at the shadows cast by the flickering torches high up on the walls.

Without warning, they heard the heavy footsteps again. "The soldiers!" Landon gasped. "Hide!"

"Where?" Rilya cast her eyes about in panic.

"There!" Landon pointed to a door that was partially ajar. Together they dove for it, tumbling into the room beyond just as the footsteps rounded into their corridor.

"O Dol, preserve us!" Rilya moaned to herself as she crouched in the darkness, her heart pounding wildly. The footsteps were nearly abreast of them when a startled female voice called out from behind, "Who's that?" Rilya cringed, more terrified than ever. Then she realized: the townspeople were sleeping in these rooms, several families together for lack of space.

"I said, who's there!" the woman cried, more shrilly.

Another voice, gruff and sleepy, answered, "Quiet there! You'll wake everyone up and we have yet to stand vigil on the third watch."

By this time the soldiers were passing so near that Rilya could have reached out and touched them. She nearly died of anguish as the shrill woman rejoined, "I hear soldiers already. Maybe they're coming to call us." But the heavy footsteps tramped on, unheeding, in the direction of the Queen's chambers.

"See that?" the gruff man remonstrated. "Now go back to sleep!"

The woman's voice subsided into treble mutterings and soon all was still. Rilya listened intently for the passing soldiers, but the blood vessels in her ears throbbed so loudly that no other sound could be heard.

"Whew! That was close!" Landon breathed. Stealthily he pushed open the door and looked about. "Let's get out of here," he added. Rilya could not have agreed more wholeheartedly, although she felt sick and faint with fear. They set out again, this time running, as fast as their trembling knees would carry them. Still, it seemed hours before they rounded the corner into the hall before the audience chamber.

Rilya would have kept on running, her eyes clouded and sightless, but Landon pulled up short. "Radin!" he exclaimed with a muted cry.

Rilya flung her eyes open wide and stared. For a moment she could not focus, but then she saw: the motionless figure of a Queen's Guardsman lying prone on the floor in a pool of wet, sticky red. Radin! She wanted to scream but no sound would come out. Landon had begun running again, pell-mell, toward the open antechamber. There was nothing for it but to follow him, blotting out of her mind the possibility that Mother was already beyond help.

Rilya caught up with Landon in the doorway and together they skirted Radin's body, without daring to look at it. The massive wooden door to the inner room was shut, but a faint glimmer of light shone from beneath it and voices could be heard within.

The children halted in front of it, panting and sobbing with fright. "O Dol," Rilya gulped, "help us!"

"Let's go in," Landon gasped, but he did not move and Rilya could see that he was pale and trembling.

"Wait!" She grasped his arm. "I think I hear Mother's voice." She listened intently. Yes, it was Mother's voice, and that of a man replying to her. Landon too was listening. Suddenly he stirred with animation.

"It's all right!" he shouted. "Captain Fandol's there! We're safe!"

"Wait!" Rilya screamed as he started to throw open the door in his relief and excitement. "Captain Fandol's a traitor." She wrenched his hand from the latch and pushed him away.

"No!" he cried, charging back again. "He's not! Let me in!"

"He is! He's here to kill Mother…oww!" Her words ended in a shriek of pain as Landon stomped on her foot with

237

his heavy boot, flung open the door and careened headfirst into the audience chamber. Rilya staggered after him, her face crumpled in agony. Desperately she forced her tear-blurred eyes to focus, to look for the Queen, but even as she did so, she heard her mother gasp, "Landon!"

The throne! Her mother was there, standing beside it on the dais, a single torch flickering near her. Fandol and another soldier had been closing in on her with swords drawn when Landon burst upon the scene. Landon steadied himself at the sound of his mother's voice and paused just long enough to take in the situation. Then, waving his wooden sword over his head and yelling wildly, he charged for Fandol's legs.

"Landon!" the Queen cried again.

"What the…!" the other soldier exclaimed.

"Never mind the brats," Fandol roared, "get the Queen! The Queen!"

Together the two men made a leap for the dais, just as Landon reached them. Rilya screamed and covered her face with her hands, unable to bear the sight any longer. But a resounding crash and a blood-curdling yell made her look up again, instantly. What had happened? All was blackness; the torch had gone out. For a moment, no sound could be heard. Then Landon began to whimper forlornly, somewhere in the dark, "Mother, Mother."

"Shut up, kid," the soldier growled, "your mother's dead. We've killed her."

Landon's whimpering rose to a wail, but Rilya felt too numb and sick to weep. She wanted only to lie down in this dismal night and die. But she did not lie down and death did not come for her. Instead she listened passively to the men groping about in the dark.

"Let's get out of here, eh, Fandol?" the soldier continued. "Curses! Where's the door? I wish we'd brought a torch! I wonder how those brats got away from the others. Do you hear them coming now?"

Yes, Rilya did hear footsteps running in the corridor. So other soldiers had been dispatched to kill her and Landon. It mattered little now. She realized that she was standing very near the door and would soon be discovered. The instinct of self-preservation urged her to run, to hide. But where? And what was the use, if Mother were dead? "Dol has abandoned us," she whispered. "I too will stay and die." So she stayed, despairing.

Behind her she could hear the footsteps coming closer and closer. To her surprise, they came from two directions at once, and voices came with them. "The Queen, tell the Queen!" one group was shouting, and "The Gelfin Tree! The Gelfin Tree!"

Above their noise rose the shrill voice of Calya. "What's this rabble? Why are you here?"

They were all at the antechamber door now, exclaiming in consternation over the body of Radin. Then, with a surge of alarm, they burst through the door, a whole crowd of draftees and townspeople holding torches aloft, and behind them, two soldiers and Calya.

Rilya quickly darted backward into the shadows, but she could still see clearly, in the flickering light, the scene before her. Standing in confusion beside the overturned throne was the soldier who had been with Fandol. His sword was still drawn. Near the base of the dais sat Landon, holding one arm and weeping disconsolately. Barely visible on the floor at the side of the dais was the dark shadow of a body and a spreading pool of blood.

"Who goes there?" the soldier demanded, glancing about nervously.

A dozen voices clamored at once, until one of the draftees stepped forward and motioned for silence. "We come in the name of the people of Arendolin," he cried, "to report to the Queen that all is well. Dol has not forsaken us. The Gelfin Tree has once more burst into flame." A motley cheer from the steadily growing crowd accompanied this announcement.

The soldier shifted from one foot to the other and glanced over his shoulder. He seemed to be looking for something. Rilya had a sudden flash of intuition that this was the mysterious rider who had carried the news of Rendil's departure to Gendol.

"Where's the Queen?" someone shouted. "Is she here or not?"

"Well, um…" the soldier cleared his throat. "You see, it's like this. When Captain Fandol and I saw the Gelfin Tree in flames, we hurried here at once to report to the Queen ourselves. But when we got here, we found that it was already too late. The Queen was dead. Stabbed herself, she did. Suicide. Yes, that's it. She committed suicide."

A murmur of consternation and sorrow went up from the crowd. "That's a lie!" Rilya shouted, so overcome with anger that she forgot her danger completely. But before she could go on or anyone could reply, a second voice echoed through the room, clear and low, its music at once chilling and warming.

"Yes, my good man, it is a lie, quite unbecoming to a soldier of Arendolin. It is not I who have killed myself, but you who have mistakenly killed your own captain."

The soldier swung around and stared in horror. Rilya too stared and all the people with her. There, coming from behind the dais, was the Queen, bathed in a light cast, not by the flickering torches, not by the dark moon, but by the enchantment of Dol shining from within.

A great gasp went up from the people. "Mother!" Landon shrieked in exultant disbelief.

"Arrest these soldiers!" the Queen snapped as her would-be murderer plunged into the crowd in a desperate attempt to flee. Several strong men immediately pinioned him along with the other two soldiers and hustled them off to the dungeon.

Rilya took no notice of this, nor of Calya slinking away, for she was still staring all the while at her mother. She felt confused, weak with relief and almost unable to comprehend what was happening. "Mother," she choked in a thin little voice. Then she tried again, calling more loudly, "Mother!" With a great effort she pushed herself out of the shadows. A draftee standing by heard her and helped her forward, until she came to rest at last in the radiant arms of the Queen.

CHAPTER 25

NIGHT OF THE DARK MOON II

Patsy caught up with Gifil after a few minutes of desperate scrambling. He waited patiently for her, his arms folded on his chest.

"Sorry for leavin' you," he remarked dryly as she stumbled to a halt beside him. "I reckoned that you wouldn't be wantin' to come."

"I...I changed my mind," she gasped.

"Good 'nuff," he grunted, "but you'll have to be puttin' out that lantern. Any light at all will draw enemies like flies."

Patsy shuddered at the thought of extinguishing what seemed her last source of warmth and comfort, but the further thought of a swarm of unseen foes buzzing malignantly about her head moved her to comply.

When the lantern was out and all was darkness, she felt Gifil reach down and take her tiny, cold hand into his huge, warm one. "Keep close aside of me so you won't be getting lost," he rumbled.

Patsy nodded mutely, forgetting that he could not see the gesture. But he started out immediately, not waiting for a verbal response, and she found herself running to keep up with his gigantic strides. Presently she could hear, louder than before, the rushing of water somewhere far below them to the right, and she realized that they must be very near the Gorge. Then she began to hear other sounds: the nervous pawing and snorting of horses, the faint clank of weapons and armor, a cough or murmur here and there. Glancing around Gifil to their left, she felt rather than saw the army of Arendolin drawn up in battle array, poised, tense, waiting.

Suddenly Gifil stopped short. Patsy also stopped, perforce, and looked up at him in wonder, but his attention was fixed on what lay ahead. So Patsy likewise turned her gaze in that direction. Her eyes had grown accustomed to the lack of light now, enough for her to make out two men on horseback, facing one another, and a third horse and rider standing off to the side a short distance away. Her heart leaped to her mouth. Rendil!

Gifil began inching his way forward and Patsy followed, still clinging to his hand. When they stopped again, they were within earshot of the two adversaries.

"So you think you can wrest control of the army from me?" Gendol was sneering.

"I know I shall," Rendil replied, "by the power of Dol and his enchantment within me. Does not the song say: 'Strong before the mighty stand, One alone the horde hold fast.'"?

Gendol laughed at these words, loud and long, his laughter echoing horribly in the uneasy stillness. "The power of Dol!" he guffawed. "His enchantment! See where they got your father, fool that he was!" Then he stopped laughing. "Sing on, little prince," he muttered in a voice mute with rage, "sing on. We shall see who is the stronger." And without further warning, he wheeled his horse for the charge.

Rendil too wheeled about and braced himself. "Light of Dol, he ain't got no spear," Gifil breathed.

"O God, do something!" Patsy whispered without thinking. She bit her lip and screwed her eyes shut as the two men hurtled at one another through the darkness. The thunder of the horses' hooves, the crash of the impact, steel upon steel, and a hard, echoless thud, told her the outcome even before she opened them again.

Rendil had been unhorsed and lay stunned upon the ground. "Light of Dol, be it the end so soon?" Gifil moaned. But then they saw him collect himself, stand up shakily and look around, bewildered. He seemed to be searching for Fendal, who had cantered off toward the camp.

"Behind you, Rendil!" Condin shouted. "Dodge him and strike at his horse!" Rendil whirled about just as Gendol bore down on him again at full gallop, this time with sword drawn.

"O God, do something!" Patsy cried aloud, grabbing for her cross. But Rendil ducked the oncoming blow in the nick of time and slashed at the hind legs of Gendol's mount. The horse screamed and bucked but kept on running.

Gifil shook his head. "Your God sure ain't doin' much."

"But he's got to," Patsy sobbed through clenched teeth. And the answer came like lightning from within: do something yourself.

"But what?" she queried in silent anguish. "I'm only a kid. What can I do?"

Gendol was closing in now, raining down sword strokes from his vantage point of height. Rendil dodged and parried and thrust back manfully, but he was obviously beginning to tire.

As Patsy looked on, horror-struck, she heard again the voice within, and this time it was the voice of the Queen: "You bear on your breast the Sign of the Great One. If you are faithful to him and cling to his love, there is nothing you will not be able to do."

"His horse! Strike at his horse!" It was Condin shouting, but Rendil could not seem to comprehend. He was on his knees now, then up again, still trying to ward off the blows of Gendol.

"Why doesn't one of the soldiers help him?" Patsy moaned. But the Queen had said that no one could help him. No one, that is, except herself, Patsy. She had to admit in her heart of hearts that she had not been faithful to her mission, had not been loving, but only self-pitying, had not been like Jesus who had died for love.

But there was still time, very little time. Rendil had fallen to his knees again and was not getting up. Gendol dismounted, laughing as he had before, and raised his sword for the finishing stroke.

"No!" Patsy screamed as she hurled herself forward, headlong, heedlessly.

"Passy!" Gifil roared in alarm, but she did not hear him. There was only just enough time. Lowering her head and running full-tilt, she slammed into Gendol from the side, throwing him to the ground and knocking his sword from his grasp. She toppled over with him, but scrambled to her feet and darted away, just as the outraged warrior made a grab for her.

"Passy!" Rendil cried out with gladness as he lifted his head and saw her there. The sight seemed to revive him somewhat. He stood up shakily and kicked Gendol's sword away, out of reach.

"Unfair!" the commander rasped, as he struggled to get up. "You are hiding behind a brat. And a girl at that," he added, peering at her closely in the darkness.

"She has been deputed by the Great One for my assistance," Rendil panted as he gathered strength. "Besides, I have not killed you, nor do I intend to, if you will only swear allegiance to me."

"I would sooner swear allegiance to the Dark Ones!" Gendol snarled.

"Then go to them, if you will!" Rendil shot back. "Since that is your choice, begone! And fight with those to whom you have already, long since, sold your soul!"

Gendol stared at him for a moment, his lips moving soundlessly. Then, without a word, he turned and began to run, fleeing toward the darkness and the Gorge. His footsteps clattered over the bridge and faded away into silence. At that very instant a trumpet sounded from across the Gorge, then another and another.

"Your Highness!" One of Gendol's captains rode up with Fendal in tow. He dismounted and saluted. "Your Highness," he said, "we men of the royal army were aware of our Lord Commander's treachery, but we had no one else to lead us into battle. Now that you are here and he is gone and the enemy's trumpets are already sounding, you must be the one to ride at our head. We pledge to you our loyalty. We will follow you as we followed your royal Father."

"Thank you, captain," Rendil answered with renewed vigor and pride. Seizing Fendal's reins, he leaped into the saddle, then hesitated for one last moment, looking down at Patsy. She gazed back at him, flushed with triumph, not knowing what he would ask, but feeling ready for anything.

"Thank you," he said quietly. That was all.

"Do you want to take my Sign?" she asked. It was for her the supreme gesture of self-sacrifice.

"No," he replied with a gentle smile. "The Sign is for you to bear. Only, you must pray for me."

Patsy wanted to answer that she would do anything for him, but before she could say another word, Gifil materialized out of nowhere and grabbed her by the arm. "It's a good deed you did, lass," he said, "but we've got to be gettin' ourselves out of here now. The battle's commencin'." And with that he began to drag her back by the way they had come.

"Wait!" she cried with anguished disappointment, but he was holding her too tightly and walking too fast for her to pull away.

"Rendil!" she heard Condin shouting, "Command the light!" This was more than she could bear. With a mighty wrench she broke loose from Gifil's grip and turned back. As she did so, Rendil's voice rang out, clearer and deeper than any trumpet call. He cried aloud in the tongue of the ancient ones and light burst forth around him, flooding the night with its radiance, driving back the shadows clear to the peaks of the mountains. He cried aloud again, and with a thunder of hooves and a mighty answering shout, the army surged forward into battle.

The two forces, of darkness and of light, clashed with a fury that shook the earth around them. Patsy watched with mingled horror and fascination as all the conflicts that had rent her soul these last few weeks seemed exteriorized before her eyes. Gifil pulled at her and shouted, then finally swept her up bodily under his arm and began to run. She kicked and sobbed, but there was no breaking away from him this time. Presently

Condin rode up and Gifil heaved her, still struggling, into the saddle behind him.

"I'm going to make for the fort," Condin called out. "We'll be safer there."

"Go on ahead," Gifil answered. "I'll follow as best what I can."

So they galloped off, Patsy clinging to Condin for dear life. Behind and all about them, she could hear the hellish cacophony of war: battle cries and trumpet blast, the neighing of horses and clashing of steel, the screams of the wounded and moans of the dying. Now she dared not turn back to look. Instead she screwed her eyes shut and began to pray, "O God, make him win!" But she knew in her heart of hearts that her prayer had already been answered.

The fort proved to be nothing more than a tall stone tower, with narrow apertures from which archers could shoot their arrows. There were no archers now, only a wild-eyed sentry who shouted, "Who goes there?" from the battlements as Burdil with his two passengers ground to a halt.

"Condin, son of Rendol, and Lady Palissa," Condin shouted back. "Let us in!"

"Wait!" he answered. With that he disappeared from view, but they could hear him calling to someone down inside the fort. A few moments later, the door opened cautiously and another soldier appeared, lantern in one hand and sword in the other.

"What would a son of the King be doing here?" he asked suspiciously. "And I don't see any lady. How do we know you're not trying to take over the fort?"

Condin laughed wearily and dismounted, helping Patsy down. "We are unarmed," he said and spread his empty hands wide in confirmation of this. "We seek refuge from the battle."

"All right," the soldier conceded. "Come in quickly. You can tie your mount over there." He gestured to a near-by hitching post. Condin hastened to comply, stripping Burdil of saddle and gear, while the soldier looked on. Then they went in and he barred the door after them.

Once inside, Patsy breathed a huge sigh of relief. The thick stone walls shut out the din of battle and, even though no fire burned on the hearth, it seemed infinitely warmer here than out there in the darkness. She thought of Rendil, bathed in light, radiating enchanted warmth and strength, and for one bitter moment she wished that Gifil had not dragged her away. But then she heard once more, dim and far off, the blast of the trumpets, and she knew that she could never endure such an experience of blood and carnage.

"You can stay here," the soldier was saying. "I'll leave you the lantern."

"Thank you," Condin replied. "An old man named Gifil was following us on foot…"

"We'll let him in," he grunted as he climbed a narrow ladder and disappeared through a trap door into the level above.

All of a sudden, Patsy felt very tired. She walked over to a rough wooden bench near the hearth and flopped down on it. Condin stationed himself at one of the openings in the wall, peering through it intently. After awhile he turned to Patsy and remarked, "I'm afraid it's going to be a long, fierce struggle. Why don't you try to rest?"

"No," she replied drowsily. "I want to be awake when Rendil comes."

"He may not be here before morning," Condin warned.

"Never mind," she persisted. "I'll wait."

But her eyelids were unbearably heavy and her whole body drooped and sagged until she finally dozed off. Still, one stubborn corner of consciousness remained, with which she heard the sound of footsteps and men's voices. "Gifil," she thought as she stirred and slept again. Later, much later, she seemed to hear rain, and wondered if this were a good or bad omen. But in the end, even this consciousness was lost to her and she simply slept.

CHAPTER 26
THE RETURN TO CELDONDOL

When Patsy finally awoke, daylight was streaming in through the narrow windows and open doorway of the tower. She stared at it stupidly, then yawned and sat up. To her amazement, she realized that she was wrapped in her own bedroll, sitting on the floor in front of the fireplace. A fire crackled on the hearth, making her too warm. "I must have fallen asleep," she thought, as she stood up and stretched.

Still feeling stiff and stupid, she looked about herself at the nearly bare room. No one else was in sight. For a panic-stricken moment she wondered if the battle were lost and they had all been killed. "No," she reasoned, getting hold of herself, "it couldn't be or else the sun wouldn't be shining." Her weeks of sojourn in this strange world had at least taught her that much.

Eventually the open doorway caught her attention. "Maybe Rendil has already come," she speculated, "and they've all gone out to meet him." She felt a pang of disappointment that they hadn't bothered to call her, but she shrugged it off and walked over to the door to see.

At first the brilliant sunlight blinded her and she could not make out anything, but she contented herself with drawing deep breaths of fresh, cool air. Voices floated to her on that air, and, with her eyes adjusted to the light, she began searching for the source of the voices.

Her search led her around the corner of the tower. There, under a tree, a makeshift table had been set up, and around it on rude benches sat a dozen or so officers, holding what appeared to be a conference. One of the officers was standing and addressing the others, but she could not hear what he was saying.

Curiosity drew her closer, even before she spied Condin sitting on a stump off to one side. He caught sight of her at the same time and motioned her over with a broad grin and a sweeping wave of his hand. Not wishing to draw attention to herself, she sidled over and whispered, "What's going on? Where's Rendil?"

For an answer, Condin grinned again and stood up to offer her his seat. She took it with a puzzled frown, while he directed her gaze toward the discussion in progress. The presiding officer, a young man with dark hair and beard, was saying, "Since all the men, living and dead, are accounted for and burial squad has finished its work, it seems that we are ready to begin preparations for the return march to Celdondol. Yesterday I dispatched a messenger, bearing the good news of our victory to her Royal Majesty and all the people of the capitol."

"Yesterday?" Patsy murmured to Condin. "But the battle wasn't even fought yesterday!"

"Sure it was, dopey," Condin retorted. "You've been asleep for three days now."

Patsy gaped at him, still uncomprehending. Then the truth began to dawn. They had left her there all that time and never said a word! "Why didn't you call me?" she demanded angrily. "You knew I wanted to be awake when Rendil came. Where is he anyhow?" She was forgetting to whisper. Condin punched her and put his finger to his lips, but too late. Glancing toward the conference table, she saw that all the men were looking at her, some with amusement, others with friendly curiosity.

"Greetings, my lady!" their leader called. "Will you not come and be introduced to these worthy officers?"

Patsy wished she could crawl into a hole and die, but Condin gave her a good-natured shove, and, willy-nilly, she went as bidden. But she did not dare raise her head as the young officer placed his hand on her shoulder, turned her so she faced the others, and said, "Men, this is Lady Palissa, emissary of the Great One, bearer of the Sign, heroine of the battle of Moldan Gorge."

All the soldiers rose as one and bowed to her. "My lady," one of them said, "on behalf of the entire army of Arendolin, we wish to thank you."

Patsy blushed scarlet with mortification. "I..." she stammered, "I'm not dressed right." She had become acutely conscious of her ill-fitting page's uniform, all stiff and wrinkled after three days of sleeping in it.

"My lady," said the presiding officer, "you would be most honored and welcome, no matter what your attire." His tone was so rich and earnest that she glanced up at him in surprise. Then she saw, not the strong, manly face, not the raven-dark hair, but the eyes, the midnight, starlight eyes, deep with majesty and strength and tenderness. Patsy found herself no longer embarrassed and confused but smiling, not just with her face but with her heart as well, and suffused with gladness too deep for words.

How long the moment lasted she did not know, but then she was back to herself again and she heard herself saying, "I didn't recognize you."

Rendil smiled too, a gentle, ordinary smile. "Yes," he said, "I have changed. I am a man now and I will be king, thanks to you. But first we must return to Celdondol."

"Where's Gifil?" His absence suddenly struck her.

"Two of Gifil's sons were wounded in the battle and he asked leave to be with them. I should like him to accompany us on our return, but I will not force him. He has been very good to us."

Patsy nodded solemnly. "What happened to Gendol?" she asked, without quite knowing why.

"Lord Gendol?" Rendil repeated, his countenance becoming grave. "When the battle was over, we found him lying dead on the field, an arrow of the Dark Ones in his breast. We buried him with honor, as his rank and dignity deserved. Perhaps he repented at the last, and the Great One has forgiven him his crimes." For a moment Rendil seemed lost in the depths of some inscrutable emotion. Then a loud sneeze from one of his officers brought him back to reality.

"Good captains," he exclaimed, looking around at them, "I beg your pardon! All this while you have been waiting for me to formulate our plans of departure." He turned to Patsy. "My lady, would you care to remain with us, or would you prefer to return to the fort?"

"I think I'd like to change my clothes," Patsy answered frankly. And with his cheery "Very well!" ringing in her ears, she darted off. She felt like leaping and dancing and singing for sheer joy. Her mission was accomplished, the battle was over, Rendil was well, all was well, very well.

Once inside the fort, she stripped off the hated uniform, washed as best she could from a bucket of cold water, and put on what was left of the rumpled but clean things in her bundle. She was in the midst of combing the snarls out of her hair when she heard a loud commotion outside – galloping horses, shouting, a trumpet call. "Now what," she thought, dropping the comb and dashing out, her curls flying.

By the time she arrived at the conference tree, two soldiers were already dismounting from their lathered horses. One of them, wearing the uniform of the Royal Guard, addressed the assembled officers.

"My Lord Captains," he gasped, "I have urgent news for His Royal Highness, Prince Rendil."

"I am he," said Rendil, rising from his seat.

The soldier stared for a moment in disbelief, then dropped to one knee in homage. "Your Highness," he said, "I have been sent by your Royal Mother to summon you to the aid of Celdondol. Rebels from Galgor have occupied the city and the fortress has lain under siege for these ten days past. Furthermore, treachery has been afoot, as a result of which Captain Fandol lies dead, three soldiers of his garrison have been cast into the dungeon, and Her Majesty the Queen has herself assumed command of all the troops defending Celdondol."

The officers all began to exclaim in dismay as they heard this, but Rendil listened gravely without uttering a sound. When the courier had finished speaking, he asked, "How many days ago did you leave Celdondol?"

"Three, your Highness."

"And if the fortress is completely surrounded, how did you manage to escape?"

"Through the old tunnel under the wall. I did not encounter any enemy outposts along the river or on the road north of Heldor."

"Very good. One more question. How did you know where to find me?"

"Your royal Mother told me that I would find you at Moldan, so I followed the Great Road northward. Late yesterday, I met this soldier bearing the news of your victory. When I told him that Celdondol was under siege, he turned about and led me here to you."

"Well done." Rendil nodded approvingly to the other soldier. "Now you must go and rest. I will expect you both to ride with me today."

The two soldiers saluted and left. Rendil turned immediately to the officers. "You heard me," he rapped. "We ride this afternoon. Captains Gordil and Diril, you will each select the half of your cavalry battalions that is freshest. Mandol, Lodon and Fendon, you will do the same with the infantry. Captain Taril, you will take command of the remainder of the army, and bring them on with the wounded and the baggage, as soon as they are able to travel. To your work! We must be ready to muster at the beginning of the sixth watch."

As Rendil issued these commands, the men in question saluted and strode off, each to his assignment. At once the camp began to be in a ferment of activity. But Patsy stood there aghast, so overwhelmed by the news of the Queen's misfortune that she did not know what to think. A few moments earlier her heart had been as bright and sunny as the air about her; now she was plunged once again into worry and fear.

"Can't we ever stop fighting?" she wailed as Condin turned and saw her there. He gestured helplessly, and, coming over to her, put an awkward hand on her shoulder.

256

A little while later, when Rendil joined them, she repeated the question. "I am beginning to understand," he answered, "that this is the way of life. But you must not be downhearted. We have had joy already and, I promise you, we shall have joy again. Now I must ask you," – he looked from one to the other – "will you ride with me one more time? Otherwise, you may stay with the rear guard under Captain Taril."

"I'm with you," Condin rejoined without a moment's hesitation.

"Me too!" Patsy chimed in, visibly brightening at the thought. Just to be with Rendil now was a joy and a comfort. She knew that no danger would ever again be so great as to deter her.

"Thank you," Rendil answered shakily. For a moment he simply gazed at them, eyes shining. Then someone called to him and he turned and strode off into the thick of the ferment.

By mid-afternoon they were ready to march, Rendil himself in the van with half his cavalry, followed by three crack units of infantry. Condin rode just behind Rendil and Patsy was positioned a little way further back, sharing the saddle with a middle-aged veteran named Rafil, whose leathery face crinkled pleasantly when he smiled. Her only regret was that Gifil had declined to come with them. "I ain't much good at ridin' fast," he had said with a shake of his head, "and I don't know them parts well enough to guide you. But you can take my two healthy lads with a right good will. And," he had added as he wrung Rendil's hand, "I'll be seein' you, young King, on your coronation day."

Patsy hoped he would keep his promise. She could not believe that the goodbye she had said to him then was really forever. "God keep him safe," she prayed in her heart.

The army moved out on schedule and rode hard all that evening and all night long. In the early morning they halted for a brief rest, then mounted up and rode again. About midday, they slowed their horses to a walk, as advance scouts reported they were approaching a town. It proved to be only a sleepy hamlet, a few houses on either side of the road, with their occupants staring curiously from windows and doorways, while chickens and dogs scattered before the advancing cavalry.

All of a sudden, a young man leaped into the middle of the road and signaled for them to halt. "I'm lookin' for the King's son," he shouted. "Might one of you be the King's son?"

"I am," answered Rendil, as he rode forward to meet him. "How may I help you?"

"You've already been helpin' me," the man declared as, to everyone's surprise, he fell to his knees and kissed Rendil's foot in the stirrup. Then he jumped up again and said, "My name's Cafil and you done freed me and my missus from the spell of the Dark Ones. Now I'm wantin' to join up and follow you like I done with your father the King."

Patsy stared in astonishment as Rendil sprang from his horse to embrace the young man. The only resemblance she could see between the vibrantly alive person now confronting them and the deathly waxen figure they had left behind only a week earlier was the splendid chestnut beard that fell down over his chest.

Rendil loosed his grip on Caf and held him back at arm's length, enfolding him in a gaze that Patsy wished she could share in. Then he said, "I would be honored to have such a loyal and courageous servant of my Father take his place at my side, but I cannot help thinking of your wife. Does she not need you more than I?"

At the mention of Tally, Caf broke into a radiant grin. "My missus, she's just fine. She birthed her babe day a-fore yesterday, the handsomest lad you'll find anywheres."

Rendil laughed for joy when he heard this, and so did Condin and Patsy and all the soldiers within earshot.

"Why, good man," Rendil cried, "I could not think of taking you with me into battle, when you have scarcely had time to see your own son! But I tell you, if in a year's time you still wish to be in my service, you may bring your whole family with you to Celdondol, and I will see that you are very well treated."

Caf was so overwhelmed by the offer that for a moment he could not speak. "Thank'ee," he stammered, "thank'ee." Falling to his knees once more, he seized Rendil's hand and kissed it. Then he leaped to his feet and bounded off the road, whooping and hollering in his elation.

Rendil laughed again as he remounted and gave the signal to ride. The last Patsy saw of Cafil, he was surrounded by village folk, slapping him on the back and offering him boisterous congratulations.

The army marched on at a somewhat slower pace until dusk, when Rendil called a halt. Patsy expected that they would spend the night there, but, to her surprise and dismay, after a meal and a few hours' rest, they rose while it was still dark and marched again.

259

Not until the following dusk did Rendil call another halt. By this time, Patsy was so weary that she could not hold her head up or focus her gaze on the passing road. One terrible mile blurred into another, until she had no idea how far they had come or how far they had yet to go. When she slid down from Rafil's horse, her legs would not hold her and she slumped like a rag to the ground. "Shame," Rafil murmured with a grim shake of his head. "This is no place for a youngster like you." He picked her up bodily and placed her near an already assembled campfire, where she sat in a daze, her head on her knees, her hands dangling limp.

She had all but fallen asleep when she felt rather than saw Rendil kneeling beside her. "My lady," he was saying anxiously, "are you all right?"

She lifted her head to look at him, but his face swam before her eyes and she had to let it drop back to her knees again.

"Are you too tired to go on?"

"No." The one word took all her strength, but she would not fall behind now, or ever again. Never. "Jesus, help me!" she prayed. Then she felt Rendil's hand on her head, warmer by far and more penetrating than the fire blazing before her. The warmth of his presence surrounded and strengthened her so that she raised herself once more to look at him, and this time she could see. He was smiling at her.

"Eat a little, if you are able," he said, "and rest for this night. Tomorrow I will tell you what I have in mind."

With that he left her, but the enchanted sense of well being remained. Patsy ate as bidden, then rolled herself in her bedroll and slept. She was awakened by Rafil just before dawn and bounced up, amazed at her own freshness and energy.

Rafil shook his head again, but this time he was laughing. "You certainly revived in a hurry," he exclaimed. "Now you get a bite to eat, then run along. His Highness will be waiting for you."

Rendil was indeed waiting when she arrived at his tent, and with him were Condin and the soldier of the Royal Guard who had brought the news from Celdondol. Condin waved cheerfully at her approach and Rendil greeted her with, "Good morning, my lady! I trust you slept well?"

"Yes, very," she answered with a grin as he ushered them into his tent. They all settled themselves in a semi-circle on the ground and waited for Rendil to begin.

"First of all," he said, "I must emphasize that while this soldier is bound to my service, you two, Lord Condin and Lady Palissa, are free..."

"We'll do whatever you want!" Patsy blurted out, before he could finish speaking.

"You can count on my complete loyalty," Condin affirmed solemnly.

"Very well, then," Rendil acknowledged, also solemnly, "I will tell you my plan. Last evening, as you, Condin, know, I sent out advance scouts toward the Fords of Heldor, which we are now approaching. They have returned already with their report: the Galgorians have not yet penetrated that far upriver. The townspeople have barricaded themselves in, fearing the worst, but one or two of the more intrepid among them have explored downstream toward Celdondol, and they were able to assure our men that the enemy is still concentrated on besieging the fortress. One of these brave men owns a boat and our scouts had no difficulty in persuading him to lend it to us. I want the three of you to

261

travel by boat down the river from Heldor to the entrance of the tunnel, and to make your way from there back into the fortress. My captains and I have agreed upon a stratagem for the raising of the siege, but it requires the knowledge and cooperation of those inside Celdondol. Do you think you will have any difficulty in finding the tunnel?" He addressed this question to the Guardsman.

"No, your Highness," he replied. "I took a good look at all the surroundings, expecting that I might have to return that way."

"Well done!" Rendil approved. "We will set out shortly and reach Heldor before mid-morning. You will embark immediately, so as to reach the tunnel before nightfall. This is what you must tell our Royal Mother. Our forces will surround the besiegers tonight under cover of dark. Those inside the fortress must prepare themselves for battle. In the fourth watch of the night, when I sound the first trumpet blast, all our men will light torches and begin to shout their war cries, but they will not move to attack. Only when I sound the second trumpet blast, will they hurl themselves upon the enemy, hoping to drive them back upon each other in confusion. Those within Celdondol must join in the attack from the ramparts. When they see that the Galgorians have been driven away from the gates and they are no longer in danger of being surrounded by fleeing enemies, they are to charge forth in whatever strength they can muster and join in the pursuit. Do you understand this?"

"Yes," answered Condin. "When we get back into Celdondol, we're to tell Mother to be ready for the fourth watch tonight. At the first signal, we remain quiet, but at the second signal we attack from the ramparts. Our troops should not leave the fortress until we're sure that all the enemy forces are in front of us and can't cut us off."

"Good. Do you have any questions?"

"What about you? Aren't you coming with us?" Patsy asked forlornly. She already knew the answer, but she had to ask anyway.

"Oh!" Condin groaned with exasperation, but he restrained himself and said nothing. Rendil looked surprised but he responded gently.

"Did you think that I would be elsewhere than at the head of the army?"

"No, but…" She felt her eyes brimming with tears of disappointment and humiliation. "I want to be with you!" she choked finally.

"My lady," Rendil answered, still gently, "I have told you that you are free. You may do as you wish. But it will be dangerous with me. You have neither weapons nor armor. And I think for this once, your Sign will be of more value within Celdondol."

Patsy was silent, struggling with her emotions. "Why?" her thoughts cried rebelliously. During all these past weeks, whenever she was reluctant to go with him, he had forced her. Now when she was anxious to be at his side, he did not want her. It seemed so cruel.

"You promised him you'd do whatever he wanted," Condin reminded her unsympathetically.

Yes, she had. And he had said that she was free. Free to do what she wanted. Why didn't he want what she wanted? She did not dare raise her eyes to his as she said, "Can I have time to think about it?"

"You may have until we reach Heldor," he answered gravely.

The army moved out shortly after this and marched quickly through the cool, rosy dawn. The atmosphere was very different now from when they first passed this way a fortnight earlier, but Patsy could not enjoy the difference. "Why didn't I just tell him that I was going with him?" she thought miserably. "He said I could do whatever I wanted and that's what I want. When we get to Heldor, I will tell him, that's all!"

Having thus made up her mind, she tried to dismiss the subject altogether. But her mind would not rest. "You promised him," the silent voice of Condin taunted. "Oh, why did I speak up so fast?" she moaned to herself. "Because you knew it would make him happy." The interior voice was not Condin's, but she had heard it before and she knew it was right. She would make Rendil happy by doing what he asked of her.

"But then I won't be happy," she objected. "I'll only be happy if I'm with him. Besides, that's my mission!" This was her trump card. But the persistent voice came right back, "You will not be happy with him if he is not happy. And he had told you that the Sign is needed inside Celdondol."

Patsy sighed, pulled out the Sign and looked at it. The figure of Jesus seemed impaled on the silver beams like some too-frail butterfly. "He certainly couldn't have liked doing that," she thought. "But he did it for love. Is that what love is like, doing what you don't want in order to make someone else happy?" There was no answer. But she went on staring at the crucifix all the way to Heldor.

They reached the Fords of Heldor shortly before midmorning. Dogs barked a raucous greeting but no human ventured from the boarded-up houses to meet them. Rendil beckoned to one of his scouts. "Where is this man whom you said would lend us his boat?"

"I gave him a signal, your Highness," he answered, "and he will come only at that signal." Having said this, he went up to one of the houses and rapped on the door, a peculiar staccato rap. Within a few moments, the door opened cautiously and a short-bearded, blonde man stepped forth. The soldier brought him to Rendil.

"You will let us use your boat to reach our destination?" Rendil asked him.

"Aye," he answered, "and I'll guide you there myself."

"Very good." Rendil turned to Patsy. "Have you made your decision?" His voice was serious but in no way threatening. "If you do not wish to accompany Condin and the others, I shall order one of the soldiers to go."

But Patsy had made up her mind and she met his gaze steadily. "You won't need to," she said. "I'm going back with them to Celdondol."

CHAPTER 27
THE RAISING OF THE SIEGE

Rays of dying sunlight slanted across the river, casting long shadows over the boat with its four occupants. Patsy closed her eyes and breathed deeply with contentment. Not for days and weeks had she known such peace; it was as if a great mountain of selfhood had been lifted off her chest. They were sailing headlong into danger, but she could not feel the least bit nervous or frightened. At last she had surrendered all.

"We'll have to cast ashore here," the soldier's voice broke into her stillness. "The tunnel's only a little way ahead of that large rock we're coming to."

Patsy opened her eyes and looked about curiously, but the terrain seemed unfamiliar. The river was growing wider now, but thick clusters of trees still overhung its steep banks. A great granite rock loomed up before them on their right, jutting out into the water. With a mighty effort at the oars, the soldier and the villager headed their craft out of the current and into shore.

"Will you be coming with us?" Condin asked the villager as he tied up to a tree and helped his passengers disembark.

"If you'll be havin' me," the villager replied. "I ain't worth much, but I'm willin' to help."

"You've done us a great service already," Condin rejoined. Then he turned to the soldier. "Lead on," he said.

Without a word the soldier turned and plunged into the forest. Skirting the rock, he led them by a narrow path parallel to the riverbank. Dusk had already fallen and the path

266

was rough. Patsy remembered their earlier passage in the rain and mud, and wondered how they had made it safely. She wondered still more when they stopped a few minutes later in front of a large shelf of rock.

"What's this?" the villager asked, startled.

"The tunnel entrance," Condin supplied triumphantly. "I know where we are now."

"I don't," Patsy remarked, looking around her dubiously.

For answer, the soldier stepped under the shelf and pulled aside a pile of brush to reveal a yawning hole, edging away and down into blackness.

"We're goin' into that?" the villager queried nervously. Patsy too felt her fears returning.

"It's not so bad," Condin reassured him. "You grasp the soldier's hand and I will follow behind with Passy."

"It's Patsy," Patsy corrected absent-mindedly. But he seemed not to hear her and she really didn't care.

"Come," the soldier said, "we must not waste time." With that he seized the villager's hand and walked straight on into the blackness. Patsy could hear the villager's vociferous protests trailing out behind them. She turned and looked at Condin.

"Well?" he said.

"I'll walk ahead of you," she said stiffly, drawing herself up to her full eleven-year-old dignity.

"All right," he said, "go on."

So Patsy went, slowly and cautiously, not feeling at all as brave as she was acting. At first she expected stairs, but then she remembered that there were none at this end, only a gentle sloping down. The riverbank must be on a much lower level than the fortress. Behind her she could hear Condin whistling and she sighed with relief. No, she would *not* hold his hand like a baby, but she was glad at least to hear him.

The tunnel seemed longer this time, or was it her imagination? She clenched her teeth, determined not to panic. Condin's whistle still sounded faintly behind her, but no voice at all could be heard ahead. Why did they never think to bring a lantern with them? At last, when her courage was wearing thinnest, a pair of black shapes loomed up before her and she stopped just short of crashing into the villager. He was trembling, panting and speechless.

"Where are we?" Patsy asked in a whisper.

"At the foot of the stairs," the soldier answered. "Where's His Highness?"

"Here," Condin said, "right behind you. Is this the end?"

"Yes."

The end! Patsy felt her heart leap. They were back home in Celdondol! The Queen would be here, and Rilya. She hoped they were safe. Suppose the enemy had already taken the fortress and they were dead? She swallowed a pang of dread as they started climbing the steep earthen steps.

Suddenly a lantern appeared at the top of the tunnel. "Who goes there?" a voice barked.

"Reldon of the Royal Guard," the soldier answered.

"Hurrah!" Patsy heard to her relief the cheers of his mates. "Welcome! Do you bring help?" As her head popped up above the floor level, she saw three of the Guardsmen, standing in the lantern glow, beaming.

"Take us to the Queen," Condin ordered as his head came up. He too was beaming.

"Right, Your Highness," one of the guardsmen answered, "with pleasure." He led the way immediately and the four of them followed, with the villager trailing behind. Patsy could not help thinking again how different this was from the way they had left.

They emerged from the stables and made, not for the castle as she had expected, but for the nearest tower leading up to the ramparts. As they reached the top of the stairs and climbed out onto the battlements, she looked about herself curiously. The castle seemed strangely darkened, as if deserted, but campfires dotted the courtyard. She wondered why all the soldiers were sleeping out of doors. Glancing over her other shoulder, she noticed still more campfires, stretching out over the fields toward the river, as far as the eye could see. The Galgorians! She chilled with the realization that they had just passed under those very enemy fires.

Their little party was all the while moving swiftly along the ramparts. Soldiers stepped aside for them with curious glances, and one or two of them saluted. At last, after passing two more towers, they came to the entrance of a third, where a group of guardsmen stood at attention. Only a small lantern burned within the tower, but Patsy sensed a luminous presence that needed no light. Instinctively she turned her gaze up to the sky. Yes, there it was, the tiny sliver of chaste silver moon, beaming its gentle smile through the darkness.

"Your Majesty," she heard Reldon saying.

"Yes, Reldon, what have you to report?" the deep, musical voice responded.

"His Royal Highness, Prince Rendil, is marching double-time to our rescue and will arrive tonight. But he has sent two others as his special envoys and has entrusted his instructions to them."

"Yes?" the Queen asked expectantly. "Where are they?"

"Right here." With a triumphant smile, Reldon stepped outside and swept Condin and Patsy into the tower.

"My son, Condin!" the Queen's low cry rang with joy.

"Mother!" Condin choked. He fell to his knees before her and she clasped him to herself. For a moment they pressed close to each other in silence. Then Condin drew away and raised his eyes to his mother's face. "Mother," he said in a trembling voice, "I am sorry for my past insolence, and for the pain I caused you by leaving the fortress without your permission. Please forgive me."

"Gladly do I forgive you, my son," she answered him. "By this one gesture you have proven yourself worthy of the royal enchantment of Arendolin." She gazed long into his face, her eyes shining like stars. Then she recalled herself. "But you have important instructions for me. And was there not another envoy?"

At this, Patsy stepped shyly into the light. "My Lady Palissa!" The Queen stretched out her hand to her as Condin rose and stood aside.

Patsy knelt also and placed her hand in the Queen's. She knew that she too should apologize, but in her heart she could feel only a quiet confidence that, in spite of all her weaknesses and failures, she had fulfilled her mission. The Queen gazed down at her and she met her gaze as steadily as she had met Rendil's earlier that day. "We did wrong, Ma'am," she said, "and I'm sorry too. But why did it turn out all right anyway?"

"Because, my little one, you have learned how to love. Is that not so?"

"Yes, Ma'am." Patsy felt her heart swell with gladness. Lifting up her face, she drank deeply from the Queen's tranquil eyes. It was as if she had never been away, and yet she had come so far.

At length the Queen released her and spoke again. "Here, now, enough of this! I have been so happy to see you that I have forgotten to ask what message you bring from Rendil."

"Rendil will be arriving tonight," Condin answered, "and this is what he plans to do." Quickly he informed his mother of what was expected of them. There followed the repetition of a now-familiar scene: orderlies being dispatched, commanding officers reporting, assignments being given, a quiet flurry of activity as soldiers began filing to their posts. Reldon left also, taking the villager with him. Patsy's heart pounded with excitement as she imagined Rendil and his army already closing in on the fortress, and she wondered what her role would be in the coming battle.

At last, when everyone was gone except her personal bodyguard, the Queen turned to Condin. "I shall remain on the ramparts tonight," she said. "You may remain with me if you wish, my son."

"Yes, Mother, I do wish," he replied eagerly.

"And you, my lady," she added, addressing Patsy, "I think you will be safer with Rilya and Landon in the castle."

"But Ma'am," Patsy blurted. Then she caught herself and bit her lip, her eyes brimming with tears.

The Queen looked at her a moment. "I understand, my child," she replied. "You are young and small of stature, but you have undergone many trials and the Great One has given you a valiant heart. This is your battle also. Yes, you may stay."

"Thank you, Ma'am." Patsy gulped and grinned a watery grin.

"You still bear with you the Sign, do you not?"

"Yes, Ma'am."

"May I venerate it?"

Patsy was startled by the request. She had never thought of the Sign as a sacred object. Now she removed it hesitantly from around her neck and handed it to the Queen, who received it with reverence. At first the royal lady gazed on its crossed form in simple wonder, then she kissed it. That too was simply done, yet Patsy fell to her knees at the gesture and remained kneeling until the Sign was returned to her. She also kissed it before replacing it under her clothes.

Abruptly the Queen rose from her seat. "Let us be off," she said. Patsy too rose and followed her, together with Condin and the bodyguard. They filed silently along the ramparts under a flawless, star-flecked sky, heading for the twin towers, which flanked the gate. As they rounded the southeast corner of the castle, what seemed like a huge bonfire leaped up before their eyes. Patsy gasped in amazement.

"What is it?" she whispered.

"The Gelfin Tree," Condin hissed back. He bowed in homage to it, as did the Queen and the bodyguard. Patsy merely stared, dumbfounded. Yes, she could see clearly amid the flames the black but unburned branches of the ancient tree, reaching upward to the heavens and outward to embrace the world with their fiery light. She stared, but she did not bow. Her Sign, although it had no magic, had a power greater than

272

any Gelfin Tree, the power of love, the power of the Great One.

They moved on from there until they reached the tower to the left of the gate and settled themselves to watch. Then the Queen spoke again. "Well, my children, tell me all that you have been doing these many days past."

So they took it in turns to tell her of all their adventures: the miserable flight in the rain to Heldor, Rendil's narrow escape, Gifil, the fangolfin forests, Caf and Tally, Moldan Gorge, the great battle, the return march. She listened to the whole tale with a gentle, sympathetic smile and many a nod of approval, but when they had finally wound down and run out of words, she merely said: "You have done well, my children, very well."

After that, silence fell once more on the little group, a long, still silence, broken finally by the cries of the sentries, "Third watch and all's well!" That meant two more hours of waiting at least. Patsy leaned her head back against the rough stone wall and closed her eyes. She did not feel sleepy or even tired, but her feelings were deceptive. The next thing she knew, a voice was crying, almost in her ear it seemed, "Fourth watch and all's well!"

Patsy's head came up sharply from its resting-place on her chest and her eyes flew open. Fourth watch already? Where had the time gone? She looked around the tower room in some confusion but no one was there except the Queen and Condin. Condin was unashamedly asleep, curled up on the floor near his mother's feet. The Queen sat on her small stool, in the same tranquil pose as Patsy had last seen her. She smiled at the little girl but said nothing.

273

Patsy wondered how she could be so peaceful when it was the fourth watch already. Rendil would be coming soon! Wide-awake and wide-eyed, she stood up and tried to see out through one of the long, narrow slits in the tower wall. But all was darkness yet. "Isn't he coming?" she exclaimed to the Queen, her voice echoing too loudly in the stillness.

"He is already here," the Queen answered. "I can sense his enchanted presence."

Patsy stared at her, agog, then resumed her lookout post with pounding heart. At first she could see or hear nothing, but then, faintly and far off, the sound of a trumpet floated through the stillness. "Is that it?" she cried, "Is that it?" She strained her eyes now and, yes, she could see lights, one after the other, flickering in a long semi-circle, north and west of the castle and southward beyond the town. A noise was beginning to rise up too, the noise of shouting, the battle cry of Arendolin that Patsy remembered from Moldan Gorge.

A sentry rushed in. "Your Majesty," he exclaimed, "the forces of His Highness the Prince are upon us!"

Condin darted up instantly and looked at his mother without a word.

"Thank you, soldier," she said to the sentry. "Now bring my helmet and breastplate. I shall be going to the ramparts."

"But Mother, you are unarmed!" Condin protested sharply.

"I shall be safe," she answered, again with serenity. "I have no wish to fight. But you and Lady Palissa must remain here, for I cannot guarantee your safety."

"Yes, Mother." He watched apprehensively as she donned her armor and left. Patsy remained glued to her vantage point. Other noises had begun to arise now: alarms from the Galgorian camp, a clamor and rush of confusion, the clash of weapons. Above it all rose, harsh and clear, the battle cry of Arendolin.

Patsy felt another wave of impatience. "When are they going to attack?" she asked Condin, who had joined her.

"They're hoping that the Galgorians will panic and attack each other," he rejoined. "And judging from the sound of things, I would say that that is just what is happening." And indeed, the clamor and confusion in the Galgorian camp was growing greater. Screams of wounded agony could be heard, mingled with the other noises of battle. Suddenly a shaft of flame shot up in the middle of the town.

"Great Dol!" Condin exclaimed. "I hope they haven't set fire to Celdondol."

"What would happen if they did?" Patsy asked in horror.

"The whole town would burn to the ground," he answered grimly.

At that moment another trumpet blast rang out, much closer now, and a second blast responded from the ramparts of the fortress.

"Rendil," Condin breathed. "He's just in time."

The battle became more intense now as war cries could be heard from the ramparts as well as from the tower. "I wish I could see him," Patsy exclaimed as she stood on tiptoe and strained her eyes.

"You had better get away from that opening," Condin warned. "You never know when a stray arrow might come this way."

"It wouldn't come in here," she argued, clinging to her post, "the opening is much too small."

"Get away from there!" Condin repeated forcefully as he grabbed her by the shoulders and pulled at her from behind.

"No!" Patsy shouted, struggling to get away from him. But as she did so, something smashed against her chest from the front, sending her staggering backward into Condin's arms. The suddenness of the movement toppled him over and the two of them landed in a heap on the floor.

"What are you doing?" he yelled as he disentangled himself and leaped to his feet.

"Somebody pushed me in the chest and knocked me over," she panted.

"There's nobody else here. Don't be silly!"

"I'm not. My chest hurts." She stood up shakily, clutching at the clothing over her heart. As she did so, something scraped on the floor under her foot. "What's that?" she asked.

Condin stooped to pick it up. "An arrow," he said quietly. Walking over to the lantern, he uncovered it and held the long, iron-tipped shaft in its glow. "A Galgorian arrow."

"But...but, I'm not bleeding," she protested in disbelief.

Condin lifted the lantern and brought it over to her. "Take your hand away," he said. She removed her hand slowly from her chest and there, in her leather tunic, a small hole could be clearly seen, and under the hole a faint silver gleam. "Is that your cross?" Condin asked.

Without a word she jerked it from under her tunic and stared, trembling at the small, bright silver dent in its somewhat tarnished surface, just under the feet of the corpus.

"O favored of the Great One," Condin whispered in wonder, "why are you standing here? Why are you not interceding for us with your God?"

Patsy shook her head from side to side, too bemused to say anything. Before she could collect her senses, a cry arose from the ramparts. "Fire!"

Instantly Condin sprang to the window, heedless of the danger. "The town is burning!" he exclaimed in dismay. "And I hear the trumpets of Arendolin sounding the retreat. We are doomed!"

Patsy frowned at him, still somewhat dazed and uncomprehending. "Why?" she asked.

"I'm not sure," he replied, straining to see. "The Galgorians appear to be rallying. A large group is breaking out toward the west, away from the town. Rendil must be cut off by the fire from the main body of his troops."

"But can't he use his enchantment to put out the fire, or something?" Patsy asked as she also returned to the window.

"I suppose he could, but what good would it do? O Dol, help us," Condin moaned as the Galgorians raised their war cry.

Suddenly Patsy felt a profound inner conviction of how she must act. The crucifix was still in her hand and now she fell to her knees before it. "God," she prayed aloud, "show him what to do. He's new at this. He needs help."

"But I love the Galgorians too."

Patsy stared at the crucifix in amazement. No, she thought, it couldn't have spoken. She looked at Condin, but he was still at the window, with his back toward her. So she tried again. "God, please help him, or we might all be killed."

"I love the Galgorians too."

It was the interior voice again, not her own, but whose she knew not. And yet she did know. "They are our enemies," she argued desperately. "Do you love them more than us?"

"They are also my children. Let them escape."

Escape? She had never thought of that, but suddenly the idea seemed plausible. "God," she cried, "if that's what you want, then tell him so. Hurry, before it's too late and all our men are killed trying to stop them."

For a moment there was no answer, no sound at all, not even the beating of her heart. Then, "The Light!" Condin shouted triumphantly. "Light of Dol! Rendil is using his enchantment!"

Patsy leaped to her feet and elbowed him aside at the window. Yes, the night had become as bright as day, illumined with a light of dazzling brilliance. In the face of its radiance, she could see the Galgorians falling down in dismay or scattering to the right and left. From across the fields a small band of mounted troops rode slowly toward them. The light seemed to emanate from their midst and as they approached the Galgorians, cries of anguish and despair could be heard on all sides. A little way in front of the enemy the small band stopped and a single splendid figure rode forward.

Patsy caught her breath and strained to see and hear, but her attention was broken by Condin pulling on her cape. "Come on," he said impatiently, "I'm going to the ramparts." With that he turned and ran from the room. Patsy, hesitated, then tore herself from her vantagepoint and dashed after him.

She caught up with him just as he reached the Queen at her station over the gate. Breathlessly the two of them stumbled to a halt at her side and looked out over the fields

278

once more. By now the lone, splendid figure had drawn up his mount within a few paces of the enemy lines and was resting there, silent and still. Then he began to speak, his voice ringing out clear and sonorous, but too far away for his words to be heard on the ramparts.

"What's he saying?" Patsy whispered.

"Shh! I can't hear," Condin hissed.

"He is offering them terms of peace," the Queen interposed quietly. "He will let them retreat unmolested if they promise never to attack us again. Otherwise, he and his men will be forced to drive them back into the burning town."

Patsy stared at her in surprise, but she knew better than to ask how the Queen could have heard what was beyond human hearing. A faint aureole of moonlight clung to her slender person.

They watched now in silence as the Galgorians conferred among themselves and one of their number stepped forward to speak to the splendid figure. Then signals were given, trumpets sounded on both sides and the army of Arendolin parted to let the Galgorians march through. Patsy squeezed her crucifix and smiled a great, glad, peaceful smile. "Thank you," she breathed. For answer, she felt the Queen's hands falling gently upon her head.

"It is well, little one," the great lady intoned, "very well. Return to the tower and rest now. I am sure that Rendil will not be here before morning."

"Will you call me?" Patsy asked in momentary panic, remembering her disappointment at Moldan.

"Of course," the Queen replied with a smile.

Patsy needed no further reassurance. Without another word, she went back to the tower, lay down on the

279

cold stone floor and instantly fell asleep. The sun was already creeping over the eastern wall of Celdondol when she felt herself being roughly shaken. "Come on," Condin was saying, "hurry, up, he's at the gate."

Patsy rolled over and tried to clear her bleary eyes and foggy brain. "Huh?" she mumbled.

"I said, hurry up. Rendil's already at the gate!"

"Oh! Rendil!" The message having at last penetrated, she jumped up and followed him. When they reached the courtyard, the Queen was already there, still in helmet and breastplate, flanked by her Guardsmen and the soldiers assigned to the fortress. Behind them, massed between the Gelfin Tree and the castle were the people of the town. Patsy was surprised to notice that the Gelfin Tree was no longer flaming. Everything seemed so quiet and ordinary compared with the upheaval of the past weeks, yet an undercurrent of excited anticipation ran through the crowd. Rilya and Landon were there too, standing just behind their mother, and Rilya hugged Patsy until she was breathless.

The two of them were still clinging to each other and giggling when, from out the walls, a trumpet sounded. On the ramparts over the gate an answering trumpet blew. "Lower the drawbridge," the Queen commanded, and the drawbridge was lowered. As it creaked into position over the moat, Patsy could see a small band of horsemen waiting on the other side. In their center were the magnificent charger Fendal and his majestic rider. Another trumpet blast rang out and the small band clattered across the drawbridge and through the great stone arch of Celdondol, coming to a halt just inside the fortress.

A loud murmur of approval went up from the crowd and Patsy bit her lip and squeezed Rilya's hand as the majestic rider slowly dismounted. Then, with a bewildering suddenness, he was no longer the majestic rider, the splendid figure, but simply Rendil, a young man kneeling humbly at his mother's feet. "Mother," he said in a firm but barely audible voice, "I have sinned. Can you find it in your heart to forgive me?"

"My son," she answered, and for once her voice trembled, "I have only prayed that you should return home safely, yet you have done far more than that. You have returned home a man and you have returned home a king. Arise, my son, and receive my embrace, for I have long since forgiven you."

With that Rendil leaped to his feet and clasped his mother in his arms. The trumpets rang out again and the crowd roared with applause as raven-dark head pressed close to raven-dark head. Patsy, unaccountably, turned away and wept.

CHAPTER 28
THE CORONATION OF RENDIL

Time passed quickly after the raising of the siege. The fire that the Galgorians had ignited had consumed nearly half the town and the task of clearing and rebuilding occupied everyone's attention for many days. Rendil himself personally supervised the work, while the troops of Arendolin labored side by side with the townsfolk of Celdondol. Even Patsy and Rilya were kept busy, sewing clothes for the families who had lost everything. Patsy had never sewn before, but after a few lessons from Galna and a bit of practice, she found to her satisfaction that she could be quite deft with a needle and thread.

In the evenings, when all their work had been laid aside, the royal family and Patsy with them would gather in the Queen's privy chambers, and the conversation would often dwell on the exploits of the weeks just past. Patsy learned with horror of the plot against the Queen and marveled at Rilya's bravery and daring. Rendil and Condin were both proud of their little brother's heroic effort to save his mother's life, while Landon, for his part, strutted about with his wooden sword and splinted arm prominently displayed.

In this way the Night of the Full Moon passed and the Night of the Dark Moon, and spring was already melting into warm and splendid summer when the Night of the Full Moon came round again. Patsy lay wide awake in her bed that night and stared at the flawless orb poised radiant and free in the deep midnight sky. She could not believe that two months had passed since she had first gazed on the moon of Arendolin.

The time seemed so much longer and so much shorter all at once. She remembered that first Night of the Full Moon, the first realization and acceptance of her mission, the paralyzing fear, the temptation to abandon it all and go home.

Now, she thought with satisfaction, she was no longer afraid. She smiled and pressed her small silver cross close to her chest, while her whole being pulsed with joy. No words could adequately express what that Sign had come to mean to her in these last few weeks. Life itself, peace, security, surrender.

Now her mission was accomplished. For tonight it was Rendil who kept his lone vigil beneath the Gelfin Tree. And tomorrow he would be crowned King of Arendolin. Her heart once more leaped and throbbed with joy.

Now she could go home. But this thought did not give her joy. True, once the atmosphere of novelty and excitement had worn off, she had begun to miss her parents and to realize, with a pang of regret, that they would be missing her. She wished that she had some way to get in touch with them, to reassure them that everything was all right. But as for actually going home, that was another matter.

"They won't understand," she thought regretfully. "I love Jesus, I love my cross, and Daddy won't let me wear it!" Tears stung her eyes at the remembrance, even after all these weeks. Yet, she asked herself, did these people understand it either? The Queen did, of course, perhaps better than Patsy herself, but Rilya did not. Patsy had tried to speak of it once or twice with her friend, and each time she had been met with a glowing panegyric to the saving might of Dol. Rilya thought she understood and her heart was filled with warmth, but these very sentiments only made Patsy all the more uncomfortable.

Did Rendil understand? She thought back over his past attitudes toward herself and her Sign: his first, almost greedy desire for possession; then his attempts to bully, manipulate, use her and her cross; and finally his humble requests for her assistance, his newly manifest respect for her freedom. Her imagination pictured for her the intimate family gatherings of the past few weeks, at which she had been so graciously welcomed: the Queen presiding as a good mother, with Rendil at her side. Everyone was easy and familiar, exchanging teasing and banter, expressions of admiration and gratitude for Palissa the Sign-bearer and peals of laughter for Passy the Page. But that was all. They had not spoken of her cross, nor had she and Rendil spoken to each other privately about anything.

Patsy felt within herself a queer sense of disappointment that she did not understand. She looked out once more at the flawless moon of Arendolin, but now its rays only hurt her eyes. She closed them and turned her face away.

The night crawled on sleeplessly and Galna's predawn summons was all too welcome. Patsy rose and dressed with care, trying not to let her hands tremble from nervous anticipation. Galna had made her gown especially for the occasion, of shimmering forest-green silk trimmed with ivory lace. Her crucifix hung proudly free on the outside of the gown, suspended from a chain of finely wrought silver, each of whose links was shaped like a leaf of the Gelfin Tree. The chain was a gift from the Queen, who had insisted that the Sign be henceforth openly worn.

Once dressed, Patsy joined the royal children and their escort for the march to the Great Hall. The way seemed short and familiar now, nor was Patsy surprised to find the corridors once again silent and empty. She knew that the people would all be massed, as for the departure of Gendol, in the courtyard in front of the castle.

Soon they reached the bronze doors at the entrance to the Great Hall, with their leaping figures and graven shields of the Full Moon and Flaming Tree. They stirred deep resonances in Patsy's soul, now that she had experienced their power and significance.

After a moment's wait the doors swung open and the little party marched in. Patsy expected to see the throne room as it had been on that earlier occasion: a blinding glare of myriad torches on bare stone walls and the alabaster throne showing blood-red in their rays. But instead, to her astonishment, the great room lay in semi-darkness. The few torches that were lit shed a soft glow on walls hung with brightly colored banners and muted tapestries, on banquet tables decked with garlands of flowers, and on the throne translucent against a background of brocaded silver draperies. The Queen in robes of midnight blue stood this time next to the empty throne, upon the seat of which were laid the scepter of royal power and a crown of pure silver encrusted with sapphires, at once massive in appearance yet delicate in workmanship.

As soon as the children had arrived, the Queen gathered up her robes and, surrounded by her attendants, swept down from the dais and made for the castle entrance. Patsy's heart pounded with anticipation as they followed after her in formal procession.

When they reached the open entrance, trumpets sounded, drums rolled, and immediately the people took up a solemn chant. Patsy recognized their strange language now as

285

the tongue of the ancient ones and marveled that even the common folk knew it so well. The song rose and swelled and sustained for a long time, then died away into silence. Then the Queen stepped forward, raised her arms aloft and began to pray, in a voice that floated, clear and lovely, above all that vast assembly. Patsy could not understand the words of her prayer, but she was not really listening anyway. She was looking for Rendil. Her eyes peered eagerly through the dim half-light of dawn and scanned the crowd in the courtyard, but she could not find him. So distracted was she in her search that the sudden flaming of the Gelfin Tree took her completely by surprise.

An upward rush of flame and light dispelled the last remnants of darkness with such force that Patsy was blinded and sickened by it. To her dismay, she heard herself scream and felt Rilya's protective arm encircling her shoulders. "Shh," the other girl whispered. "I told you that Dol was all powerful."

Patsy nodded dumbly as she struggled to get hold of herself. When at last, with a great effort, she had forced her eyes to focus, she was amazed to behold Rendil striding up the steps toward his mother. He moved straight toward the Queen, seeming not to notice anyone else, and knelt at her feet. As she laid her hands on his head and began to pronounce the solemn blessing, Patsy devoured him with her gaze, memorizing every detail of his midnight blue tunic and cloak, his ebony hair and beard, his handsome features in the repose of prayer. The blessing too was in the tongue of the ancient ones, but now she strained to catch every word. When it was ended, he kissed his mother's hand, looked for a moment into her eyes, then turned resolutely to face the Gelfin Tree.

Drums began to beat again, a slow, somber beat, and the people once more began to chant, in rhythm with the drums. Patsy wondered what was going to happen next. Then Rendil moved forward, quietly and deliberately, down the steps and across the courtyard toward the flaming Tree. And Patsy remembered Lord Gendol and the ordeal by fire that had somehow failed. Was this what was going to happen to Rendil? "No," she whispered fiercely between clenched teeth, "No!"

"But he has to do this," Rilya hissed, her arm tightening about Patsy's shoulder. "It's part of the ritual."

"No!" Patsy murmured again, shaking her head violently. But out of the corner of her eye she caught a glimpse of the Queen, standing still and serene, without the least sign of fear or protest. So the great lady too thought that this cruel ordeal must be. Then the least that she, Patsy, could do was face it like a woman. She wrenched free of Rilya's embrace and stood stiffly upright, gripping her cross in her fist, as Rendil approached closer and closer to the source of the flame.

The drums beat louder and faster now and the singing rose to a mighty crescendo. Rendil reached the low stone fence encircling the base of the Tree and hesitated for an instant. "No!" Patsy screamed this time, but her scream was lost in the roar of the crowd. To her despair, he leaped over the fence and plunged headlong into the flaming branches of the unburnt Tree.

The roaring noise reached such a pitch that it drowned out every other sound except for the sound of the "no" welling up from the depths of Patsy's being. Then, "Get up, my lady," the Queen's voice breathed very close to her ears. She opened her eyes slowly and realized, in confusion, that she was crouching on the pavement with her arms thrown protectively over her head.

"We should have explained in advance the meaning of the ceremony," the Queen went on to say. "I am sorry."

Patsy stared at her, dull and uncomprehending, then rose unsteadily to her feet with the help of the Queen's gentle hands. She saw, to her horror, that the Gelfin Tree was no longer flaming, but stood peacefully, as it had for centuries, its leaves rustling in the early morning breeze, its monstrous appetite apparently sated by the sacrifice of Rendil. Her mind was racing now from shock, so wildly that she did not notice coming toward them, up the steps out of the thronging and jubilant crowd, the majestic figure radiant with a light from within more brilliant than a thousand flaming trees.

Not until he stood directly in front of her did Patsy see him. Then she looked up into his face and gasped with terror. Who was this super-human being, so utterly transformed, so blazing with glory? She wanted to turn away, it hurt so to look at him, but mingled fascination and awe held her gaze fast. He reached out and touched her head gently, very gently. Recognition flooded her then and a kind of relief, but it was not a peaceful relief. Something inside her recoiled, protesting the suddenness and the totality with which the old familiar Rendil had been torn away forever. She looked up solemnly into his face, without smiling.

He did not smile either, but withdrew his hand from her head and swept past her, preceded by the royal guards, into the Great Hall of Celdondol. Trumpets split the air both within and without the castle, as the Queen and the children moved to follow him. Slowly they proceeded up the Hall toward the dais and the throne, while the radiance of his glory reached even to the soaring vaulted arches overhead.

Patsy found herself walking as if in a dream, with the majestic figure before her, Rilya beside her and the joyful noise of the throng flooding the Great Hall behind her. When they reached the dais, the children took up positions on the steps, while the Queen continued on up to the throne. There, amid trumpeted fanfares and shouted acclamations, she placed the silver crown upon her son's head and the royal scepter in his hand, proclaiming him Rendol Clarendil the Fifth, Sovereign Lord of Celdondol, Heir to the Might of Dol, King of Arendolin. Then he took his seat upon the throne and she knelt to kiss his hand, as he in the past had so often knelt to kiss hers.

After this, the royal children came forward, one by one, to do him homage, Condin, Rilya, Landon, and last of all, Patsy. With leaden feet and leaden heart she dragged herself up the steps of the dais and thudded to her knees before the throne. Not daring now to lift up her eyes to the majestic face of Rendol Clarendil, she took his outstretched hand and kissed it. It was warm, very warm, and strong, and she felt like sobbing; only her pride kept her from doing so. When she rose to leave, to her confusion he did not release her hand. Instead, he helped her gently to her feet and she heard him saying, "My lady, may I venerate the Sign?"

Caught off guard, she fumbled, not knowing what to do. "My lady," he asked again, "may I venerate the Sign?" This time she managed to remove it from around her neck and hand it to him. He touched it to his lips, cradled it in his palm, then looked at Patsy in such a way that she could no longer avoid his gaze. "My lady," he said, as his great midnight eyes sought entrance to her soul, "I thank you once more, and I thank the Great One who sent you and who has claimed you for his own. May you always be faithful to him as he has been faithful to you."

"May it truly be so," Patsy heard herself stammering as he replaced the crucifix about her neck. With a great leap, her soul finally opened to his gaze and was filled with strength and surrender and peace. But not a strength and peace that came from Rendol Clarendil; instead, in the depths of his eyes, she met, face to face, the reflection of the Crucified.

Gentle hands took her by the shoulders and drew her aside, and there she stayed next to the Queen, while the Royal Guard and the officers of the army of Arendolin came forward to present arms to their newly crowned King. Following them came the nobles of the realm in slow and stately procession, bearing in their hands rare and costly gifts. On their way down from the dais, they all bowed to the Queen and many of them had a special smile for Patsy. For her name and the fame of her exploits had spread far and wide through the land. But she took scarcely any notice of them: her mind was still on the Crucified. She had said yes to the Queen, yes to Rendil, yes to her mission. Had she really, all along, been saying yes to Jesus? And what would that yes mean for her now? That she did not know.

A warm, familiar sight in front of her stirred her back to the present moment. It was Gifil, coming up the steps toward them, with Melna at his side. So he had kept his promise! Patsy grinned in recognition. The old couple were dressed in their rustic best, yet they seemed strangely out of place in that glittering assembly. Gifil knelt to kiss the hand of the King, but as he rose, Rendol too stood up and embraced him. "My good man," he said, "what can I give you in reward for your services? Name it: though it be half my kingdom, it is yours."

"Now that would be a right foolish request, young King," Gifil rumbled, his face suffused with pride and gladness. "All I'll be askin' of you is to let me and my missus and my young'uns live out our days on our land in peace."

"You are as wise as ever," Rendol nodded approvingly. "I could grant you no boon greater than that. But I must present you to my Mother." With that, he led them over to where the Queen was standing, and Patsy next to her. "Mother," he said, "this is Gifil and his wife Melna. They were like the messengers of Dol to us all along our journey."

The two of them bowed awkwardly and the Queen laid her hands on their heads. "You have my profound gratitude and blessings," she said.

"It were our pleasure," Melna spoke up, taking confidence in the feminine presence. "We knowed you would be worryin' for your young'uns, so we took good care of them."

"Thank you," the Queen responded with her deepest smile.

Then Gifil turned a sad face to Patsy. "Reckon it's the last we'll be seein' of this little gal," he said.

Patsy was startled by the pronouncement, but she knew in her heart that it was true. "Thank you for everything," she gulped, her eyes filling with tears.

"Now don't be cryin'," Gifil soothed, although his own voice was hoarse and Melna was dabbing at her eyes with a huge white handkerchief. "You'll be much happier home with your own folks."

Patsy was not so sure of that, but she kept her fears to herself. Instead, she stammered shyly, "May I kiss you?"

"Why, reckon you may," Gifil answered, his face creasing with gladness.

So she threw her arms about his neck and kissed his leathery cheek, then hugged Melna hard. Tears were trickling down her face as the two of them left the dais. On the way down the stairs, they stopped to give Condin a friendly greeting. Patsy felt a sharp pang of envy as she realized that he would be seeing them often in the future.

The rest of that day passed in a glorious whirl of feasting, singing, dancing, talk and laughter. Patsy shared in it to the full, glad to forget for the time being her own perplexities and to relish the almost ecstatic joy of these people in their new King. Not until after sunset did the royal party leave the Great Hall, and then only to repair to the southwest tower of the castle, where they were treated to a breathtaking fireworks display.

Patsy sat on a cushioned window seat next to Rilya, leaning out the open casement and thrilling to the gigantic pinwheels and sprays and stars and showers that flashed before her eyes. It was a perfect warm summer night, with the moon of Arendolin rising in the east and a smattering of stars overhead, daring to compete with the fireworks for space in the velvet sky. Rilya chattered gaily on between the bursts of pyrotechnics about what they would do tomorrow and the next day, now that they were together again. Patsy nodded and smiled, but she knew it was not to be. "Maybe tomorrow and the next day," she consoled herself. Yet an aching sense of finality had begun to weigh upon her heart.

At last the fireworks were over and Rendol Clarendil stepped out on to the balcony, bathed in the splendor of his own inner light, and raising both arms aloft, blessed his people. With the sound of the enchantment song ringing in his ears: "Ride on, Rendol, King to reign," he stepped inside again and closed the casement, cutting off the echo. The day was ended.

"Rendol, will you bless us too?" Rilya cried eagerly as the King turned to face them.

He smiled. "Little sister, I fear that you are greedy. But come." He held out his hands and she ran to him. But instead of blessing her, he hugged her and kissed her shining silver curls.

"Me too!" Landon cried when he saw it. So, laughing, Rendol made room for him also in his embrace.

After a moment he released them and gestured to Condin. Condin came forward and received a strong arm about the shoulders. Patsy noticed that his hair was beginning to turn black at the temples. He too was on the road to manhood. "One day you will be chancellor of the Kingdom," Rendol said to him.

"I only pray that I may be worthy of it," Condin answered humbly.

Now Rendol was looking at Patsy. Her eyes dropped to the floor, then raised to his face, then dropped again. "My lady," he said with an oddly wistful smile, "the time has come."

She nodded.

"Do you want to go home?"

"No," she answered frankly, looking up at last. "I'm happy here and I wasn't at home. And I'm afraid they won't accept my Sign. But I don't belong here anymore, do I?"

"No," he answered quietly. "Your mission is accomplished and you belong where the Great One wishes you to be. But you must go freely."

"I will go." Somehow, what God wished meant more to her now than anything did. She knew that his love would give her strength.

"Come then," he beckoned.

Still she hesitated. But Rilya intervened. "Where are you going?" she asked in alarm.

"Home," Patsy answered.

"You mean you're leaving us? Forever?" Rilya wailed.

"Yes," Patsy said woodenly.

"Oh, no!" Rilya sobbed, throwing her arms around Patsy as if she could prevent her friend from leaving by sheer force. Patsy squeezed her comfortingly in return. In a way, she was relieved by the outburst of emotion, even though she dared not let herself join in it.

Rilya lifted her tear-streaked face and murmured brokenly, "I'll miss you very much."

"I'll miss you too," Patsy answered.

"Where's she going?" asked Landon who had not been following the conversation.

"Home," said Condin.

"Oh. Well, then, goodbye." Landon thrust out his hand to her solemnly. Patsy shook it with equal solemnity. Then she turned shyly to Condin.

"Thank you for everything," she said.

"You are welcome," he answered with a gracious bow. Much to her surprise and embarrassment, he took her hand and kissed it.

The Queen was next. She enfolded Patsy in her arms and pressed her close to her heart. "I shall miss you too, my little one," she said, "but I cannot detain you any longer, knowing that your own mother is waiting for you. Only do not be afraid. The Great One will be with you at home just as much as he was here."

Patsy actually smiled as she kissed the Queen on the cheek. "Goodbye," she said, "and thank you."

"Goodbye," the Lady answered.

Now Patsy stood where, a few minutes earlier, she had dreaded to stand: directly in front of Rendol. She looked up at him expectantly. He smiled at her again with the same oddly wistful smile, then cupped her face in both his hands and, bending down, kissed her on the forehead. As he straightened up, he took a deep breath and said something very strange, which she did not understand. Then he said it again and she realized with a shock that he was addressing her in plain American English. "Patricia Morgan," he was saying, "go home, Patricia Morgan…"

CHAPTER 29
HOME

"Patricia! Patsy!" The man's voice was urgent. "Patsy, can you hear me? Wake up, Patsy!"

Patsy opened her eyes in bewilderment and looked up, wondering why Rendol was suddenly addressing her in this way. What met her gaze was the distraught face of her own father, his hair disheveled, his beard unshaven.

Quickly she closed her eyes again. "I'm dreaming," she thought. "What's he doing here?" Then she heard the man's voice again, unmistakably her father's.

"She's coming around. Kate, don't you see? She's coming around. Patsy!"

Patsy opened her eyes again and saw not only her father but her mother as well, and behind them the face of another man, wearing a white coat and a stethoscope.

"Where am I?" she asked in confusion. Her voice sounded ghostly in her own ears and far away.

"You're right here with us, honey," her mother answered reassuringly, "in the hospital. You're going to be okay now. Don't worry about anything."

Patsy closed her eyes once more and strained to remember, back beyond Rendol, beyond Celdondol, beyond Moldan, beyond the Queen. Where had she been that last morning at home? With painful effort, she managed to recall the tense scene with her father, the walk to school, the last-minute dash to cross the street before the light changed. Had something happened to her in crossing the street? Is that when some unknown power had transported her into the far-off

296

world of Arendolin? But then why was she now lying in a hospital bed? She groped for her cross, seeking for an answer in its familiar touch. But her fingers sought in vain for it, on her chest, about her neck.

"My cross!" she gasped frantically, struggling to sit up. "Where's my cross?"

'It's all right, honey, it's all right." Her mother's arms immediately encircled her shoulders to support her.

"Here's your cross," her father added, picking it up from the bedside table and holding it out to her. "I'm sorry I raised such a fuss about it. You can wear it from now on if you want to. I promise." His eyes were filled with tears.

Patsy hesitated for a moment, then reached out a trembling hand, took it from him and placed it around her neck. But all the while she was doing this, her eyes never left his face. Suddenly her whole being seemed to split for sheer joy. "Daddy," she sobbed, "I'm glad to be home!"

She felt him enfolding her in his embrace, holding her and rocking her as he had never done before, but she was too overcome to wonder at it. "Thank you, God," her heart pounded, over and over. "Thank you." After a few minutes she felt her mother's gentle hand taking her from him and laying her back in the bed.

"You've had a hard time of it, honey," she heard her saying. "You'd better rest awhile now."

Patsy did not understand how her mother could have known, but the last day at Celdondol had been exhausting. Gratefully she relaxed and closed her eyes and let the waves of fresh bittersweet memory roll over her until she slept.

When she awoke some hours later, her mother was sitting quietly by the bedside reading. Patsy watched her for awhile without moving. "The Queen was right," she thought, "she is my own mother, better than strangers, however good they are." Nevertheless, a pang of regret pierced her heart as she realized that the Queen could never again be considered a stranger.

Just then Mrs. Morgan looked up and saw her. "Why, hello Patsy dear," she said. "Are you awake?" She got up and leaned over to kiss her and stroke her forehead. Patsy lifted a hand to her mother's cheek but let it drop again almost immediately. She felt so weak, and she could not understand why. "Mom," she asked, "am I really in the hospital? How come? What happened to me?"

Mrs. Morgan hesitated, then drew a long breath and let it out slowly. "We're not quite sure, honey, what happened to you. Apparently a hit-and-run driver struck you as you were crossing the street in front of school. There were witnesses who saw the man put on his brakes, then swerve, hit you, and drive right on. But no one got his license number. And for some reason they couldn't find you. It was as if you had vanished. They called the police and they called us and we searched and searched for hours before we finally turned you up unconscious under the neighbor's hedge. The police figure that you must have been thrown by the impact, but they can't understand how. Anyway, miraculously, except for a few bruises and a concussion, you were unhurt. But you wouldn't come out of the coma. We've been sitting here by your bedside for ten days now, waiting and watching…" Her voice broke and she turned away quickly, but Patsy had already seen the tears in her eyes, the worry and care etched deep into her face. She felt ashamed for having stayed away so long with hardly a thought for her and her father. But how long had she stayed away?

"Mom," she asked with a puzzled frown, "how long did you say it was before you found me?"

"About four hours, I guess, but it seemed much longer. Why? Do you remember anything after you were hit?" Mrs. Morgan wiped her eyes and leaned forward eagerly to catch Patsy's every word.

"I remember trying to cross the street," she began slowly, "and I remember the sound of brakes real loud, and then I went black. And when I woke up, I wasn't there anymore."

"You weren't there any more? Where were you?"

"In Arendolin."

"Arendolin? Where's that?"

Patsy hesitated, groping for an answer. "I don't know," she admitted finally, "but I was there a lot longer than a few hours. It was weeks and weeks. And I wasn't lying there hurt, either. I was doing all kinds of things. I even learned to ride a horse, at least sort of. And I'm awfully sorry, really, for not trying to get in touch with you and tell you I was okay."

Mrs. Morgan looked startled for a moment, then she smiled gently. "Never mind, dear. I'm glad you were having such pleasant and exciting dreams while you were away from us."

"Dreams?" Patsy cried in hurt tones. "But it wasn't a dream! It was all real!" Or was it? The question stabbed her to the core. She had been hit by a car, thrown into a hedge, left ten days in a coma. Was it all just a dream: her cross, her mission, Rendol, the Queen? "No!" she sobbed aloud, tears gushing down her face. "No, it was real, it was real!" Her

299

voice trailed off in wracking anguish as her mother pressed her close. Eventually a nurse came in and went out and returned with a needle and gave her an injection that she did not feel. As the sedative began to work, her sobs died away and once again she slept.

The next time Patsy awoke, the room was dark and neither of her parents was there. For a long time she lay still, staring wide-eyed into the blackness, too drained to weep, to dazed to think. "All a dream, all a dream," the words mocked her over and over again. At last, as she began to revive, she groped for her comforting cross. It was gone. "So it was all a dream," she thought bitterly. But after awhile she remembered the bedside table and that her father had taken the cross from it and handed it to her and promised her that she could wear it from now on. Maybe he had just changed his mind and taken it back again. That thought was scarcely less bitter than the first one. Nonetheless, she twisted over to the edge of the bed, stretched her arm as far as it would go and began to feel along the tabletop. Yes, there it was – a cold little pile of metal – the chain and the cross. She scooped it up quickly, rolled back into the center of the bed and jerked it down over her head, hiding it underneath her hospital gown.

"They're not going to take it away from me again," she determined fiercely as she pressed it close to her flesh. "Never!" At least that much was real. Then her mind began to seek for further realities. Mrs. Denton was one. And if she were real, then her words about Jesus and how he had died to save all men and had risen from the dead, overcoming all evil by his power, were probably real too.

But what about the Queen? If she were only a dream, then what about her words: that love was more powerful than any science or magic; that if she, Patsy, would only cling to God's love there would be nothing that she could not do or endure; and that God would be with her as much at home as he had been in Arendolin. Could she really believe those things now? Or were they only part of the beautiful dream? How could she find out? How could she know for sure? Maybe Mrs. Denton would know. Maybe.

Presently morning dawned and a nurse came in to give her routine bedside care. It did not take her long to spy the chain around Patsy's neck. "I'm sorry, sweetheart," she said as she put out her hand to remove it, "but you can't wear necklaces in the hospital. I know you like this one, but if you just have it here on the bedside table, you can look at it any time."

Patsy's eyes filled with tears, but she let the nurse remove it without protest. "That must be what happened last night," she thought. "Daddy didn't take it away from me after all. The nurse did." The realization brought profound relief. She could trust her father; his promise also was real. There was hope yet.

The nurse let her sit up and eat breakfast, then the doctor came in and examined her, pronouncing her strong enough to get up and walk around for a few minutes. Patsy thought that rather cautious and silly until she actually got up and her knees wobbled beneath her weight and the nurse had to support her. She was glad to be back in bed again when her parents arrived a little later.

Her father was groomed and shaven and looked his usual self. He came up to the bed and kissed her, but he was holding something in one hand behind his back.

"What's that, Daddy?" Patsy asked with an impish grin, guessing that it was for her.

He smiled broadly. "Just a little something for my favorite patient." With a grand flourish he produced his surprise, a white plush teddy bear with a huge red ribbon around its neck and a red heart appliqued to its chest.

"Oh!" Patsy exclaimed as she grabbed it and hugged it. "Thank you!" She grabbed her father and hugged him too. Both of them were laughing. As she let go of him, his eyes fell on her crucifix on the bedside table.

"You removed your cross," he observed with some surprise.

"They told me I had to take it off," she explained. "They said I couldn't wear necklaces in the hospital." Then a thought struck her. "Daddy," she asked, "what made you change your mind? About my cross, I mean."

Her father's smile faded into seriousness. He looked down at his fingernails, then over at her mother, who had been standing quietly by the bed all this time.

"Well, honey," he said finally, "I guess it was your accident. When I got to work and found your mother already on the phone about you, I was pretty annoyed. But I came anyway and joined in the search. We couldn't find you – I suppose Mom told you all this – and I got kind of scared and was sorry for having blown off at you before you left for school. Then you turned up under the hedge and they took you to the hospital and I breathed a sigh of relief, thinking everything was all right now. But you just went on in a coma and wouldn't wake up. The longer you lay there, the more anxious and ashamed and guilty I got. Finally…" He faltered and looked down at his hands, then up at Patsy again. "I don't

302

know whether you'll understand this, but I ended up cursing the God I said I didn't believe in."

Reaching over, Jim Morgan took his wife's hand and squeezed it hard. She bit her lip, then covered his hand with her free one, her wedding ring plainly visible.

"Your mother had some pretty hard things to say to me then," Mr. Morgan went on, "all of them true. I guess her words brought me to my senses. Patsy, honey," he looked at her with a sad smile, "I've done a lot of things wrong in the past and I'm sorry. It's going to be different from now on, I promise."

Patsy was not sure she really understood but she nodded solemnly. "Daddy," she said, "and Mom, I'm glad to be home. I love you. I love you," she repeated, flinging her arms around both of them. For a long time the little family held each other very close.

After that they talked for awhile, about her new teddy bear and about when she could leave the hospital and about school and how she would possibly have to miss the rest of the term. An aide came in with a lunch tray and they continued to talk while she ate. At last the nurse returned and suggested that Patsy should rest. Only then did she realize how very tired she was, yet how loath to let her parents go. It was as if the happiness she had not felt in so long would disappear if they went away. But when she clung to them wordlessly, her mother smoothed her curls and said, "We'll be back, honey. Just rest now like they want and we'll see you this evening." So she fell back into the bed, closed her eyes and slept.

When Patsy woke, the window curtains were drawn and the room had a late afternoon dimness. She could hear the hustle and bustle of hospital noises in the corridor, but around her bed all was still. She lay there, not wanting to move, while the feeling of happiness washed over again. "I love you," she heard herself saying, over and over, and her father's words, "It's going to be different, I promise." Love: isn't that what the Queen had said? That love was more powerful than anything else? That God's love would be with her at home as much as in Arendolin? After her experience with her parents that morning, how could she doubt the truth of her words? And if what the Queen had said was real, then maybe the Queen was also real. She reached out for her cross and gripped it fiercely. With her other arm she squeezed the teddy bear, clinging to them both as she clung to hope.

The rest of that day passed quickly in exercise and eating. By evening, Patsy could walk unaided all around the room and sit up in a chair in her robe and slippers. The nurse had even relented and allowed her to wear her cross when she was not in bed. So, when her father popped his head in the door some time after supper, he found her enthroned like a princess in her chair, with the teddy bear in her lap and the crucifix proudly displayed on the front of her robe.

"Well, hi there!" He positively beamed with delight. "Don't you look beautiful tonight!"

Patsy grinned at his blarney. "Hi," she said.

"I have another surprise. We've brought your teacher friend to see you. What's her name? Mrs. Denton?"

"Oh!" Patsy's heart leapt and quailed at the same moment. She hastily shoved the teddy under the covers on the bed, straightened the blanket over her knees, and ran her fingers through her rumpled curls. "Do I look... presentable?" she asked, fumbling for her most grown-up words.

Her father laughed. "I told you that you look beautiful." He picked up a brush and smoothed out her hair, then kissed her on the forehead. "She has been very worried about you during these past weeks, calling every day to find out how you were. So we asked her to come over with us tonight. She's a much less forbidding woman than I imagined," he added reassuringly. With that he left the room and a few moments later returned, ushering in her mother and Mrs. Denton.

The little woman came up quietly and took Patsy's hand. "Hello, Patricia," she said. "I'm glad to see you sitting up and looking so well. We were all worried about you."

"Thank you," Patsy gulped. "I'm glad you could come," she added, remembering her manners.

"Why don't you sit down," offered Mr. Morgan, drawing up another chair for her.

"Yes, thank you," she replied and settled herself, while Mr. and Mrs. Morgan remained standing near the door. Patsy was at once grateful and embarrassed by their presence.

"Your classmates have sent you get-well cards," Mrs. Denton announced with a smile and a flourish, holding out a bulging manila folder. Patsy accepted it and looked inside. It was stuffed with homemade greetings and crayon-drawn pictures. She smiled briefly and an awkward pause ensued as she struggled for a way to begin saying what was really on her mind.

"Patricia, your mother has told me that you had a wonderful adventure while you were gone from us."

Patsy was startled, but relieved. "Yes," she began eagerly, then stopped. Did they believe her or did they bring Mrs. Denton just to talk her out of it? Did Mrs. Denton believe it? Did she herself believe it? "Mrs. Denton," she began again, her mouth as dry as cotton, "it's…it's about my cross. About what you told me about it, I mean. You did tell me, didn't you, that Jesus died on the cross to save everybody and that he rose from the dead and that by the power of the cross all evil would be overcome?"

"Yes, Patricia, you have a good memory. That's exactly what I told you."

"Then it's true," Patsy said with relief. She was beginning to relax now.

"I believe that it is true," Mrs. Denton replied, "and I'm willing to give my life for that belief. But you must come to that same faith for yourself, with God's help."

"Then this is also true," Patsy plunged on impatiently, "that Jesus died because he loved us, that love is more powerful than magic, that God's love will help me to do anything, that he will be with me now just as he was…just as he was before!" Patsy hesitated to mention Arendolin, in case it wasn't real after all.

But Mrs. Denton was looking at her with astonishment. "Why, yes, Patricia, that is quite true! But who has instructed you so thoroughly? One of the nurses?"

"No!" Patsy almost shouted in her triumph. "The Queen told me that. I couldn't have dreamed what no one told me. So it must have been her."

Mrs. Denton frowned slightly and behind her Patsy's parents eyed one another and shifted uneasily.

"Would you like to tell me about the Queen? Where is she from?"

"From Arendolin, of course. That's where I was when you couldn't find me. I don't know why the time was shorter

u when it was weeks and weeks for me, but never mind.
sn't a dream, it was real."

"But, Patricia…" Mrs. Denton began.

"Patsy, dear," her mother intervened, "could you show Mrs. Denton your cross?"

Patsy had the sinking feeling that none of them believed her, but it didn't really matter now. The important thing was that God truly was with her, had truly called her, and she could go on trusting in him. Obediently she took off the crucifix and handed it to Mrs. Denton.

"Is that the cross you gave her?" Patsy's mother asked.

"Yes, certainly," answered Mrs. Denton. "I see that it was damaged slightly in the accident. And where did you get such a lovely and unusual chain for it? The one I had for it was quite plain and a bit tarnished I'm afraid."

"I don't know," Mrs. Morgan answered. "Jim and I were admiring it ourselves, but we assumed that you had given it to her with the cross. Patsy, dear, tell us, where did you get this chain?"

For a moment Patsy could not answer. She was staring at it, unable to believe her eyes or ears. Why hadn't she thought of it sooner? But there it was, the gleaming silver chain, gift of the Queen, each link shaped like a leaf of the Gelfin Tree. Her heart swelled and throbbed with a joy impossible to contain.

"The Queen gave it to you, didn't she honey?" Mr. Morgan asked her quietly, his face earnest and serious.

"Yes," she cried at last, "yes, she did! Oh, thank you, God! Thank you!" No more words needed to be spoken.

for yc
It w

Made in the USA
Middletown, DE
23 December 2017